ALCHEMY UNFOLDING

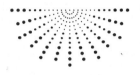

M.L. BROOME

TERRACOTTA DRAGON ARTS

Digital Edition JUNE 2020 ASIN B089XPGHVB

Print Edition ISBN: 978-1-7338964-9-8

Cover Design

Suzana Stankovic, LSDdesign

DEDICATION

Dedicated to love, in all its glorious forms.

"You'll climb as high as you dare believe you are capable. The stars are only as far as we imagine them to be, and time is neither friend nor foe. Magic is everywhere. Life is a thing of beauty."

CHAPTER ONE

BEST LAID PLANS

*Y*ou know the scene in movies where the hapless female stumbles upon her lover in the arms of another? I'm living that scene. Right now.

I always wondered what my reaction would be in that situation. Would I recoil in horror? Hurl obscenities—and heavy household objects—in their direction? Turn on the waterworks as I followed their fleeing, naked bodies?

The answer? None of the above.

"I always thought you were a natural blonde, Debra."

At the mention of her name, Debra flies off my boyfriend's naked body, his dick bobbing from her sudden dismount. "Addy, you're here."

I feel almost sorry at the sight of her deer in headlights appearance. Almost. "I live here, Debra. Come to think of it, so does the man whose dick you were just riding."

With a yelp, Debra grabs the bedsheet, wrapping it around her like a toga of shame. She spends the next few moments scampering around the floor like a deranged rabbit, gathering every article of discarded clothing before hightailing it out of the room.

I remain silent until I hear the slamming of the apartment door. Debra must be opting to dress on the fly. Bold decision. I turn my narrowed gaze to my boyfriend of four years, certain I'll burst into tears at any moment. That's how you're supposed to respond in this situation, isn't it?

To his credit, Clint doesn't appear guilt-ridden over my discovery. The pompous ass likely believes he deserves a hall pass. I scan over his still naked body, wondering what I ever found appealing about him.

Granted, on paper, the man is perfection. Squared. He's classically handsome—even if he spends more on manicures than I do—and he's a well-respected emergency physician. But any hint of the man I met four years earlier on an overnight shift is long gone, replaced with an air of entitlement and arrogance.

I wait for Clint to open the conversation, but the big chicken isn't saying a word. What a man.

I glance toward the door before releasing a sigh and roll of my shoulders. "If you hurry, you might catch Debra. Give her those orgasms you were promising."

Clint sends me a withering look, but he needn't bother. My armor is intact and battle-ready.

"Don't glare at me for interrupting your fuck fest. Go get her, Casanova."

"Stop it, Adelaide."

Ah, there it is—my full name. Clint only uses it in conjunction with his most condescending tone. It's a trait he picked up from my mother, lovingly dubbed Ice Queen by her only daughter. It usually elicits a submissive response from me, another symptom of my years of training in the art of people-pleasing.

But not this time.

"*You* stop it. Stop pretending to care, stop pretending you're concerned that I caught you, and please, for the love of God, stop pretending my emotional well-being means a damn to you. Go. Now."

Clint releases a mirthless chuckle as he snatches his boxers from the floor. How quaint. I selected that underwear for our upcoming European vacation. I guess he needed to break them in first. "I'll leave, but this discussion isn't over. I'll be back later today."

I nod my head, crossing my arms over my chest in a defiant manner. It really is shocking. Not one tear has fallen. Not one. I wonder if Clint is afraid or appalled by my calm demeanor.

I don't have to wait long for my answer.

"Don't stand there looking self-righteous, Adelaide. This doesn't even bother you, does it? You're like that with everything. No emotion. No feeling. Even our sex life was dry as dirt."

"You are *not* pinning your indiscretions on me, although I agree with your observation about our sex life. Granted, it might have something to do with the fact we never deviated from our weekly schedule or missionary position."

"I deviated from missionary with Debra."

The smug, son-of-a-bitch. His holier than thou attitude is so ridiculous, I'm forced into the only emotion that makes sense in this mess.

I burst out laughing.

"I'm so proud of you, Clint, for trying new things." I motion toward the door, my laughter increasing at his slanted glare. "I meant what I said earlier. Go catch your little secretary. Give her the orgasms you never gave me. I'm disappointed, though. I expected something less predictable from you. Screwing your secretary is terribly trite."

"Leave Debra out of this."

I tap my chin, clearing my throat. "Considering she was screwing my boyfriend in my bed, I'd say she's more than an innocent bystander."

Clint throws on his shirt and shoes. The man is moving with record speed now. "I won't stand here and listen to this garbage."

"By all means. Don't let the door hit your ass on the way out of the relationship."

Clint grabs his coat from the changing bench and storms out the door with a final glare, rattling the hinges as he departs.

FIFTEEN MINUTES LATER, I'm standing in the kitchen with dry eyes, a glass of vodka in one hand and my mobile in the other.

I should call someone. That's what you do when you walk in on your boyfriend humping his secretary, right? After all, it's a tragic occurrence. Okay, tragedy is too strong a term. That word needs to be reserved for plane crashes and bombings. Regardless, this is still a crap situation.

"If it's such a horrible situation, why aren't I more upset?" I ponder aloud, directing my question to the upwardly mobile pieces of furniture strategically positioned around the apartment.

Then it hits me.

I despise that chaise lounge. The color is putrid, and it's lumpy as the old recliner at Grandma's house, minus the charm.

In fact, there isn't a piece of furniture in this place that I like. My mother selected everything, in her quest to mold me into a woman befitting proper society. I'm as attached to these sticks of wood and fabric as I am the rest of my life.

Marching into the bedroom, I fling open my closet. It's chock-full of designer labels and hand-tailored garments. And I want to burn every single stitch.

"This isn't my life. I never wanted this life," I mutter, as my eyes fall on a sweater perched on a back shelf. Grabbing it to me, I breathe deeply and almost smell the faint whiff of my father's cologne. "I miss you, Daddy."

With those words, the tears arrive. I sink to the carpet, grasping his sweater for dear life. If my father had survived, I would have grown up middle-class and loved, instead of my mother marrying into money and forcing me into a lifestyle I despised.

"What am I supposed to do, Dad?" I sniffle against the rough wool when an odd sense of peace falls over me.

I can almost hear his dark-timbered voice and feel his arms wrap around me. "Addy, my darling, it's time to go live *your* life."

The simple truth screams too loud to ignore.

When Clint returns—*if* he returns—things are changing.

Namely, me.

GOOD TO HIS WORD, Clint returns that night with my mother in tow. I giggle behind my hand as I watch them enter the apartment. He must have heard the news from someone at the hospital and realized he needed reinforcements.

"Adelaide, get in here right now." My mother's voice reaches me from my vantage point down the hall.

With a resigned—and bemused—sigh, I slip into the role of a dutiful daughter. "Yes, Mother. What a surprise to see you here."

As always, Claire Perkins is the picture of perfection. Not a hair out of place, despite the 20 mph winds blowing outside the window. She was built for this life.

Me, not so much.

"I want an explanation." Her dark brown eyes bore into mine.

Externally, we are carbon copies. Same chestnut-colored hair. Same ivory skin. Same petite frame.

But that is where any similarity ends.

"If you'd like an explanation, I suggest you speak to the man who was fucking another woman in my bed." I jerk my head in Clint's direction, pleased that the man has the graciousness to appear sheepish.

"Language, Adelaide. I did not raise you to speak in such a manner."

I'm not sure why this statement, of all the coldhearted comments my mother has made over the years, snaps my last thread of patience. "Mother, you didn't raise me. My father did until his death. After that, an assortment of nannies took over any maternal role."

"I see what you mean, Clint." She aims her comment over my head, one of her usual tactics.

"You see nothing, Mother. You never did." I gesture around the apartment, now in all manner of disarray, thanks to my erratic packing. "As you can see, I'm quite busy."

"That's why we're here. You gave Clint the shock of his life earlier today."

"The poor baby," I grit out, glaring at my ex-lover. What a total louse. "I suppose turnabout is fair play. He shocked the hell out of me earlier, as well."

"Have you seriously resigned from Good Hope?"

I nod, my foot drumming the floor. Their visit is throwing quite a kink in my packing timeline.

"What in the world for?" My mother's calm facade is wearing thin, and the real Claire is about to make an appearance.

"I took a job elsewhere. I didn't think working alongside my ex-boyfriend was a smart idea."

"So you took a nursing job across the country? What were you thinking, Addy?" Clint finally jumps into the conversation, his frustration evident as he paces the carpet.

"I was thinking about *my* well-being. Something I haven't considered in a very long time." Tears prick my lids, but it's not from grief. How funny. The idea of escaping this life makes me so overwhelmingly happy, my body can't contain the emotion.

"Why San Diego?" my mother presses.

I wipe my eyes with the heel of my hand. "Dad used to travel to San Diego all the time. Don't you remember, Mother? He loved the city."

"Are you telling me you're moving 2,700 miles away from everything you know because of some beach tales your father told you?" My mother joins Clint in pacing. Much more of this, and they'll wear a hole in the Persian.

Someone has to be the adult in this situation, and that someone will be me. They can't talk me out of leaving, but I would like to go with their blessing. Apparently, certain facets of my people-pleasing personality are still intact. "I need a change. A big change. I need to start over."

"You're throwing away four years with Clint and over a decade working at Good Hope. You were in line for the nursing director's position, Adelaide. I don't understand your reasoning."

God help my mother. She can't understand anything beyond appearances.

I run my hands through my long hair, giving it a good tug. "You don't understand my reasons? Mother, Clint slept with another woman! You could try seeing my side in this situation."

Her shoulders sag, and she grasps my hand. Whether it's a genuine attempt at camaraderie or a meaningless gesture, I can't be sure. But for the moment, it feels good. "I see your side, Adelaide."

I chew my lower lip, uncertain how to make her understand. "You don't even know my side, Mother. I need to do this. I have to go find myself, and I can't do that staring at the same walls, surrounded by the same people. Please understand."

For the next thirty seconds, the silence reverberates with tension. Then, with a sigh, my mother reaches for her purse, pulling out her checkbook. "Let me give you some money. San Diego is not cheap."

"You're letting her go?" Clint demands, earning a side-eye glance from my Mother.

"She's thirty-nine years old, Clint. I can't make her stay."

I don't know if I'm relieved that she isn't fighting me on my decision or hurt that her reasons for caring have nothing to do with missing me. I suppose it doesn't matter.

"I don't need your money, Mother. Thank you, but I need to do this on my own." I pull her to me, wishing that just once she would return the embrace. "Could you give me a few minutes alone with Clint?"

She nods before turning her gaze to my ex-boyfriend. "You have my number." She strolls to the front door but pauses with her hand on the knob. "I hope you know what you're doing, Adelaide."

"I don't have the first clue, Mother."

"That's what frightens me."

Her barb bounces off me. "Don't be. I'm excited. How often do you get to begin again, to search for the magic you lost somewhere along the way?"

She chuckles softly. "You are so much like your father. Both of you, total dreamers. I know you don't think so, but I miss him, too. Call me when you arrive in San Diego."

After my mother departs, I turn my attention to Clint, still shocked by my composure regarding our relationship's demise. "You can keep the apartment."

"We're supposed to be moving into the condo next month, or have you forgotten? That's what you said you wanted, Addy."

"I only said that because I knew it was what *you* wanted. I wanted you to be happy."

"And now?"

"I want to be happy."

He grabs my shoulders, forcing me to look at him. "You're throwing away four years because of a single indiscretion?"

I meet his emerald gaze and feel my resolve strengthen. "You and I both know it wasn't a single indiscretion, Clint. I've suspected for a long time."

"We can get past this, Addy."

"Why would we want to? You're not happy. You can't be. No man who's happy with the woman he's involved with shags every eligible nurse under the age of thirty."

His square jaw clenches as I speak the words I never wanted to admit. "I don't know who you've been talking to—"

"Despite what you believe, you are not that slick. Everyone knew. I knew, too. I just didn't want to face what that reality meant."

"What does it mean?"

"That I don't make you happy."

"Addy—" he interjects, but I wave off any further discussion.

"And you don't make me happy. I'm leaving. In a week, I'll be on a beach in San Diego."

"You really think moving across the country is the answer to your problems?"

I shrug, offering a rueful smile. "All I know is that staying here sure isn't the answer." I stand on tiptoe, pecking his cheek. "Goodbye, Clint."

CHAPTER TWO

A BRAND-NEW ME

"My father wasn't kidding. San Diego is paradise." I'm planted on the sand of Pacific Beach, letting the waves lull me into a zen-like state. I haven't felt this calm in...ever.

"Your father is a smart man." Melissa hands me a beer from the cooler before settling back into her beach chair.

"Yes, he was."

I've been a California resident for two weeks, and I understand why people never want to leave. It has its challenges, but they're minor compared to the glory of the area. The people are far more laid back than Manhattan—a genuine, beach community vibe pervades the entire region—and for me, it's a welcome respite.

"I'm glad you're enjoying California. Everyone loves you at work. You're running circles around the rest of the staff." Melissa is a fellow emergency nurse at Memorial. She was the one who got me up to speed in the department after my arrival, and it only took one shift to feel like I'd known the woman forever.

"I love it here. I'm so glad I came."

"No buyer's remorse?" she adds with a wink, waving at a figure making his way across the sand.

"None at all. Who's that?"

"Remember the respiratory therapist I told you about the other night? The one who resembles a young Richard Gere and is newly single?"

"Please tell me this isn't a piss poor attempt at a setup."

Melissa feigns shock, her eyes widening. "Would I do that?"

I laugh at her stilted expression. It's impossible not to smile around this woman. "I don't know, but probably."

The Richard Gere doppelganger finally arrives at our blankets, tossing his backpack into the sand. "Nice spot, Melissa." He turns his gaze to the water. "Some bombs out there today."

"Bombs?" I scrunch my nose at the term, searching the beach for anything remotely bomb-like.

"Waves, big waves. You must be Addy from New York." He extends his hand, a smile lighting up his face. Melissa wasn't far off —the guy definitely has 'An Officer and A Gentleman' vibe about him.

"That's me. And you are?"

"Melissa, you're a terrible hostess," he jokes before turning his gaze back to me. "Sean."

"Nice to meet you, Sean." I motion to the beach, in awe of the giant waves—I mean bombs—crashing onto the sand. "You surf?"

"Everyone surfs, Addy. It's San Diego," Melissa sends me a wink before tossing Sean a beer.

"I love surfing. I'm not very good at it, but it's a hell of an experience. There are some guys out here that live and breathe for the ocean. You ever been surfing, Addy?"

I shake my head, swallowing down a mouthful of beer. "No. I love the ocean, but I don't think I'm that brave. Besides, surfing isn't nearly as popular in New York as it is here on the West

Coast." I pull my camera from my bag, kneeling in the sand to snap a few photos of the water.

"That camera is never out of your sight, is it?" Melissa inquires.

I shake my head, shooting a few more frames before stowing it safely away. "I've always loved photography. And the ocean. But Clint and I worked so much that we never had any time to visit the water, which is pretty pathetic considering Manhattan is technically an island."

"Who's Clint? Your husband?" Sean's question is innocent, but Melissa shakes her head at him, begging him to drop this conversation train.

"We don't talk about Clint," Melissa interjects, popping out of her chair. "I'm heading to the concession stand. You two want anything?"

I shake my head and laugh as I watch her wind around the other beachgoers. "Clint was my boyfriend, right up until I caught him in bed with his secretary."

"Shit. That sucks."

I'm not sure why Sean's response is so welcome. It's not trite or full of forced optimism. "Yep. Good times."

"I know the feeling."

"Your wife slept with Clint's secretary, too?" It's a joke, but I realize I'm not far off the mark when Sean's face hardens.

"No, but she did sleep with my cousin." He polishes off the beer, grabbing another one from the cooler. "Next month was supposed to be our wedding."

I rest my hand on Sean's forearm, trying to convey empathy. The trouble is that this poor man is broken up about his failed relationship; I'm relieved about the demise of mine. "I'm so sorry."

"Why does everyone say that?"

"Say what?"

"I'm sorry for things that aren't their fault. I'm not judging. I do it, too. But I don't understand why we apologize for things beyond our control."

"It's a way of reaching across the chasm of self-inflicted isolation we put ourselves in after our relationship dies a slow and torturous death. We feel terribly alone in the aftermath, and it helps to know that others think the behavior is equally screwed up."

Sean smiles, clinking his bottle against mine. "That might be the greatest explanation in the history of man."

"Thank you. Stick around, and I'll explain life on Mars next."

"Can't wait." He picks up a handful of sand, letting it drift through his fingers. "You know Melissa is trying to set us up, right?"

I laugh and nod in agreement. "I know. I think she feels like she owes it to the world since she has the happiest marriage on the planet."

"They are pretty damn happy."

I know Sean brought up Melissa's idea for a reason. I hear it in the tone of his voice. Even if I were interested in him in that manner, he's not emotionally ready. Time to put his mind at ease. "I think dating so soon after ending a long-term relationship is counterproductive. We should be wild and free, at least for a while. See how the other half lives."

His face relaxes at my statement. 'Operation I Don't Want to Sleep with Sean' is a success. "It always looks so glamorous. Going out to all the newest clubs, dancing all night, tons of photos and videos on social media—"

"Different man or woman every night..." my voice trails off as I chew the inside of my lip. "Actually, that doesn't sound very appealing at all."

"You're right. I can't imagine dating multiple people after being with the same woman for two years."

"I got you beat. I was with Clint for four years, and we were nowhere near saying I do."

"What did I miss?" Melissa inquires, plopping into her beach chair, a tray of nachos balancing precariously in one hand.

Sean and I exchange glances and burst out laughing.

"We don't want to sleep together," I remark, snatching a chip off Melissa's tray.

"Bloody hell, how long was I gone?" She releases a sigh, her eyes on the ocean. "Fine. I tried."

"You've done your due diligence," I remark, stealing another chip.

Melissa holds the tray away with a smirk. "You know, Addy, you and your camera should head to the beach at dawn if you want to see something spectacular."

"Amazing sunrises?"

"Yes, but I'm referring to the surfers. They're usually up and at it by first light. You could get some terrific shots of the local talent."

"I'll have to check it out. My experience with surfing is nil, so I'll take any recommendations you can give me." I stash the beer bottle, offering up a smile. "So, team, are we still on for the club tonight?"

"Hell yes," Melissa replies, sending Sean a glare. "Don't even think of bailing out."

"Can't wait," Sean mutters, maintaining his focus on his phone game.

"Melissa, you can't force him to go out. Maybe he's not up for it."

"He's up for it. He just doesn't want to admit it right now. Besides, we are going to have the best time. You'll see."

CHAPTER THREE

THE BEACH AT DAWN

"We're here, miss."

The Lyft driver's voice jolts me from my nap. I fell asleep? In a stranger's car? Bad idea #5918, and that's only since the start of last night.

"You sure you don't want me to take you home? You seem pretty tired." The driver is an older gentleman, and I can feel his fatherly concern wash over me. Sadly, it's one of the most comforting feelings I've had in months.

I smile and shake my head, grateful that he's a kind-hearted soul and not southern California's latest serial killer. "I want to watch the sunrise. I need some peace and quiet after the night I had."

"I guess you weren't enjoying yourself?"

"That's an understatement. I'm too old for this crap," I grin as I exit the vehicle.

"Aren't we all." With a wave, he drives off, and I head in the direction of the waves. This is a more desolate area of the beach, but I see hints of the sun rising above the horizon. Peace and quiet. Thank God.

I glance around for an open coffee shop but soon realize I'm in the wicked in between—those hours when nothing is open, and I might be the only one awake. "Fuck," I mutter, rolling my shoulders and trying to loosen the array of kinks that have taken up residence there.

My new friend Melissa is a wonderful person. Lovely in every sense of the word. She is also a liar. I did *not* have fun at the club last night. Neither did Sean, but he stole the 'I have a headache' excuse before I had a chance to use it. He was home and snoring by midnight.

I, on the other hand, was subjugated to a club full of beautiful people, all sweating and grinding against each other as their drinks splashed like liquid confetti.

I'm not trying to sound ungrateful. I wanted to hit up the club scene—it was yet another experience I hadn't gotten around to in between school and work—and this club was gorgeous. But the shiny newness of the night wore off within an hour, with my skin sticky from spilled alcohol, my feet throbbing from four-inch stilettos, and my ass groped more times than a porno flick.

Melissa may be happily betrothed, but she adores the bright lights and thumping bass. It's her outlet as a married person. For a single person, it's the best place to meet a local shag. Ever since one drunken evening saw me confessing the entire history of my relationship with Clint, Melissa is on a mission to get me laid properly.

"Ahh." I release an audible sigh of relief when I pull off my torture devices, also known as shoes, and wiggle my toes into the sand. It's nice and cool this early before the sun has an opportunity to heat it up.

I traipse toward the water, damn near falling multiple times in my over-exhausted, too many fruity cocktails state. I really want some coffee. Or water. Or my bed.

With another sigh, I plop onto the sand, feeling my body meld into the moving piece of mother nature's art. As I gaze out to the ocean, I see a few people surfing the larger waves. One, in particular, catches my attention. There's a fluidity to his movement as if the line of demarcation between him, the board and the sea cease to exist. He remains standing along the crest of one particular wave, while his buddies crash into the surf. Even from this distance, I can see the lean muscles underneath the wetsuit, the neatly trimmed beard, and long hair. The man looks as good as he moves. What a deadly combination.

I spend the next several minutes staring at the man, enthralled with his movements, before digging out my phone as it buzzes. Melissa is ensuring I arrived home safely. I opt not to tell her that I took an early morning detour, as the maternal side of her just might come to fetch me.

Tucking the phone away, I close my eyes and focus on my breath. I suck at meditation. I'm good for about ten seconds before my brain comes knocking with a thousand and one questions. But at the beach, my mind is usually quiet, lulled by the crashing of the waves.

This time, though, my brain is not content to sit idle. My thoughts start swirling around my sudden move, my failed relationship, and the state of my life—all set to the thumping of an EDM beat.

"That's quite the internal monologue playing in your head."

"What?" My reverie from hell broken, I swing my head to the right, catching the gaze of the delicious surfer I was ogling not five minutes earlier.

"It looks like you're contemplating a life-changing decision."

"Splitting the atom, actually."

He smiles, and my breath catches. He's the kind of good-looking that makes women forget their own names. The kind that can remove a woman's panties with the snap of his fingers. "Would you like some coffee?"

"That was quite the conversation leap."

"I'm not usually so forward, but you look like you could use some."

My minor high from flirting with Mr. Universe crashes back into reality. I likely do look worse for wear after a night on the town. Knowing my luck, I've got eyeliner smeared down my face and lipstick covering half my chin. "It was a late night."

"Night ended hours ago. You made it to morning, sweetheart."

"Go big or go home," I mutter, feeling the last vestiges of my self-confidence dive at his pointed accusation.

"Come on, everything looks better after coffee."

I run my hand over my hair, in a futile attempt to smooth it down. I can feel his gaze on me, and it's intense, to say the least. Knowing that I likely resemble roadkill, I keep my eyes locked on the ocean. "You sound like a nurse."

"No, just your standard California surfer. I take it that you're a nurse?"

I nod, uncertain how much information I should be giving this stranger. This-melt-in-your-mouth, delectable stranger. "I work in emergency at Memorial. I just moved here from New York."

"Big move."

"Big decision."

"You need to stop talking so much. You and your long-winded answers."

I giggle. The man is nothing if not direct. "Considering you know more about me in five minutes than most people do in a year, I think I'm saying plenty. Besides, my life is not that interesting."

"I think you're fascinating so far."

His words are muted on the breeze, but I swear the man just called me fascinating. And it wasn't dripping with sarcasm, either.

Addy, the man looks like a Calvin Klein cover model. You look like a suicidal aardvark. No chance—in hell or any other location.

Willing up my last morsel of courage, I pivot in his direction, meeting his gaze at last. If I thought he was gorgeous in profile, the man is even more so head on. He's definitely younger than me, by at least five or six years, and in prime condition.

I extend my hand in greeting. I figure if I'm subjecting the poor man to my life story, he might as well know who to send the therapy bill to later. "I'm Adelaide, but everyone calls me Addy."

His grasp is warm and calloused from hours in the surf. But it's how his fingers slide around my hand, enveloping me, which makes my body flush with heat. "It's a pleasure. You're my first Adelaide."

"Popping your cherry, huh?" For some reason, despite his awe-inspiring looks, the man is ridiculously easy to talk to.

Another grin splits his face, but this one is accompanied by a deep laugh bubbling up from his chest. Holy shit, this man is sex on a stick. "That you did. It's a pleasure to meet you, Adelaide. I'm Josh."

I return the smile and try to pull my hand from his grasp. But my new surf buddy has other ideas as he pulls me to a standing position, almost knocking my halfway inebriated ass back into the sand.

"Whoa, easy there, killer." He steadies me, those warm digits stroking along my upper arms. "I don't want to break you before breakfast."

I know his statement is innocent, but the sexual connotation sticks in my craw anyway, making me flush. "Are we having breakfast now?"

"It's been known to happen at this hour."

He's still touching me, even though my feet are now firmly planted in the sand. "We don't know each other."

"Sure, we do. I'm Josh, and you're Addy." He points at a small cottage on the beach. "You see the yellow house? That's where I live. Your coffee is right there."

I nod, biting my lower lip nervously. First falling asleep in the cab, now considering breakfast in the house of a stranger. I must be losing my ever-loving mind.

He picks up on my energy, giving my hand a squeeze. "You don't have to come inside. We can sit on the patio. Or, I can go make us coffee and bring it back here."

I raise my chin, meeting that azure blue gaze. "I've never seen eyes that color before." What the hell am I thinking? Why would I make such a personal and sexually laden observation? Ugh, I suck.

"I got them from my Mom. She always said they matched the sea."

"They do."

"Come have coffee with me, Addy. I have breakfast food, too. All able to be carried onto the patio."

"Do you serve coffee to all the stragglers you find wandering the beach?" Then it hits me. Perhaps I look so pitiful he feels obligated to be friendly, similar to how we approach a wounded animal.

"Not hardly, but I like talking to you. Simple as that."

Funny thing is, nothing in my life has ever been that simple. But Josh's reasoning holds merit, so I follow him back to the beach cottage, noting he moves as effortlessly on the sand as in the water. Even while lugging a board that's taller than him.

Once inside, I make a beeline for the bathroom. Time to assess the damage. To my surprise, I don't look half bad. My lipstick is long gone, and my eyes are a bit puffy, but overall, not bad for thirty-nine. I splash some water on my face and finger comb my hair, pulling it into a braid before returning to the kitchen.

I stop dead in my tracks. In the thirty seconds I've been gone, Josh has removed his wetsuit, leaving only a pair of skin-tight shorts wrapped around his lean frame. He glances up when the floor creaks, offering up that signature smile again. "Your coffee is ready, my lady. I'm going to jump in the shower, rinse off the salt. Make yourself at home. I'll be done in a few."

My eyes trail him as he strolls down the hall and into what is presumably the bathroom. I didn't mean to look at his package—I swear, I didn't—but it was right there. The shorts leave nothing to the imagination, and all I can say is Clint's an underachiever in at least one area.

I bet I'd have no issue with orgasms from Josh.

I giggle under my breath at my internal monologue. With Clint, I rarely thought about sex—it was more a perfunctory act—but with Josh, all manner of sexual ideas flood my brain.

Brushing off my lascivious fantasies, I sip down my first steaming mouthful of the divine nectar. Holy hell, but that is beyond delicious. I stroll the small living area, stopping to examine the myriad of photos littering his table. There are several of Josh surfing, group shots with other surfers and beach bunnies, and a few that must be professional modeling shots. All are enticing, but one jumps out at me, demanding my attention.

"Eyes the color of the sea," I whisper, lifting the photo for a closer look. The picture is of Josh as a teenager, sitting next to an ethereal blonde woman with matching eyes. There is such a connection between the two, it emanates from the photo. I guess it's true what they say. Pictures are worth a thousand words.

"That's my Mom and me," Josh remarks over my shoulder, his breath tickling my hair.

I turn, noting his proximity. As a New Yorker, I'm used to

limited personal space, but in intimate situations, I prefer to maintain a three-foot distance. One that Josh has invaded and one that I'm seriously okay with. "She's exquisite. You two are really close, aren't you?"

I'm struggling to come up with normal conversation when he's standing this close. My mind blanks, and all I know is he smells fantastic. I'm sure it's just soap mixed with him, but the combination is intoxicating.

"We were, yes. She died several years ago."

My practiced response is to apologize for the loss. Standard, right? But nothing with Josh is standard. "You, too?" I look down as soon as I blurt out the words.

So much for possessing any tact, Addy.

"You lost your Mom?"

"My Dad. I was as close to him as you were with your Mom."

"Daddy's little girl, huh?"

"Absolutely. Still am."

"I'm lucky that I still have my father. Even though losing my mother broke my heart, it shattered my dad's soul. He's never fully recovered."

"He lost the love of his life. At least, that what it sounds like."

"That he did." Josh takes the photo from my hands, a small smile playing on his mouth. It's the same expression his mother is wearing, and I can't help but wonder in what other ways they're similar. "Your mother lives in New York?"

Oh, joy. The topic of my mother. "Manhattan."

"She must have hated you moving so far away."

I have a choice. I can lie and agree with Josh, ending the conversation. Or I can admit the nature of my relationship with Claire. My screwed-up, demented relationship.

With a sigh, I opt for the second choice. "We aren't close."

Those turquoise orbs focus on me, and I swear he's reading my thoughts. "And you put on a brave face and act like it doesn't bother you."

"It doesn't."

"Your body language says otherwise."

Well, that was unexpected. I consider myself a master of hiding my emotions, something I learned from watching my mother. If you wear the mask long enough, you forget what you look like underneath. "It's funny. We look exactly alike, but personality-wise, we are polar opposites. Couldn't be more different if we tried."

"She must be a very beautiful woman, then."

My heart thuds against my chest. Did he intimate I'm beautiful, as I stand here covered in dried alcohol and teetering in ill-fitting heels? "I...I...I don't know how to answer that without sounding conceited."

My breath catches when Josh pushes a strand of hair behind my ears. It's innocent but so very intimate. And I suck at intimacy. "You said she looks like you, right?"

I nod, unsure if the lightheadedness is due to his touch or the rush of caffeine.

"Then she's very beautiful."

My jaw drops as I fumble for a response. Finally, I manage to mutter, "thank you."

"How's the coffee?"

Thankful for the topic change, I take another mouthful of the liquid gold. "It's the most delicious beverage I've ever had. What kind of coffee is it?"

Josh laughs, going to the kitchen to retrieve his own mug. "I can't tell you that."

"Why? Is it a family secret?"

"No, but if I tell you then you can buy it."

"Right...kind of the idea."

"If I don't tell you, then you have to come back here to get more." He winks at me over the mug, nodding in the direction of the patio. "Let's go sit."

"You've been wonderful, but I really need to get home and sleep. I'm going to call a Lyft driver." Maybe I'll get lucky, and the same guy will pick me up. He'll be glad to know I'm still in one piece.

"No need. I'll take you home."

"I can't ask you to do that."

"You didn't, Addy. I offered. Let's finish our coffee, and then I'll drop you off. Deal?"

I think I'd agree to set myself on fire if this man asked me. "Deal."

* * *

An hour later, good to his word, he pulls up outside my apartment.

"This is a nice area, Addy."

"I like your cottage better."

Josh turns partway in his seat, leaning back against the door and offering up a smile that upends my equilibrium. "You can't beat the location. So, what are your plans for the rest of the day?"

I stretch in the seat as the effects of the coffee begin to wear off. "Sleep. Well, a shower and then sleep. More like passing out for the next several hours. I have to work tonight."

"Ah, the dreaded overnight shift."

"Yeah. It's fine, though. I work with a terrific bunch of people." I'm not sure what to do now. I'm stalling, but I get the impression he isn't in a rush to kick me out of the vehicle. I wish I possessed some level of moxie to ask for his number, but I don't think he and I run in the same social circles. "What are you doing for the rest of the day?"

"I'm headed up the coast with a few buddies."

"Looking for bombs?" I inquire, using the surfing term I learned from Sean.

Josh laughs, ruffling my hair. "Are you a surfer?"

I return the giggle. "No. Sadly, that's the only term I know."

His hand slides along my hair, his fingertips brushing my neck, and another wave of sparks rush through my body. "We'll have to change that, Addy. Surfing is an institution out here."

"I'm not that brave. Or graceful. It wouldn't be pretty." Trying to maintain a regular breathing pattern is damn near impossible with his hands anywhere near my body. With any part of him anywhere near me. What is wrong with me? I've regressed to a bumbling high school student.

"I beg to differ." His mobile rings, breaking into the moment. He glances at the number and shakes his head, his damp blonde hair curling around his shoulders. "My friends are wondering where the hell I am."

I grab the door handle. That's my cue. "I won't keep you then. Thanks for everything, Josh." I jump out of the vehicle with the speed of a gazelle, somehow managing to remain upright on my torture devices.

"You don't have to run off."

I lean in the open window, reaching out my hand. "You have friends waiting. I have a shower calling me. The coffee was delicious. It was a pleasure meeting you."

His hand envelops mine, and the sparks turn into a fan of flames. I can't seem to control my hormonal urges in his presence. "I'd like to see you again, Addy."

"You would?"

"Don't look so surprised. I slipped my number into your bag. I really hope you use it."

I'm tempted to climb through the window and straddle him. That mouth of his is begging to be kissed, and I'm a more than willing participant. But my social training kicks in, mentally reminding me of my place. "Be careful today, Josh."

I stand up from the car and head up the walk to my apartment. After a few steps, I stop to remove the stilettos from my feet. My body demands comfort now. I glance back and notice that Josh's pup truck is still idling, his gaze zeroed in on me.

"You're still here," I mumble as a flush rushes across my cheeks. Great, did I just show off my ass on top of everything else?

"I'm making sure you get inside safely since you won't let me walk you up." His smile widens. "That was one hell of a view, though."

"Oh, crap. You didn't see anything, did you?"

Now he's laughing. The bastard. The sweet, hot-as-hell bastard. "Like I said, it was one hell of a view."

Normally, I would find offense with his blatant statement, but I don't detect a hint of malice in his tone. With a smile and shrug, I toss my shoes over my shoulder, holding them by the strap. "Glad I could provide some form of payment for the coffee."

I know he's watching me as I walk the rest of the way to my apartment, and I can't help but throw a tiny extra hip shake in for kicks.

Who knew being hungover on the beach could be so much damn fun?

CHAPTER FOUR

YOU'RE ADDY?

*E*veryone thinks nurses love quiet shifts. That is a crap concept. First, we never utter the dreaded "q" word because no sooner has it left someone's mouth, then all hell breaks loose. Second, a slow night means the time drags, and although friendly banter is fun, it's tiresome after twelve and a half hours.

Tonight was perfect. Busy enough to keep the hands moving on the clock, but not so insane that I don't have time to pee the entire shift.

"Hey, Addy, admit in Bay 5." Melissa hands me the chart, and I look it over with a glance before heading for the suture cart. A man suffered impact injuries while reef surfing. Fairly standard in this area.

Of course, mention of the word surfing brings up memories of Josh, not that he's been far from my thoughts the last few days. In fact, his number is burning a hole in my purse, not that I've had the guts to call it.

I wonder if he's thought at all about me since our chance encounter on the beach.

He probably doesn't even remember me, I chide myself as I reach for the bay curtain. A hand closes over mine, and I jump, whipping around.

Speak of the devil.

You know when you meet someone and think they're attractive, but the next time you see them, you realize your beer goggles weren't properly focused? Seeing Josh again is the complete opposite. He's even more gorgeous than before, his long hair pulled back, showcasing that oh-so-kissable mouth, his beard neatly trimmed to highlight his square jaw, those turquoise waters that he calls eyes. He's delectable, and I haven't even moved south of his neck.

Then he smiles, and I lose the last vestiges of my cool factor. "Addy." It's only two syllables, but it's the way he says my name, along with the grin that lights up his face, that slays me.

"Hi. You don't look like an injured surfer."

"My friend, Frank. How are you?" He shoves his hands into the pockets of his low-slung jeans, drawing my attention to the ever-present bulge down south.

"Better. Sober." I laugh, but it feels forced. I'm not sure what to say, how to act. Any chance at decorum flies out the window when our eyes meet.

"You look fantastic. I like you without makeup."

Oh, wonderful. He noticed. Why didn't I bother to throw on some eyeliner and lipstick tonight? "Ah, but makeup hides a myriad of sins."

"Only if you have them." His hand reaches up, and I know what he's going to do. It seems to be his trademark move where I'm concerned—tucking my hair behind my ear and setting my body to tingling at the same time. But a doctor walks past, interrupting the moment, and his hand falls back to his side.

"Let me go check on your friend. It won't take long. Do you want to have a seat in the waiting room?"

Josh nods, a small smile flitting across his lips. "I want to know why you haven't called me."

There's that directness again. "I didn't think you were serious."

"Addy, I gave you my number because I want you to call it." He crosses his arms, sending me a fake glare. "But you failed miserably in that endeavor, so now you have to give me yours."

"You want my number?"

"You have no idea how much."

Grabbing his hand, I scribble my number onto his palm. "I guess it's on you now."

That smile. God in heaven, that sultry smile, and those lips. He's got the fullest lips I've ever seen on a man. "Challenge accepted. I'll be in the waiting room. Don't let Frank give you any shit."

"I'm from New York, remember? I'm the queen of handling shit." With a wave, I watch him stroll through the double doors.

"Who was that delicious hunk of burning love?" I should have known Melissa and her eagle eye would notice me speaking to Josh. "Please tell me you're shagging that gorgeous man."

"I am so sorry to disappoint you, my friend."

"You'd better get on that. And quick. A man who looks like that has his pick of women."

Her words reopen an old wound. People say the same thing about Clint. What a catch. How lucky I am to be dating a hot, eligible doctor. I'm sure they mean well, but all it does is stoke the fires of my inadequacies. "We're just friends."

Melissa sends me a withering stare. "Right. Because I look at all my friends like that."

"How was I looking at him?"

"Like you want to eat him with a spoon."

I wave my hand at her, shooing her from the curtain. "Go away. I'm busy. Don't you have something to do?"

Melissa laughs, giving my shoulders a squeeze. "Maybe I'll go chat up your friend, learn more about him."

My eyes widen in horror. She's kidding. I think. "Don't you dare."

"No promises."

I pray my glare is enough to deter her, but I doubt it. With a sigh, I open the curtain, coming face to face with Josh's injured surf buddy.

"Hi there, Frank. I hear you and the reef had a bit of a disagreement."

Apparently, all surfers are hot as hell. This man is no exception, but his good looks pale when compared to Josh.

"One could say that. Unfortunately, I didn't get the last laugh."

"There's always next time." I pull on gloves to inspect his injured paw. "Some of this will have to be cleaned and bandaged; it's too jagged to suture."

"How do you know Josh?"

I jerk my head up, surprised by his blunt question. I didn't realize he'd heard us conversing. Granted, curtains provide little privacy. Blushing, I resume my examination of the rest of his body. "I met him on the beach a few mornings ago."

"You're a surfer?"

A laugh escapes my lips. "Definitely not. I can't walk and chew gum."

"So, what were you doing at the beach?"

God, he asks pointed questions. It's as if no one can set foot on the sand if they don't surf. Maybe it's some unwritten credo in San Diego. "I was walking off a night in the club."

His gaze narrows as he reads my name badge. "Shit. You're Addy?"

His question surprises me, since my badge only has my full name listed. "How did you know that?"

Frank laughs, but it's less amusement and more sarcasm. "Interesting."

"What's so interesting? My name?" I don't like the way he's looking at me. His narrowed gaze trails up and down my body, making my insides clench. And not in a good way.

"Josh has been rattling on about this woman he met the other day. Said her name was Addy."

My face flames at Frank's statement. "Likely a different Addy."

I know my statement is crap, and so does Frank. "I doubt it. How many women named Addy do you know?"

"I was pretty pitiful the other morning. He probably had a good chuckle at my sorry state." I'm not sure where this conversation train is heading, but I'd like to disembark. Now.

Frank, however, is more than happy to keep the train moving. "You and I both know that's bullshit." His eyes narrow as he squints in my direction. "Robbing the cradle, huh?"

His question rams into me like a fist. I should have expected it. I knew Josh was younger, I just didn't realize I looked *that* much older.

Brave face, Addy. Slide that mask on.

"What the hell is that supposed to mean?"

He holds up his uninjured hand in mock surrender, and I'm tempted to mangle it like the other one. "Don't get me wrong. You're hot as hell. But isn't Josh a bit young for you?"

I roll my shoulders and remove my gloves with a scoff. "While I appreciate your observation, Frank, my dealings with your friend are none of your business."

"I hit a nerve."

Now it's my turn to scowl. "You meant to. The doctor will be in shortly. Can I get you anything while you wait?"

I don't know why I expect an apology—half-hearted or no—but Frank isn't offering one. "Can you send Josh back in?"

I bite my lip so hard that I'm shocked blood isn't pouring from my mouth. "Of course."

I storm out of the bay, making a beeline for the break room. I pace the floor of the renovated closet, trying to find my center before I explode in front of some hapless patient.

"What happened?" Melissa pokes her head in the door, her face questioning.

"Don't fucking ask," I hiss. I keep my tone low enough that the patients don't hear, but loud enough that she catches my drift.

"Whoa, what in the world?" Melissa closes the door and grabs my shoulders, ending my ceaseless pacing. "What crawled up your ass and died?"

"You know the guy I was talking to before? Well, his friend reminded me in not so subtle a fashion, how much older I am."

Melissa smiles, pulling me into a hug. "So? Who cares?"

I push back, my mouth agape. "Who cares? I care. He claimed I was robbing the cradle."

"He's an asshole. But this came from hot guy's friend and not from hot guy, right?"

I laugh at Melissa's nickname for Josh. "His name is Josh."

"Hot guy works equally well. Did Josh say that you were too old?"

"No. He wasn't there. His friend went off when he discovered I was the woman Josh met the other morning."

Melissa shrugs as she tries to hold back a grin. "Why should he care? More importantly, why should you?"

"I don't want to be a cradle robber! I knew Josh was younger, but apparently, he's young enough to be my grandchild."

"Not hardly, Addy. Ignore what his friend said." Her expression changes as she watches me. "I thought you hadn't slept with him."

"I haven't. I've had coffee with him. That's it."

"So my original argument stands. His friend is an asshole."

I pull at my braid, my emotions a rollercoaster. "But it was the way he intimated that I was doing something wrong by even talking to Josh."

"Stop caring what other people think."

"Sure, I'll undo thirty-nine years of training." I bury my face in my hands with a groan. "Can you get Josh from the waiting room? I don't want to see him again."

"What did Josh do, besides being hot as hell and making you coffee?"

How can I explain this mounting feeling of embarrassment and inadequacy brewing in my core? How do I admit that Frank is right, and I'm probably way too old for Josh? "I just don't want to see him. Can you please help me?"

Melissa chews her lip, sighing in resignation. "You're acting like an idiot. But I'll go get him. Where will you be hiding, in case I need you?"

I send her a withering glare. "I won't be hiding. Just... otherwise engaged."

"Girl, you sure like making your life harder than it has to be. Get a cup of coffee and take a break. I'll watch your patients."

I'm not sure why people drink coffee during times of crisis. It doesn't instill emotional calm. But after fifteen minutes, I'm feeling ready to face the world...and avoid Josh and his asshole friend.

I glance at the board and notice that Melissa has changed my assignment. God bless the woman. Then I make a decision. I grab my bag and pull out Josh's number, tearing it into tiny pieces. It's for the best. Really, it is. That's my story, and I'm sticking to it.

I grab my workstation and wheel it to the appropriate bay. Time to get my head in the game.

"Hey."

I jump, finding myself less than a foot from the man I'm trying desperately to avoid. So much for the easy route. "Oh, hi." My only remaining card is to downplay the entire situation, putting everything—my age, especially—into glaring perspective. "Is there something I can help you with?"

"I didn't see you when I got back. I wanted to make certain you were okay."

Christ, did his friend mention our discussion? Correction, his pointed accusation? My pale skin flames at the thought. "I'm fine. The patient assignments were changed, so I won't be caring for your friend."

I hope that's enough to end the conversation.

It's not.

Josh releases a lengthy sigh. "Did Frank say something?"

His astute observation catches me off guard. Time to downplay the entire scenario. "Only about his hand." I return my gaze to my workstation, but Josh isn't taking the hint. "You're making me nervous, Josh."

His eyes widen. "Why?"

"You have an intense stare."

"You mean the one you're avoiding?"

I shrug because I'm not sure what to say at this point.

"I didn't mean to make you uncomfortable, Addy. I just love looking at you."

His words are so honest, his tone so genuine that any wall between us falls away.

He didn't do anything, Addy. There's not a reason in hell the two of you can't be friends.

"You've never seen a nurse in action before?"

"I haven't seen you in action before." The double entendre hangs between us, confusing my jumbled brain further.

"If you or your friend need anything, I'll let your nurse know." I figure that my reserved tone and stance will keep a safe distance between us.

But instead of moving away, Josh edges closer. "Do you always do that?"

"Care for patients? It kind of comes with the territory."

"Deflect when you think someone's getting too close." This time, there's no one to interrupt as his hand strokes against my hair, tucking a stubborn strand behind my ear. "Too intimate."

"I'm not deflecting. I'm just busy."

His hand remains against my skin, and I'm trying desperately not to read into his intentions, especially after Frank's pep talk. "Why don't you come over after your shift?"

My eyes widen at his offer. "Why?"

Josh smiles and bites his lower lip, and my mind immediately heads to naughty territory. "I've missed you."

I could ask how that's possible, but the truth is that I've missed him, too. "I don't have anything but my scrubs."

"I'll lend you some clothes. I stocked up on that coffee you love. Just in case."

"I'm pretty tired. I worked all night."

"I've spent most of the night here with you, so I understand being tired." He quirks his lips. Those gorgeous lips I want all over my body. "We could sleep first and then have coffee when we wake up. Are you working tonight?"

I shake my head, mesmerized by the magnetism of this man. "I'm off the next four days."

Josh glances around the unit before grasping my fingers. Holy hell, but even this simple touch feels incredible. "Come over. Just stay. I can show you all sorts of things. We'll have an amazing time together."

I stare into this man's gorgeous face and realize—I want to. I really want to partake in a sleepover at his place for the next few days and get to know his every intimate detail.

"Hey there," Melissa remarks as she enters the conversation. "Sorry to intrude, but I'm headed out."

I nod at my friend, who is way more interested in the blonde sea god next to me. "Get home safe."

Melissa extends her hand in Josh's direction. I knew she wouldn't let me off that easy. "We weren't officially introduced before. I'm Melissa."

"Josh." There goes that smile again. I swear it lights up the damn room.

"How do you know, Addy?"

"He's friends with one of the patients," I mumble, hoping the answer will suffice.

It doesn't.

Josh shoots me a strange look before turning his attention back to Melissa. "I met her the other morning on the beach. We shared a cup of coffee."

My eyes plead with Melissa to let the topic drop, but it goes unheard. "You're *that* guy!"

Now the smile returns in full force while I'm looking for a linen bin to jump into. "I'm that guy. It's nice to know Addy mentioned me."

"She did more than that."

I'm going to kill her. I may be a foot shorter than Melissa, but it won't stop me from murdering the woman.

Melissa laughs at my glare. "I'm leaving. It was nice meeting you, Josh." Her gaze turns to me. "I'll see you tonight."

"Tonight?" What is she talking about?

"The club? I bought us VIP tickets."

I close my eyes and let out a small groan. "Oh crap, that's tonight. Okay, I'll see you then."

"Feel free to join us, Josh."

"I'm sure he's busy, Melissa," I grit through my teeth.

Thankfully, Josh picks up on my distress. "I'm actually not a big fan of clubs. But thank you for the invitation."

"Anytime." My friend shoots me a 'we are discussing this man in more detail later' stare before turning and walking out the door.

"Sorry about Melissa. I didn't say anything about you. Nothing bad, anyway. I—"

"Addy, I like that you mentioned me. When you didn't call, I figured you weren't interested in another coffee date."

The light above one of the bays illuminates. "I have to get that."

"Okay. I was really hoping you didn't have plans tonight. Or you had ones that you could cancel."

If he only knew how much I want to cancel them. I reach over and give his arm a squeeze. "I'm really sorry. It slipped my mind."

His face falls, but he nods, forcing a smile. "Be careful tonight, okay? Call me if you need me."

"That's really sweet. Thank you."

The curtain to Frank's bay opens, and he nods to Josh. "That's my cue. Remember, call me for anything."

I nod, noticing Frank's annoyed expression as he glowers in our direction. True to my New York roots, I glower back. "It sounded amazing, spending time with you." The words slip out before my mind can reel them back, and once again, my pale skin turns the shade of a blood orange.

His lips move near my ear, apparently not caring who might see at this point. "It's an open invitation, Addy. Just say the word."

Josh steps back, turning in Frank's direction, and for the first time, I'm grateful for the distance. I was close to melting into a hormonal puddle. "Goodbye, Josh."

"Goodnight, Addy. I'll see you soon."

As he leaves the hospital, I can't help but hope that he's right, no matter what his friend thinks. I return to my patients, pausing only to snatch my phone from my scrub pocket when it buzzes.

I don't recognize the number, but I know who it belongs to.

I know it was in the emergency room, but I'm so glad I saw you tonight. Be safe, Addy.

CHAPTER FIVE

NEVER SAY NEVER TO DRUNK TEXTING

"*D*o you honestly need a pros and cons list?" Melissa swigs back the shot, slamming the glass on the table with a triumphant flourish.

The VIP section is tiny, but at least it's less packed than the rest of the club, which resembles a tin of sardines if the sardines were still alive. Not a pleasant visual either way.

"Why would I need a list? Clint and I are over, and I'll never see Josh again."

Melissa and Sean shake their head in unison at my statement. So glad they disagree.

"You need to get shagged properly. That man, that hunk of surfing love, would be perfect for your first real shag." Melissa's voice increases in decibels with every word.

"You make me sound like a virgin," I counter back, sipping down my alcohol-filled coconut.

"You are," she replies. "An orgasm virgin."

"Melissa!" I hiss, my gaze moving to Sean. "Can we not dredge up every dirty piece of my history?"

"Doesn't sound like much of it was dirty," Sean teases, chuckling at my vexed glare.

"I know Clint is an asshole for what he did, but we did date for *four* years. That's a long time."

"To be miserable," Melissa adds, downing another shot.

"I suppose you're right, but the singles scene sucks." I'm not kidding. I've only been a part of it for a few weeks, and I despise it. "I can call Clint, at least see how he's doing."

Melissa is shaking her head so hard I fear it might fly off her neck. "Clint is a misogynistic pig who's more interested in your mother's bank account than you."

"Who also failed to ever give you an orgasm." Sean is so helpful.

"I don't know. Maybe he did?"

Melissa sputters her drink. "Honey, if you don't know, he never did. Trust me."

"I'm like the forty-year-old virgin. All I need is a collection of action figures."

"What you need is to get laid, and I nominate Josh."

"Why is Josh such a good idea?" I counter, although I can't disagree with her observation. Sex with that man is likely an orgasmic volcano.

"You come closer to orgasming when Josh is within ten feet of you than you ever did when Clint was inside you."

Thanks for that accurate—and mortifying—description, Melissa.

There go my cheeks again. "I do not."

Okay, that statement is not entirely true. Proximity to Josh does do all manner of naughty things to my nether regions.

"I've seen your face when you look at him." Melissa waves down the server, ordering another round. At this point, I've lost count of the number of drinks we've consumed. Is it five or fifty?

"I'm that obvious?" When both my friends nod in agreement, I hide my face in the safety of my hands. Maybe I can remain in this position indefinitely.

"Sorry, my friend, it's that obvious. But Addy, it's obvious on both ends. Josh is seriously hot for you, and personally, you're letting us all down by not shagging the hell out of him."

Sean shakes his head, hiding his laugh behind his hand. "I don't personally care if you sleep with him."

"Shush, you're not helping," Melissa downs another shot, and I'm amazed she's still making sense. Wait, is she making sense?

What the hell, it's all in good fun, right? It's not like Josh is going to show up and follow Melissa's advice.

"So," I inquire, sipping more of my drink down, "you consider having sex with Josh to be a public service? I'm doing it for the greater good? Taking one for the team?"

"Whatever you want to call it. I know what a difficult undertaking it would be for you, Addy."

I send Melissa a cheeky wink as I drain the last of my drink. Surprisingly, I feel fine. Nothing like overpriced, watered-down alcohol to make a girl feel sober. "Some might consider the task monumental, but he is a challenge I'll gladly get on top of—or under. Maybe both."

"Who are you getting under?"

I whirl in my seat, my mouth falling open. Josh is here, and I've no idea how much of the conversation he's heard.

Before I can voice my surprise, Melissa pats the chair next to her. "Hey there, glad you could make it. Have a seat."

My gaze moves between Melissa and Josh. Have I entered the twilight zone? How is he here? And why doesn't Melissa seem the least bit surprised?

"Would you like a drink?"

Josh shakes his head, his eyes focused on me. At least I look better than I did when I stumbled across him on the beach. I hope. Tugging at my skirt, I drink him in through lowered lashes. He certainly cleans up well. His long hair is pulled back, his button-down shirt exposes just a hint of taut, tanned muscle, and those jeans certainly showcase his assets.

The alcohol chooses that moment to start seeping into my system, and I let out a slow exhale. One that Josh notices, much to my dismay.

"Addy? Are you okay?"

I nod, my mouth dry as the Sahara. Grabbing my coconut, I take a futile pull on the straw. Empty. Where the hell is that next round, anyway?

"We were just talking about you, Josh," Melissa exclaims, giving Josh a friendly wink.

She didn't. Dear God, please don't do this to me. One look at my friend solidifies my fear. Alcohol loosens her lips, and I can only hope she keeps quiet on the specifics of our conversation.

"What were you saying?" Josh knows Melissa is drunk. It's obvious by the joking smirk on his features. But he's playing along, likely spurred on by morbid curiosity.

"How you and Addy should actually have sex because you eye fuck each other every time you're in the same room."

I hate my friend. Next time, I'm bringing duct tape to ensure her yap stays shut. With a groan, I cover my face. "You did not just say that."

From the safety of my hands, I hear Sean release a surprised guffaw. Apparently, Melissa's statement shocked the hell out of him, too.

"Anyway, Sean and I are off to dance. I bet you two have tons to discuss."

I grumble a reply, my gaze locked onto the tabletop.

"See you, Addy." Melissa leans in, giving my shoulders a squeeze. "You can thank me later for texting him."

Say what now?

My head flies up as their forms are swallowed by the crowd, right before catching Josh's amused smirk. With a strangled laugh, I wave a hand in my friend's direction. "Ignore her. She's drunk."

He nods, but the smirk stays firmly planted across those delicious lips. "So, you don't want to fuck me every which way since Sunday?"

My jaw drops, and I lack the wherewithal the close it. Did he actually say what I think he said? With a shake of my head, I pull one of my standard moves—I change the subject. "What are you doing here?"

"Should I leave?"

"I didn't mean it like that. I thought you hated the club scene."

"I do."

"You decided to give it another chance?"

"I wanted to see you." His fingers push a lock of hair behind my ear as tingles rush across my skin. This man is trouble, and not with a capital T. With *all* capital letters. "You look beautiful, Addy, but I still prefer the no-makeup look."

The server arrives, setting down a tray of drinks. I see Josh's eyes widen at the sheer number of beverages littering the table.

"These are not all mine." I grab a glass and take a long pull. Thank God, this bartender is a bit more heavy-handed. I need all the help I can get. "Help yourself. Melissa won't care."

I hand the server some cash, but she doesn't know I'm alive at this point. Her gaze is locked on Josh. And why not? The man is an entirely new level of beautiful. "I can you get you whatever you like, handsome. On the house."

I roll my eyes as she pushes her breasts together. Subtle.

"Just water, please." To his credit, his eyes stay focused on her face. Her lovely, young, sex kitten face. Why does every woman—but me—look like a damn Barbie doll out here? Is it something in the water?

"Are you sure? We have all variety of delicious beverages."

"Positive. Thank you." She leans across the table to fetch an imaginary straw, her body rubbing against Josh the entire time. I'm tempted to grab her by her extensions and yank her to the ground. I know the man isn't mine, and he's fair game but holy hell, I'm sitting right here.

Instead of inciting violence, I take another pull on my drink, feeling the warmth spread through my belly. I glare at her retreating form, secretly hoping she catches her stiletto in a pothole.

"You didn't answer the question."

My gaze swings back to Josh, my eyes narrowing. It's surprising, he didn't even turn his head to watch our server's illustrious exit. "You didn't answer yours, either. What are you doing here?"

Josh leans back in the seat, studying me. "You texted me, remember?"

My eyes widen as I grab for my purse. "I did what now?"

Josh pulls out his phone, showing me the screen. "Texted me. See?"

I close my eyes, wishing the floor would open up and swallow me whole. The text is innocuous enough—thank God—but it's also not one I composed. "Melissa texted you. That must have been why she borrowed my phone earlier."

Josh sits up, putting his elbows on the table. "She texted me for you? Why would she do that?"

Another swig of alcohol. At this rate, I might be able to finish off all the drinks by myself. Sucking in a deep breath, I lay it all out on the table. "Well, you are insanely good-looking, and your body is amazing, and Melissa thinks that I should sleep with you immediately."

Josh takes a moment to process my verbal onslaught, but at least he hasn't run away screaming. Yet. "Melissa has a lot of opinions."

I finish off my drink, having lost count as to how many I've consumed. "That she does."

He takes my glass and returns it to the table before scooching closer to me. I can't be sure if it's because of the club's noise level or because he's enjoying this amenable torture. "What do you think, Addy?"

I want to look away, but I'm tethered to that blue stare. "About?"

"Your friend's opinion...of you and me."

My mouth turns to soot as my body tingles from the inquiry. "I told you."

His fingers trace along my arm as the blood pounds in my ears. It's a million degrees in here. "No, you didn't."

The server returns, draping herself over Josh as she delivers his water. I swear, she must moonlight as a stripper with those moves. I see red, and I'm not the type to see red, but that woman touching him makes me want to break every bone in her body.

I can't sit here and watch this unfold.

"I—I need fresh air." And an escape route. The last drink hits me with the power of a jetliner, and I turn and stumble towards the exit. Any exit.

I squeeze through the crowd, tensing as countless sweaty bodies rub against me. Tonight was such a bad idea. Josh is right. The club scene sucks, and now, I'm another one of its nightly victims.

With a heave, I push open an exit-only door and suck in a lungful of air, before leaning against the cold brick. "Thank God,"

I murmur, my eyes closing while I focus on breathing. At least I won't have to watch that little tramp canoodling with Josh.

I hear the door creak open and heavy steps on the wooden deck approach me. "Jesus, are you okay? You scared the hell out of me, running off like that."

My eyes fly open to find Josh in front of me, not more than a foot away, concern creasing his brow. "Sorry. I needed air. Also, I didn't want to be a third wheel."

"What are you talking about?" His hand brushes my hair off my face, and I know I'm clammy, sweaty, and gross. Wonderful. Beach monster, part deux.

With a groan, I lean my head back against the wall. "What am I doing here, Josh?"

"Having fun?"

"I'm not, though. I'm thirty-nine years old. I bet you didn't know that. Hell, I'm almost forty. I'm too old for this shit."

His arm slides around my shoulder, easing me off the brick. "You want to get out of here?"

I turn away from him, stumbling a couple steps. At this rate, I'll be on the ground in no time. "How are you here? You had to have better plans tonight."

"You texted. Well, I thought you did. I thought...you might need me."

I pivot back in his direction. There's something so earnest about his words. Could he actually be for real? With a laugh, I move closer, tapping him on the chest with my finger and holding back a rising desire to fan out my hand and rub him all over his body. "You're like a knight in shining armor, you know that? Riding in to save me from a night of drunkenness and sin."

Josh's arm loops around me again, turning me in the direction of the exit. "I'm going to forget I heard that last part of your statement. But Addy, maybe you need a knight in shining armor."

CHAPTER SIX

BREAKFAST OF CHAMPIONS

I peel open my eyes to light streaming through the window. Funny, I always keep my blinds drawn. With a start, I sit up, ignoring the throbbing in my head.

Where the hell am I?

I spy a picture on the wall and repeatedly blink, trying to focus my vision. With a low groan, I fall back against the pillows. The photo is of Josh, which means only one thing. Unfortunately for me, the end of the night is a blur, but judging by the pounding in my brain, it wasn't pretty.

"You're awake."

I struggle back to a seated position, offering a rueful smile as Josh lounges in the doorway, clothed in only a pair of board shorts. "Hi there. This is your bed, isn't it?"

Josh nods, perching on the corner of the mattress. "You needed the bed more than I did last night."

I struggle to remember the end of the night, and then it hits me. Oh. My. God. I kissed Josh last night. The memory floods back in a painful, embarrassing rush. He brought me here, and I kissed him. But instead of kissing me back, he pushed me away.

Wow, that's a memory I'd have been happy never recalling. Time to get the hell out of here—and Josh's life—for good. Rubbing my face, I clear my throat while planning my exit strategy. Hopefully, he'll let escape with some shred of my dignity intact.

"I think we should talk about last night."

Or not.

"Why? Are you a therapist, too?"

But Josh isn't in the mood for jokes this morning. "I'm concerned, Addy."

God, that's even worse. Pity. Lovely. Rolling my shoulders, I summon my best hangover smile. "I'm not an alcoholic, believe it or not."

"Could have fooled me last night. You were slamming those drinks back."

I stare at the photo over his shoulder. It's of him on a surfboard at dawn, the pinks, and orange reflecting off the water and the planes of his face. He really is a striking man. "I guess I'm looking for something."

"At the bottom of a bottle? In a club with a ton of other lost souls? I don't know if that's the best place to look."

It's funny. Anyone else, I'd be furious. Who are they to judge me? But Josh's remarks are spoken without malice. How do I respond to a stranger who just hit the nail on the head about the status of my life?

"What are you looking for, Addy?"

I shrug and swing my legs out of bed. "My youth, I guess. I sometimes feel like I cheated myself. All those years in school and working. For what? I spent my twenties with my nose in a book and most of my thirties pulling down overtime shifts. I forgot to have fun. Maybe I never knew how in the first place."

"Did you have fun last night?" His sea-blue eyes search my face.

"I thought that's what fun was—drinking and dancing and being manhandled by sweaty guys." I rub my eyes and release a sigh. "I'm a mess."

"No, you're not. I just don't think you actually know who *you* are. You know who your mother told you to be, who your ex told you to be, who your friends told you to be. But you forgot to check in with you."

He stands suddenly, averting his eyes, and I realize I am wearing only a T-shirt and panties.

"Hmm, I don't recall getting changed last night." I shoot Josh a confused glance, and I swear his cheeks redden.

"You ruined your dress, so I gave you a shirt."

My eyes widen as I try to wipe the fuzz off my brain. Then I remember. Christ, I remember everything. I tripped over a guard rail and bloodied my knee. Pulling my leg forward, I verify the damage. "I'm so sorry, Josh. God, I'm sorry. I'm leaving now. I've wasted enough of your day."

Josh holds up his hands, slowing my roll. "Relax. I made breakfast." He hands me a pair of boxers, that same studious expression on his face. "You can wear these."

"Thanks. You didn't have to make me food, Josh."

"I don't mind, and I think you could use it. Go freshen up, and I'll meet you on the patio."

I stagger into the bathroom and make a futile attempt to look presentable. Oh, who the hell am I kidding? I kissed the man, and he pushed me away. It doesn't matter what level of hell I resemble at this point.

With a resigned sigh, I push open the bathroom door, my eyes darting around for my clothing. And shoes. And purse.

What in the world happened to all my stuff?

"Your clothes are in the wash."

Apparently, mind-reading is another of Josh's talents. "You're washing my clothes, too? Can I hire you to clean my house?"

He grins, and I wish it didn't upend me so much. I wish I was numb to him like I am most men. "I'm sure I can be convinced. For an additional fee, of course."

"Of course." I stand in the kitchen, clothed in an ill-fitting t-shirt and boxer shorts belonging to a man I drunkenly—and unsuccessfully—kissed last night. Oh, what a night. I'm not sure where to look, so I focus my gaze on the cabinets. What an exciting shade of...wood. God, I suck at appearing disinterested.

Josh steps between me and the row of cabinets, handing me a bowl. "Here. You might even consider it a *good* morning afterward."

I take the bowl from him, a tingle rushing up my arm when his fingertips graze mine.

Oh stop it, Addy, you're covered in day-old makeup and bar spunk, not to mention he's significantly younger. Significantly. And let's not forget how he had to fend off your unwanted advances last night.

Here I thought the server was brazen. She was tame compared to me. "What is this?"

"Açai bowl."

"A what?"

"It's a berry. The berry is mixed with banana and coconut, and there is granola and fresh berries on top."

"Is there a side of bacon hiding around here somewhere?" I'm not trying to sound ungrateful, but fruit is not going to cut this wallop of a headache.

Josh laughs, swallowing a spoonful. "I'm vegan."

"Of course you are. Let me guess, Buddhist, too, right?"

He waves his spoon at me, a smile crossing his face. "Right on the money."

I stare at the bowl in front of me. It's definitely pretty with all the colors and textures, even if my body is screaming for animal fat.

"It works better if you actually put it in your mouth."

"Thanks, smartass." With a smirk, I dig in. As soon as it hits my lips, I release a soft moan. "Oh, my God. This is delicious." And it's on like Donkey Kong. I shovel the contents into my mouth, scraping the bowl like a five-year-old holding cake batter.

Josh watches me with obvious amusement. "See? Not so bad."

"Mmm. I could eat that all day. Thank you."

"My pleasure. I'm heading out for a hike. Care to join me?"

A hike. I think I'd rather die. Actually, I likely am dying, considering how I feel. Never mind that I don't really want to spend *more* time with the man who doesn't want me touching him. "That's a really nice offer, but I think—"

Josh takes the bowl from my hands and sets it in the sink before pulling my clothes from the dryer. "Actually, I'm not asking."

"Huh?"

"I'll take you home, and you can change. The fresh air will do you good."

"My bed will do me good."

Without warning, he grabs my hands. "I'll make you a deal, Addy. Let me introduce you to *my* California. Let's put the club scene on hold and try things my way."

"Why would you do that?"

"I enjoy spending time with you."

"Oh, sure. Babysitting me, watching me stumble around—I'm a bundle of fun."

His hands squeeze mine as his stare drives his words home. "I enjoy spending time with you."

I can keep arguing how ridiculous it is that this gorgeous, younger man wants to spend his time with a thirty-nine-year-old woman who's suffering an apparent early midlife crisis. But I choose to remain silent. Arguing requires energy I don't have, and the faster I get home, the faster I can take some aspirin.

As if by magic, he hands me a glass of water and two white pills. "Here. I figure these, and the food will calm the banging in your brain."

"Are you a mind reader?" I ask, accepting his offering with a grateful smile.

"Not even close. I never know what you're thinking, Addy. It's all a shot in the dark."

I'm not sure if that's a lead-in for my drunken, clumsy pucker attempt, but I'll take it. "I'm really sorry about my behavior last night."

There's that striking turquoise gaze again. "Which part?"

"All of it. I'm not normally so badly behaved. I'm usually very well-mannered."

A grin breaks across Josh's face as he ruffles my hair. "You weren't ill-mannered. But I also think you're tiptoeing around it, instead of addressing it."

"I'd rather not talk about it, if at all possible," I mumble as my face, once again, flames with the memory.

One arm slides around my shoulder, the other grabbing his keys. "Fair enough. For now."

CHAPTER SEVEN

HOW OLD ARE YOU?

I step out of my shower, feeling at least half-human. One glance in the mirror, however, reminds me that I don't look it. With a sigh, I pull my hair into a messy bun and slather on some moisturizer and lip gloss. God, the morning after is never pretty.

I silently hope that Josh has changed his mind about hiking the Oregon Trail while I showered, and I would emerge to an empty apartment and a nice, fresh bed.

No such luck.

Josh's gaze tracks me as I wander back into the living room. It's incredible how he can appear laidback yet smolder all in the same moment. I sneak another glance in his direction, averting my eyes when they lock on his. Holy hell, but he's pretty.

"How old are you?"

A small chuckle escapes his lips. Those lush, full lips. "I wondered when you might ask that question."

I shrug, attempting to appear nonchalant and failing

miserably. "It's a valid question. I do remember telling you how I old was last night."

And I'm reasonably sure there are several years between us.

"You told me that, among other things."

I hate blackout drunks. Now, I understand why I never hung out at those college parties. You wake up feeling like death, looking far worse, with holes peppering your memory. Some people call it a good time. "I think I verbally vomited on you about Clint, as well. Am I close?"

"Yeah, you told me about the asshole." Josh sits up, adjusting himself. I know it's unintentional, an involuntary reflex, but holy hell, way to wake up my hormones.

"Is that what I called him?"

"No, it's what I call him." His jaw twitches under the neatly trimmed beard, and for a brief instant, I recall the feel of it against my face. The feeling of those full lips beneath mine.

"You want coffee?" I ask, holding up the coffee pot before pouring myself a mug. "You're avoiding the question, you know?"

His brow furrows. "What question?"

"Your age. I'm likely being silly, but you look so young in that light. Any light, really."

"I'm not that young."

I release a sigh. "Thank God. I worried you might be twenty-seven or something." With a giggle, I open a sugar packet.

"I'm not twenty-seven."

"Whew. Now I feel better." Apparently, he just looks really young. He takes care of himself, so it's not unlikely.

"I'm twenty-six."

What. The. Fuck.

The mug never makes it to my mouth as I grasp the counter, feeling the world skew sharply to the left.

"Addy, are you okay?"

I exhale slowly as I try to figure out my next move. Hide under the sofa? Move to Minnesota with no forwarding address? Instead, I practically jump through the ceiling when Josh's fingers brush across my back.

"Easy. It's just me. How are you feeling? You look a bit pale."

I manage to mumble, "I'm fine," all the while maintaining my staring contest with the counter.

His fingers stroke small circles along my spine. Why does he have to keep touching me? It feels way too good, and that is way too dangerous. "With that reaction, I *almost* believe you. Let's go sit down."

Josh leads me to the couch, and I sit like an obedient wooden soldier. My body is rigid, but my mind reels.

He's twenty-six.

Twenty-six.

Holy shit, I was a teenager when he was born. A freshman in high school. And I kissed him last night. Worst part? I loved every blurry moment of it, up until he pushed me away.

"Addy. Earth to Addy."

His hand waves in front of my face, and I slam back to the reality of my situation. I'm not sure why he's even still here, outside of some karmic debt he's paying off, obliging him to hang out with hungover middle-aged women.

Rubbing my hand across my brow, I release a shaky sigh. "Sorry. Just tired."

Josh leans forward, running his fingers along my cheek. "Liar." There's no anger in his word, solidified by the wink at the end.

"What am I lying about?"

"You're freaked out about my age."

"You're a lot younger."

"So?"

My eyes bug out of my head. "So? That's it? Just so?"

Josh shrugs and offers another grin. "I don't think it matters. I have friends of all ages."

There it is. I should feel relief, but instead, that sinking feeling hits me right in the gut. Josh is smooth, sliding in that friend comment to offer reassurance while simultaneously putting me in my place. Hell, at least now I know how he felt about the kiss. And why he stopped it.

"Right," I manage to eke out. "You're absolutely right."

I spring to my feet, feeling oddly at peace. Josh's reaction isn't a surprise. On some level, I expected it. He's too young, and we both know it. He likely looks at me like a mother figure. Ugh, that puts a whole new spin on the kiss. "I think I'm going to skip the hike, Josh. I'm really beat, and I don't bounce back the way I used to. You'll know when you're my age."

Many, many moons from now.

Josh remains silent, so I blunder forward. "I want to thank you for everything. You have gone above and beyond in the kindness department." Scampering to the table, I grab my purse, fishing into my wallet to pull out a fifty. "Here. It's the least I can do."

Josh stares at me and then the money but makes no move to take it. "Put your sneakers on, Addy."

"Excuse me?"

"You're not missing this hike."

"Josh, I'm tired."

"No, you're embarrassed because you suddenly think what happened last night shouldn't have happened because you're a few years older."

"A few? More than a few." I choke on a mixture of laughter and nausea. "Besides, it isn't like you actually enjoyed the kiss. You stopped it. That much, I clearly remember."

Instead of appearing sheepish, Josh surprises me by pulling me against him and wrapping his arms around my waist. "I don't think you remember much clearly from last night, and I don't give a shit if you're fifty years older."

"I'm not—"

"My point," he interrupts, his lips hovering at my ear, "is that I like you way too much to let something as insignificant as age come between us."

I pull back, confusion creasing my brow. "You like me as a friend?"

His thumb reaches out and traces my bottom lip, a smile pulling up the corners of his mouth. "Can you finish getting ready?"

My jaw slackens as I gape at him and his blatant disregard of my question. I open my mouth but bite back any additional questioning. Josh mentioned not five minutes ago that he has friends of all ages. Friends.

End. Of. Story.

"Do I have to?" Wonderful. Now I'm whining like a seven-year-old girl.

Josh shrugs, grabbing his keys from the table. "You can go willingly, or I can turn you over my knee. Your choice."

I'm obviously still drunk. And hearing things. "Are you threatening to spank me?"

Josh leans in, his lips centimeters from mine. "Not at all, Addy. It isn't a threat. It's a promise."

My new friend just threatened to spank me, and I hate how tempting that idea sounds. I shake my head, hoping to clear the cobwebs from too much alcohol and lack of sleep. You would think that in thirty-nine years, I'd have a firm grasp on human behavior, but if the last month is anything to go on, I'm a greenhorn.

With a grumble, I plop into the chair, throwing on my sneakers. "I don't really think I'm up for a spanking right now." If he's going to force me to trek with him up a mountain, I don't want him to think I'm drooling over him. No matter how little he believes me.

As per usual, the man—boy—is one step ahead of me in our verbal spar. "Too bad. Maybe later, you'll be in the mood."

He walks out the front door with a wink and shake of his keys, leaving me gaping after him.

Again.

What a friendship this is turning out to be.

CHAPTER EIGHT

A HIKE TO REMEMBER

I have to give it to him. Mission Trails Park is beautiful, and the fresh air is restoring my joie de vivre. That, and the company isn't half bad. Josh is a natural guide, far more at home in nature than any club.

He seems to take great pleasure in pointing out the various flora and fauna, and he knows the trails like the back of his hand.

"You come here often?"

Josh nods, his gaze focused on a distant point. "Not as often as I'd like. Surfing takes up most of my time."

I join him in drinking in nature, my breathing finally—*finally*—reaching a calm rhythm. "Tell me about that."

"I got on my first board when I was three."

"Three? Were you even out of diapers?"

Josh grins, offering me his water bottle. "Barely. I was a scared kid. Afraid of the dark and the bogeyman. But I never feared the ocean. The first time I sank my toes into the wet sand, I knew I'd found home."

"Twenty-three years of surfing. No wonder you're so good. Are you professional? Is that a thing in surfing?" I likely sound like an idiot on the subject, but let's be real. I am an idiot on the subject. One who is willing to learn, however.

"It's not that cut and dried. You have to surf all over, collecting points. Once you've finally amassed enough points—if you ever do —you're invited to the WCT, the World Championship Tour. But it requires a ton of money, dedication, and travel. You need a sponsor to help allay those costs."

"Is that what you want to do, join the tour?" It's hard to explain, but my heart hurts at the idea of him leaving to travel the globe. Selfish and silly, but present, nonetheless.

"I did. Sometimes I still do. But I love teaching. I help run the surf school, and we work with veterans. It's an amazing honor to watch those heroes come alive in the waves."

"I didn't know you were an instructor. I think that's an amazingly noble cause. I'll bet surfing is fun."

I feel his gaze on me. He's been getting more brazen with his stares in the last hour, and I can only hope I don't have a tree branch sticking out of my hair like a deranged Rudolph. "I could teach you, Addy. I'm pretty qualified."

I shake my head, offering up a small smile. "I adore the water, but I think I'll stick to swimming."

"We'll see about that."

The man always speaks his mind. With anyone else, I'd be aggravated, but with him, it's endearing. I release a small groan as I stretch, flipping my heavy braid over one shoulder and fanning myself. "It's beautiful, but it sure is hot."

"Here." Josh places his hand, wet from the water, against the back of my neck. I know he thinks he's cooling me down, but in truth, his touch has me all kinds of fired up. "Is it true what you said last night?"

"I said a lot of things, Josh. Care to be more specific?"

"You said you'd never had an orgasm."

I bury my face in my hands with a groan. I really must learn to sew my mouth shut when I drink. Apparently, the man now knows my entire life history—in all its pitiful glory. "Ugh. To be fair, I didn't say that. My friend said that."

"She said it about you."

I shrug, my eyes widening as I search for a retort. "Yes, but— "

"What?" His eyes are so unnerving. And he knows it; I can tell by the glint as he bites back a smile.

"I'm not sure she's right. I might have had one. Once."

The smirk wins as Josh leans forward, yanking on my braid. "Addy, if you don't know, you never have."

"Maybe?" I am so not winning this argument.

"Definitely not."

I groan and throw my hands up. This has gone from bad to worse. First, I kiss him. Then he pushes me away. Next, I find out he's thirteen years younger, and now I top it off with my declaration that I'm an orgasm free zone. I'm just the banner party friend.

I jump to my feet. It's time to finish this walk. Fast. "Ready to get going?"

Josh's hand snakes up, grabbing my wrist. "Sit down, Addy."

"We should get moving."

"We will. Soon. But first, we need to finish our conversation."

I'm shaking my head before he completes his sentence. "No. I emphatically disagree. We do not need to talk about this ever, *ever* again. Trust me, with everything that has happened in the last twelve hours, I feel stupid enough."

"Because you've never experienced an orgasm? That's not your fault."

"Actually, it probably is. Especially if I haven't had one at my age. I must be broken down there or something."

"You're not broken." I wish I possessed 1/100th of Josh's confidence. I'd be unstoppable.

I throw up my hands as I shrug. "But every time? Every guy? Wait, that sounds terrible. I haven't slept with many men." I close my eyes, feeling the burn climb my body. I am the antithesis of cool. "Forget it. Can we please go?"

But the golden-haired surf god is intent on ignoring my request. "My opinion? If a man doesn't make you come, you haven't been intimate with him. You might have gone through the motions of the physical act, but sex is far more than physical."

There are two equally bad things about Josh's statement. One is that I know he's correct. The other is that I'd never experienced sex on anything beyond a physical level. It's hitting way too close to home. He's hitting way too close to home.

It's time to put some emotional distance between us. I push myself to a standing position because this conversation is over. "Can we please stop talking about my sex life—or lack thereof? I'll beg if I have to because this is the most mortifying conversation of my life. Why did I have to say anything last night? Me and my big, drunken mouth."

Josh tips his chin up, offering me a reassuring smile. "I'm glad you did."

"So, you can have a private joke?"

"Never. Addy, please sit down."

With a huff, I plop back on the blanket, drumming my nails across my thigh. I've moved from mortification to pouting. "What else would you like to discuss about my apparent lack of experience?"

Instead of answering, Josh clasps my wrist, exposing the underside of my forearm. His long fingers trail along my skin, but his eyes remain laser-focused on my face. "Women aren't like men.

They don't turn off and on like a switch. Men know this, but many don't care, so long as they get off."

"So, men are pigs?"

"Some. Some men love women, not just for their beauty or sex appeal, but their capacity to love and nurture."

"Which one are you?" Why am I asking such personal questions? Then I realize it might have something to do with this flaxen-haired man inciting more feelings from stroking my forearm than most men accomplish fondling my breasts.

Josh chuckles. "I think you know which one I am. Some of the most sensitive places on the body aren't the ones men generally think of first. They've got their big three, and many don't venture beyond those."

"I blame Playboy," I mumble as I avert my gaze, trying to focus on anything other than the fire building inside me.

Josh lets go of my arm, shaking his head. "You need to relax."

"I'm relaxed."

He chuckles, cupping my face. "You're wound up tight as a drum. You are the complete opposite of relaxed. Close your eyes."

Instead of obliging, I widen them. "Why?"

"I promise you're safe with me. Do you trust me?"

The funny thing is, I do trust him. Implicitly. I close my eyes, jumping slightly when his fingers grasp my arm again.

"I want you to feel. Don't think. Just feel." His voice is low. Insistent. It's a gentle but firm order.

I release a slow breath and nod. For several breaths, Josh's hands remain still, gently encircling my arm. Maybe he's right. I need to be in the moment and expect nothing.

A small, surprised cry escapes my lips when his beard tickles my inner arm, nuzzling the sensitive flesh. "Just feel, Addy." His tongue glides along my skin, and I bite my lip as my core sizzles. Breathing is becoming significantly more difficult as I'm teased with an intermingling of soft nips and gentle licks. Who knew the forearm was an erogenous zone?

His hand cups my face again, and I open my eyes, my breath slowing to normal. "There's nothing wrong with you, Addy."

I scan my brain for something to say. Shelves and shelves of memories, witty retorts, and knowledge in my mind and I can't figure out how to verbalize any of it.

The worst part? Josh knows it. He can see how tied up in knots I am, and he knows he's the reason. Bastard.

With a grin, Josh hands me a water bottle. "I've never seen you lacking a witty comeback."

"Forgive me, I wasn't prepared for forearm fondling this morning. Better be careful. You could get drunk off my sweat."

His smile widens, a laugh echoing through his chest. "I'll take my chances."

I'm so confused by his behavior, and I hate feeling confused. Time to clear the air, maybe that will help the situation. I reach into my bag, pulling out a tin of trail mix and offering it to Josh. "It's vegan."

"Thank you."

Staring at the natural beauty surrounding us, I rack my brain for how to start. Finally, I realize there is only one place. "I'm sorry."

His eyes narrow in confusion. "For what?"

I meet his gaze, tamping down the smoldering fire he stoked earlier. "Kissing you. I'm so embarrassed about my behavior, some drunk woman who's way older than you are making a pathetic play for attention. I never thought I'd be a cliché, but here I am."

Josh leans back on his elbows. "Your age was never a factor, Addy. You were drunk. I wasn't taking advantage of that, no matter how tempting. And trust me, you were exceptionally tempting."

As kind as his words are, I find his reason hard to fathom. So in true Adelaide Perkins fashion, I take the only route I've ever taken —the safe one. I hold out my hand in his direction. "Can we start over?"

His hand wraps around mine, so warm and firm. "Absolutely."

"Good. Here's to friendship."

His grip tightens ever so slightly as his eyes widen. "Friends, huh?"

"I might have behaved like an utter ass last night, but I have a ton of redeeming qualities. I'm actually a kick-ass friend. The kind that bakes cakes for your birthday and holds your hair back when you puke." Why do I sound like I'm interviewing for a dream job?

Josh grins as he releases the grip on my hand. "Those are redeeming qualities, Addy. Highly desirable in the friend category. There's only one problem, besides the fact that I haven't puked from alcohol since I was eighteen."

"What's the problem?"

He leans in, closing the distance between us. "Friends don't normally kiss the way you kissed me last night."

What are the chances an earthquake will open up the ground beneath me and swallow me whole? I already apologized for the kiss, I have no desire for a play-by-play. I force a smile, trying to make light of the situation. "How would you know? You stopped me, remember?"

"Because you were drinking." His blue eyes hold me captive. "But, you're not drinking now."

My heart, beating so erratically the last few minutes, stops in my chest. "What are you implying? That I should kiss you again?"

"Yes."

I force a laugh and look away as my cheeks flame. "Oh, of course. Great idea."

"I think it is a great idea, unless you didn't really want to kiss me last night. Chalk it up to inebriation attraction." Josh leans back on his elbows, offering up a sexy smirk.

He's laying down a challenge. I've known him less than a week, and he's calling my ass on the carpet.

"Which is it, Addy?"

"I meant to kiss you last night," I mumble.

His fingers push back the strands of hair that have fallen, covering my face. "What was that? I couldn't quite hear you."

Bastard. Clearing my throat, I meet Josh's gaze. "I meant to kiss you."

"Good to know."

"Is it? Do you feel better now?"

"I think you should try again."

A shower of sparks run through my body. Is he serious? He can't be serious. "You stopped me last night, and now you want me to try again?"

"Exactly." Josh smiles, brushing his thumb across my lower lip.

"No way. I have a fear of rejection, buddy."

His smile widens so that his dimple is just visible under his beard. The beard that felt so amazing caressing my skin. "So, it's up to me this time?"

"How am I supposed to answer that?" With a shrug, I lean back against a boulder. "I suppose if you want to kiss me, then you're going to have to make the first move."

"I'll keep that in mind." Josh jumps to his feet, offering me a hand up.

Not what I expected.

With a grin, he bends down, his breath warm against my ear. "You didn't think I was going to kiss you right now, did you?"

"I don't know what to think with regards to you, Josh."

Without warning, he pulls me in front of him, my back pressed to his chest. "Addy, when I kiss you, which I will, I want the element of surprise on my side and"—his lips brush against my nape—"I want you as hot for me as I am for you."

I want to scream how that won't be a problem. Not around him. But I can't say a word. I have to focus on breathing. That and not melting into a puddle in his arms.

His lips dust across my skin. "Because it won't stop at a kiss, Addy. Not by a long shot."

It's close to ninety outside, but my body is nearing nuclear temperatures. "You sound pretty confident in your abilities."

I expect a cocky retort, but once again, Josh surprises me. "I'll let you be the judge. But I am an eager and willing student, so I'll keep practicing until I get it perfect."

"Don't forget, I'm broken in the sex department. You might want to run while you have the chance." There. That should be enough to scare him off.

Wrong again. Josh's arms tighten, bringing me closer to him. "Don't ever think, for one moment, that there's anything wrong with you because the idiots you let into your heart didn't bother to care for it. You just need someone to take their time"—his lips brush my shoulder—"build it up"—a nip at the back of my neck —"and coax you out to play. I feel you quivering, Addy, and I'll bet money that you're soaking wet right now."

I release a gasp when his hand slides past the waistband of my shorts, his long fingers sliding between my legs.

A soft mewl escapes as he skims his fingers along my slick skin. I couldn't hold it back if I tried. It doesn't matter where he touches me. It's magic. Every time.

"Knew it." His lips hover at my ear as his fingers strum my body into a frenzy. "I wish we were somewhere more private because I want to lick you until you can't stand. Feel you come all over my tongue."

His salacious words heighten the heat, and I clench as one long finger slides inside me, my body jerking involuntarily.

Josh pulls me tighter against him, his arm encasing me. "You see? There's nothing wrong with you, and I can't wait to prove it to you. Again and again." His finger dips deeper, and I moan, leaning my head against his chest. "That's it. I got you, Addy. Just let go."

Voices down the trail cut into the moment, startling me back to reality.

"To be continued, beautiful." With a final kiss to my nape, Josh slips his hand from my shorts and takes a step back.

I give myself credit that I'm able to remain standing when he moves away. That has to count for something, right?

I force a smile as the hiking duo passes us, offering a wave. If the blissfully unaware hikers had been thirty seconds slower, I'd have been blissfully orgasming. I was that close. With Josh, it was that easy. A fact that scares the hell out of me.

With a slow exhalation and a roll of my shoulders, I turn to face him. How does he do it? The heat and the hike have only made him look more beautiful. His sweat glistens. I swear to God, he glistens. That old wives' tale about women glowing? Total crap.

"Did that just happen?"

Josh offers up a smile as he swigs back some water. "That was just a preview, Addy." Another smirk as he hands me the bottle.

With a smile, I accept the water bottle. The liquid runs down the back of my throat, but nothing can tamp down the fire that Josh has stoked in my body. Judging by the satisfied grin on his face, he knows it too.

Time to play it cool, even if the man knows it's a load of shit. I close the distance between us. "If that was just a preview, this will certainly be the most interesting friendship I've ever encountered."

"You keep using that word, Addy. But it doesn't suit us." Another smile. This man's dimple will be the death of me. He grasps my hand, threading our fingers together before bringing it to his lips. "I should have known you'd be my greatest challenge."

I wrinkle my brow, wondering what the hell he means by that statement.

"Friends is a suitable starting point, but it's not the end goal."

"What's your end goal, then?" I might not want to know. Maybe he wants to add a fuck buddy onto his rotation, and I fit the bill. Would I even consider something like that? Short answer—yes.

"Us. The two of us so interlaced that you can't tell where I end, and you begin." His tongue licks along the side of my index finger, twirling the digit into his mouth. I couldn't look away if my life depended on it. It's one of the most erotic moments I've experienced, and he's only touching my hand.

Holy hell. I've gone almost forty years without another person bringing me to orgasm, and this young guy almost manages it twice —inside of five minutes. So, either I've got some weird finger fetish, or he's damn talented. I'm reasonably certain which situation is correct. "Your goal is us? Together?"

Josh nods, his eyes never leaving my face. "That's the end goal. But I'll take it one step at a time, Addy." He leans in unexpectedly, pressing a kiss to my forehead. "You're worth it."

CHAPTER NINE

CLINT'S TEXT

"*S*pill it. I want to hear all the dirty details." Melissa winks at me over her food. She insisted I meet her at the downtown cafe for lunch, raving about the sheer size of the salad.

Looking down at my plate, I have to agree with her. I think there's enough food here to feed a family of four. "I'm sorry to disappoint you, but I don't have any scandalous sex stories to share."

"You didn't sleep with Josh? You two left together the other night. Thanks for leaving without telling us, by the way."

"Sorry. I was a bit hammered." I sip my water, my gaze on the waves beyond. I wonder if the golden boy is taking advantage of the ocean's gift.

"You're thinking about him, aren't you?"

I flush but shake my head. "No. I mean, I am, but it's stupid."

Melissa pops a tomato in her mouth, offering me a curious look. "Why? Is he married?"

"No."

"Drug addict? Homeless?"

"No and no. He lives in a cottage by the beach—"

"Fancy."

"And he doesn't do any drugs, from what I can tell."

"He's a terrible kisser." She taps her chin, shaking her head. "No. There's no way a man with lips like that hasn't learned how to use them."

My flush brightens as I recall how talented his lips—and fingers—were the day of our hike.

"Ha! I knew it. So, what's the problem with Mr. Wonderful?"

"He's young."

Melissa shrugs. Apparently, this is not news.

"He's *really* young," I repeat, trying to drive the point home.

"He's at least twenty-one. He was in the club."

"God, could you imagine?" I cough out a laugh. "He's twenty-six."

"I do not see the issue."

"I'm thirty-nine. I'll be forty soon."

Melissa swirls her fork around in her salad, stabbing indiscriminately at the veggies. "Is your age an issue for him?"

"He says it's not, but we've only hung out a couple times. It's not like he wants to date me or something."

"I beg to differ. I think Josh very much wants to date you."

"Maybe add me into his rotation. You have seen him, Melissa. The man must have legions of women."

Another shrug, as her expression turns toward annoyance. "He's gorgeous, but I don't get that vibe off him. Have you asked him?"

I pause with the fork halfway to my mouth. "Asked him what?"

"If he wants to date you or date you and several other women."

I set the fork onto the plate, my appetite gone at the idea of Josh with another woman. I know I have no right. He's not mine, but that hasn't stopped the little green monster of jealousy from rearing its ugly head. "I can't do that."

"Addy, I think you're amazing, but you need to get your head out of your ass."

"What the hell is that supposed to mean?" I flag down the waiter and ask for a glass of wine. I need it for this conversation.

"Clint was an asshole. He treated you terribly. But that doesn't mean every guy out there is like Clint. Don't paint them all with the same brush."

"Josh is thirteen years younger, Melissa. I think that's a bigger problem."

"I don't think that is a problem at all. It's just numbers."

I hate when people try to simplify situations that are anything but simple. "I don't want to be a—what the hell do they call us —cougar."

"That is such a bullshit term. Why shouldn't we date whoever the hell we want? We're attractive, successful, and disease-free. If we want to bang a twenty-one-year-old cabana boy, it's our damn right. And no one else's damn business." She waves her fork at me, her eyes narrowing. "It's only going to be an issue if you allow it to be one. I don't think he rushed down to the club the other night because he hoped you two might end up being best buddies."

"I kissed him."

"You waited this long to tell me?" Her voice increases with each word until everyone is looking at us.

"Shush. I kissed him when I was drunk, and...he stopped me."

"He stopped you? Huh." I catch her expression before she turns away. "So, you haven't seen him since?"

"I have. I stayed at Josh's house. Passed out, really."

"After he stopped the kiss?"

I nod, taking another sip of wine. "Then we went for a hike in the mountains. It was nice."

"You're not telling me everything."

I smile and shake my head at my friend. She is incorrigible. "I don't have to tell you everything."

"Come on. What a gyp."

I hate to be a letdown for my friend, but I really don't kiss and tell. That and I still have trouble believing whether the mountainside scenario was real or a figment of my dehydrated, hungover mind.

"So, has he texted you since the hike?"

"He has. I'm dropping by his place later this afternoon. On my way home."

Melissa sends me a withering stare. "Maybe you can manage to have nothing to tell me again tomorrow."

My phones vibrates, and I grab it, hoping it might be the golden god himself. I feel the blood drain from my face.

It isn't Josh.

"Hey, are you okay?" Melissa inquires, reaching across the table to squeeze my arm.

"It's Clint."

Her brows shoot upward. "Really? What does the asshole have to say?"

I scan over the message. Holy hell, it's more than he wrote in all the cards during the duration of our relationship.

I can't believe it's been almost a month since I've seen you. I really thought it wouldn't bother me, that life would continue with some level of normalcy. I even tried dating Debra, which lasted all of a week. No one understands me like you. No one gets my sense of humor and ridiculous taste in footwear.

I know I messed up. I spent a lot of our relationship messing up. I'm trying to do better, and I'd really love the chance to talk to you. I'll fly out on the next plane if you'll speak to me for five minutes.

I miss you, Addy.

My hands shake as I reread the message, my heart a tossed salad of emotions. Not once in our relationship did Clint ever apologize. Although this isn't the standard, 'I'm sorry,' it's closer than ever before.

Melissa snatches the phone. The woman has no concept of privacy. She reads through the message, the shaking of her head more pronounced with each line. "No way, Addy. Screw him. Do not mess up a good thing to return to something you know is bad."

"First, I'm not getting back with Clint. He lives in New York. Second, what good thing am I messing up?"

"Josh."

"I'm not with Josh! The only time I ever kissed him, he pushed me away. Let's keep that fresh in our mind, shall we?"

"Yes, but something else happened during the hike. You just won't tell me."

I tap my foot, my patience wearing thin. "What should I do?" I inquire, holding up my phone.

"Don't answer him. At least, not yet. If you answer right now, he's going to think you're still on his hook."

She has a point. A good point. Another point is that I've barely thought of Clint since I met Josh. Who am I kidding? I always think about Josh. But Josh is a dangerous and unrealistic concept. Clint makes sense on paper, at least. "I'll let it lie then. I've got to get going."

"Heading to Mr. Wonderful?"

"Just dropping something off."

"Maybe you'll get lucky." With a wink, Melissa shoos me away from the check. "My treat. Go see your man."

My man. It sounds ridiculously good to my heart, but my head is not getting with the program. I slide into the driver's seat and glance at the ceiling. "So Universe, how about sending me a sign? Am I supposed to pursue Josh even though it makes no sense? Oh, and I'm fairly dense, so you might have to clock me over the head a few times."

With a laugh, I pull away. This time, I'll let fate decide.

CHAPTER TEN

I'VE NEVER SEEN SO MANY ABS

I quickly learn that the Universe has a warped sense of humor. I'm not one step out of the car when a shadow blocks the sun hitting my face. A human-sized shadow.

Glancing up, I steel myself. Time for round two, I suppose. "Hello, Frank. How's the hand?"

Josh has a brilliant, warm smile. Frank's smile is equally brilliant but with an icy edge that cuts deep. "Better than it was a few days ago. Are you making house calls now?"

With a sigh, I step out of the car. "No, although I can look at it, if you like."

"What are you doing here, Mrs. Robinson?" His smile now borders on a sneer.

Oh, isn't he cute? So cute, I'd like to duct tape his mouth shut. "Mrs. Robinson? I'm shocked you even remember that movie."

"But you do."

"Actually, it was before my time as well. You might want to work on your math skills."

My snappy retort seems to have shaken his confidence a smidgen. "What can I do for you?"

"You? Nothing. I'm here to drop something off to Josh."

"Well, isn't that interesting?"

"So glad you think so." I can tell that Josh's prick friend has no intention of letting me past him. What a banner afternoon this is shaping up to be. "Are you going to let me by?"

He crosses his arms over his shirtless chest, his jaw muscle jumping. "I'm thinking about it."

Tossing the bag onto the hood of my car, I throw up my hands in true New York fashion. "What is your problem with me? I have done nothing to you—except examine you when you were injured."

"Are you aware that Josh is twenty-six?"

"I am aware of that fact," I seethe between clenched teeth.

"How old are you?"

I want to kick him. Hard. Square in the balls. But if I do that, he wins.

"Frank, leave her the hell alone."

I send a grateful glance to my protector. There's something familiar about the lithe, tanned blonde hanging over the railing. Then it hits me. She's in some photos littering Josh's home, and I'm not getting a family-friendly vibe from her, either.

She takes a sip of her beer, shooting me a look that is part curiosity and part threat. "Can we help you?"

I grab the bag off my hood, praying to escape as soon as possible.

Thank you, Universe. Message received.

"I wanted to return these to Josh."

"Are you a surf student?"

Great. Another one with the inquisition. "No. I can't walk and chew gum."

She holds open the door, letting me pass. At least she hasn't tripped me. Yet. "Grace is far different on land than in the water. I figured if you had paperwork, I would take it. Josh and I work together, among other things."

And there it is. Staking her claim. It is Sunday. Maybe this is her day in the rotation. "Good to know, but I'm not here about surf lessons. I'm a... friend," I fumble, uncertain what I am at this point.

"What did you say your name was?"

"Adelaide. Addy. Is Josh here?" For God's sake, does he always have this many watchdogs?

"He'll be back in a few minutes." She turns back on her heel without warning, her eyes narrowing with suspicion. "Wait a minute. Did you say your name is Addy?"

Wonderful. Here we go again. "Yes."

Using her height to its full advantage, she crosses her arms, peering down at me.

I feel like a disciplinary case in the principal's office. Meeting her downcast gaze, I try to appear nonchalant. "Has he said something about me?"

But instead of answering me, she responds with a question of her own. I hate that habit. With a passion. "Aren't you a bit old for Josh?"

That's it. I've been polite long enough. "It's funny. I didn't know there was an age requirement for friendship in San Diego. My mistake."

"You're not friends. You and I both know that. But Josh can have any woman he wants, and he often does. Don't assume you are anything beyond a one-night stand."

Universe, now you're just being a bitch.

I shake the bag I'm holding before setting it on the table. "I'm leaving this for Josh. Please see he gets it."

"I'm just trying to warn you. You don't have to get huffy."

Now it's my turn for some righteous indignation. "Warn me against what? Dropping by here? Impeding on your territory? What's the warning?"

"Yes, Mariah, what is the warning?" Josh's voice cuts into the tension, and if his clipped pace is anything to go by, he is not happy.

At least now I know the bitch's name. Mariah shrugs, offering a slight smile. "We were just talking."

"Actually, I was just leaving." I turn to the door, but Josh's large frame blocks my passage. "I'll talk to you later, Josh."

His hands rest on my shoulders, his gaze narrowing at Mariah. "Don't you have somewhere to be?"

Unexpected.

"I thought you'd like to come along. Your...friend can come, too." What an actress. Her anger slides away on cue, leaving a sweet, well-intentioned liar.

A liar that Josh has no issue seeing through. "Thanks, but we'll pass. Have a good evening." His grip on my shoulders remains firm until Mariah closes the door behind her.

I can only imagine the hissy fit she's throwing. Glancing upwards, I mouth a silent prayer and hope the woman isn't keying my car out of frustration.

I try to roll my shoulders out of Josh's grasp. "I have to go, too."

"Why?"

Is the man seriously asking me why? Let's see. There are so many options. Mortification at the hands of his friends? Impeding on another woman's territory? Feeling like a complete ass? "I—I have things to do."

"No, you don't."

Is he serious? I plant my hands on my hips, glaring up at him. God, he's even better looking than I remember, which is not helping me. I need to remain firm and angry, and that grin spreading across his face is knocking me off my game.

"Okay, stop glaring. I get it."

"Doubtful," I grumble.

"Mariah can be a total bitch, and I will speak to her. Trust me on that."

"What about your shark bait buddy?"

The grin widens. "Is that your nickname for him?"

"Oh no, that's my politically correct version."

The smile fades from Josh's face. "Did Frank say something, too?"

"Yep." I wave my hands, trying to dispel the tension. "They are not fans of you and I being friends."

"They don't have a say." Josh releases my shoulders, placing a hand on my back. "If you really have to leave, I understand. But please don't run out of here because of my imbecile friends."

I should run. I can already see how this situation with Josh and I will pan out if we continue—and it's not pretty. But one look into those earnest sea-green eyes and all reason shrivels up. When he starts stroking my hair, it's all over.

"You look beautiful."

Now I'm fighting back the tears. Tears of frustration or embarrassment, I can't be sure. But it's new and unwelcome territory for a woman who's used to hiding every emotion she ever felt until she no longer felt any. "Funny thing? I felt beautiful driving over here. But after the way your friends questioned me, I just feel pathetic."

His hands frame my face as his lips press against my forehead. "You are gorgeous, and they are first-rate assholes for making you feel anything but gorgeous. I will speak to them. I won't tolerate them treating you poorly."

I force a laugh because this situation is past the point of

ridiculous. "Don't bother. It will only make it worse. I'll just wear stronger armor next time."

"See, that's the problem. I'm trying to get you to remove the armor, not reinforce it. Will you stay? I have to take a shower because I stink, but I'll be out in a minute. Would you like a glass of wine?"

"Wow, it is bad, isn't it? You're offering me alcohol."

Josh laughs, pulling a bottle from the fridge. I can't help but wonder who helped him drink the first half. Mariah's words circle in my head, like a shark circling prey.

She's right, of course. Josh can have any woman he wants. I uttered the same words to Melissa. But holy hell, it's gutting to hear it from someone else, validation of what I foolishly hoped was my own insecurity talking. "Here, you've earned it. Make yourself at home, Addy."

I take the glass with a mumbled thanks before leaning against the edge of his breakfast bar. I've no desire to examine his home or many pictures. The less I know about his life, the better. Part of me wants to escape while he's showering, but I can hear my mother's voice echoing in my head about how rude it would be.

A few minutes later, Josh walks out of the bathroom, a towel slung around his hips. Holy shit. The man is wearing a towel. Only a towel.

I force my gaze upwards and meet Josh's amused expression. Busted. The man knows what I was ogling, and it wasn't his surfboard. "I told you to make yourself comfortable."

"I'm comfortable." It's a total lie, as I shift my weight from one foot to the other.

"Come here. I promise I won't bite." He sits on the edge of the couch, patting the cushion next to him.

Does the man seriously expect me to sit next to him when he's clothed in only a towel? A thin towel doing little to disguise the rippling muscles and tan skin from hours in the sun? Is he insane?

I arch my brow, motioning to his attire. "Don't you want to get dressed?"

Instead of appearing flustered, Josh leans back against the sofa, his arms resting on the back of the cushions. "Do you really want me to, Addy?"

I release a huffed sigh and grab my purse. After his friend's not-so-subtle innuendos that I'm just another lay for Josh and Clint's halfhearted apology, I'm over men. All of them. Even blonde Nordic surfer types. "Well, that's my cue to leave. Have a good day."

"Addy, wait." Josh is on his feet, his fingers locking around my arm. "Please don't go. I was only kidding. Trying to lighten the mood and make you laugh."

I want to be angry at him. I should be angry at him and his presumption that his looks entitle him to an easy lay. His drop-dead gorgeous looks. But the remorseful smile on his face calms me down.

The surfer bitch Mariah's glare skates across my mind. She's right. He's far too young for me and likely only interested in a onetime lay. Figures I'd feel this level of attraction for someone so far out of my reach.

With a sigh, I rub my brow. It's my go-to nervous habit. "I don't know why your friends have it in their heads that I'm here to screw you. I'm not here for that reason, Josh. I don't do the whole casual sex thing."

"Addy, I know that. I was just fooling around."

I study his face—high cheekbones, full pink lips, eyes far too blue to be natural, blonde hair that is way lighter than I thought. Then my eyes move down. Bad idea. The hours working out on the waves shows in his muscled chest and arms. "Granted, you in a towel makes me question my decision."

"Glad I have some effect on you."

"I'd have to blind for you to not have an effect on me. I didn't realize a person could have so many abs," I grumble while trying to look anywhere but his sculpted physique.

When the man smiles, it rivals the sun. "I had them throw in a few extra for good measure."

I return the laugh, but when I meet his gaze, he appears almost embarrassed. I expected a knowing arrogance, but it seems his looks are not something Josh plays on. Shame, considering he resembles my personal version of Neptune. "You're ridiculously good-looking. You know that."

He regards me with a shy smile, those surreal blue eyes studying my face. "I'm glad you think so. Really glad."

"I'm sure all your women think so."

The smile slides from his lips, a muscle jumping in his jaw. "All my women?"

I shrug, trying to play off the statement as no big deal. "A man like you is bound to have several women at his beck and call."

I expect a knowing wink or a 'you caught me' laugh from Josh, but I get neither. Instead, he turns serious. Deadly serious. "Is that what you think of me?"

My hand rests against his bare chest, my fingers warming from the heat emanating off his skin. I know it's a forward gesture, but Josh appears so perturbed by my innocent observation that I want to provide some reassurance. Okay, maybe I'm digging, too. A woman needs to know these things, right? "I didn't mean it as an insult. How could you not have women lined up? You are seemingly unaware of your effect on the female population."

His hand rests over mine, but the smile has yet to return. He's softening, but it's obvious I hurt his feelings, something I would never intentionally do. "I'm single, Addy. But I'm working on that."

Don't read into it, Addy. You two are friends, remember? F-R-I-E-N-D-S.

"I didn't know. I mean, I wasn't positive. Mariah indicated—"

"Please don't listen to anything Mariah tells you regarding me. I thought she had grown up in the last couple of years. I was mistaken."

"It's obvious she has a thing for you."

Josh shrugs, tossing his blond hair over one shoulder. "It's not mutual."

"Well, I can't blame the girl. You are the quintessential definition of incredible." My face flames. I meant to lighten the mood. Instead, I step right into a giant, steaming pile of self-mortification, fawning over him like some groupie.

Lucky for me, Josh appreciates the compliment. "So you do like me."

"Much more than I should." Why can't I lie to him? I'm used to protecting myself, but with Josh, I open my mouth, and the truth falls out.

Before he can retort, I switch to a safer subject, snatching the bag off the table. "I wanted to drop these off."

His eyes narrow as he peers inside. "What's this?"

"The clothes you lent me the other day, and a gift card."

"A gift card?"

"To a local restaurant. A token of my thanks."

Josh scoffs, tossing the bag on the table. "Addy, I refused the money the other day, remember? I'm getting the distinct impression you're paying me to go away."

I chew my lip, unable to meet his azure gaze.

"Are you?"

"What?"

"Trying to make me go away." Before I can reply, he tousles his fingers through his long hair and smirks. "It won't work, you know. Trying to get rid of me. When I see something I want, there's no stopping me."

"Is that so?" Why is it so hard to breathe in here?

His fingers trail along the top of my dress, dancing along my cleavage. "And, I want you."

"Josh, we agreed to be— "

"I'll settle for being friends. For now. But Addy, you will be mine. Sooner rather than later."

Even if this is his MO, Josh is beyond smooth in his delivery. "Does a woman ever tell you no?"

His cheeks flush under his tan. "I've never said those words to another woman. Just you. It's always been you."

Seriously, who turned off the air? It's stifling, and my pounding heart isn't helping the situation. "Huh." It's all I can manage, and even that is an effort.

"I think deep down, you want the same thing, but you're afraid to admit it. You think it's wrong, but feelings like these are never wrong. They come around once in a lifetime if we're lucky. I'd be insane to let you slip through my fingers."

CHAPTER ELEVEN

GUESS WHO'S BACK?

My mind has replayed Josh's statement a million times. Despite everything—the age difference, his friends' opinions, my own hang-ups—I believe him.

And that idea both amazes me and scares the ever-loving hell out of me.

Any chance of further intimacy that evening was broken by a knock on his door, but this time it was a friendly face. A fellow surfer at the ripe old age of seventy-five, dropping by for an unscheduled lesson.

There's something so real about Josh, so brutally honest. He might be more than a decade younger, but emotionally, he's in far better shape than me.

"Did you see your man the other day?" Melissa inquires, leaning against the mobile workstation and sucking down a can of soda. The woman must have caffeine running through her veins instead of blood.

"Only for a few minutes. Can I ask your opinion?"

"Yes, you absolutely should sleep with him immediately."

I giggle as I stroll to the break room for my own caffeine fix. "Sorry to disappoint you, but we haven't even kissed. Not where it was a mutual action, anyway."

"Really? What's the holdup?"

Her question fires up one of the insecurities bobbing around my brain. Why hasn't Josh kissed me?

"I'm not sure. I was only there for fifteen minutes or so the other day. One of his students dropped by, in need of his expertise. The man is seventy-five and just started surfing last year. After his wife died, he decided to do all the dangerous things he'd avoided because of her fears. He said the worst that can happen is he gets to see his wife a bit sooner. Isn't that sweet?"

"Very and way to dodge the question about you and Josh. You haven't kissed?"

I shake my head, feeling my cheeks flush. "I know it seems odd to you, but we did agree to be just friends, so I can't expect overt demonstrations from him. Not that I'd mind." The last sentence is muttered under my breath, but my friend has no issue hearing it.

Melissa's brow shoots upward. "Hell's bells, Addy. I would have shut my mouth if I knew he initiated the friend-zone talk. I'm sorry."

"He didn't. I did."

"Why the hell would you do that?"

"I think it's safer this way. He's so much younger and—"

She shakes her head, disapproval radiating off her in waves. "Your head is up your ass, again."

Shooting her a scathing glare, I slug back half my coffee. Caffeine jolt, here I come. "Josh told me that he was okay with being friends. For now. But that one day soon, he would make me his. I'm sure it's just a line, but it sounded good."

"You don't believe him?"

"Am I stupid to believe him?"

"I don't think so. Has he given you a reason to believe he's anything but honest?"

I shake my head. I miss him, and it's been less than forty-eight hours. "Never. But that's not all that happened."

Melissa rubs her hands together with devilish glee. "Now we get to the good stuff. I knew you were holding out on me."

"Not hardly. When I got to his house the other day, his friends were there. The one from the other night with the injured hand and this gorgeous surfing buddy." I clear my throat, the memory of their disapproving glares still fresh in my mind. "They both let me know how unwelcome I was in Josh's life."

"Holy fuck. Jealous much?"

"I'm not jealous." Okay, that's not entirely true, but Melissa doesn't need to know that piece of information.

"Not you. Them."

"They're not jealous. They're hateful. Both of them told me I'm too old for Josh."

"What does Josh say?"

"He said he would have a discussion with them both. And for me to never listen to anything they say with regards to him."

Melissa shakes her empty soda can in my direction. "I like this guy, Addy. Aside from the no kissing situation, he's doing everything right. Then again, you did toss his pretty ass into the friend-zone."

"I don't think it's a deterrent for him. He's used to having any woman he wants."

"Apparently not." She sends me a pointed glance. "Maybe he *is* a horrible kisser. Stranger things have happened."

I recall the memory of his mouth on my finger, a smattering of sparks racing through my body. "Not a chance. He's too perfect to have such an obvious flaw."

Melissa peers over my shoulder to the central nurses station. "Looks like our new doctor has arrived."

"We have a new doctor?"

"Yeah. All the way from the East Coast. Quite a looker, too."

I pivot to catch a glimpse of the hot new commodity, and the coffee cup slips from my useless fingers.

Standing not six feet from me, is Clint.

"ADDY, ARE YOU OKAY?" Clint rushes to my side, grabbing my hands and checking me over for burns.

"What—what are you doing here?" I stammer, shocked I haven't lost all ability to speak.

"I work here now."

What. The. Fuck.

Melissa finishes cleaning up the spilled coffee, her face purposely neutral. "Hon, I'm going to run and fetch you some new scrubs."

I nod, feeling as dazed and confused as the accident victim wheeled in earlier that evening. I return my gaze to Clint, my shock evident. "I don't understand. Why do you work here?"

Clint grabs my elbow, steering me further into the break room. "I transferred. I wanted to be near you, Addy. I know I made a huge mistake, but I can't fix it if you're thousands of miles away."

I can't speak. My mouth has turned to sawdust. I sink into a chair, rubbing my forehead and praying I wake from this crazy dream.

His hand strokes my back, and I tense. I'm not ready for this level of personal contact. Hell, I'm not even prepared to see him, much less have his hands on me.

"Can I get you some water?"

"Why? So I can chuck it at you?"

He sinks into the chair next to me, grabbing my hands. "I understand that you're still mad. You have every right to be. But at least now, we can work towards a reconciliation."

I glare at him, not believing the crap spouting from his mouth. "We're reconciling now? Do I get a say in this? Why would I? I never got a say in anything else."

"You're right, and that will change, too. I just want to be near you, but we will play this by your rules."

My rules. He's got to be joking. "How kind of you."

"I'm willing to do whatever it takes." He sounds so charitable, but it's a control move. One that Clint is famous for. "I'm assuming my mother knows all about your transfer?"

Clint nods. "I had to keep her abreast of the situation. She's glad I'm out here and near you. She's worried about you, Addy. You haven't returned any of her phone calls."

"If I'd known that ignoring her calls would mean working with you again, trust me, I would have answered the phone." I throw up my hands, my aggravation mounting. "What happened with Debra?"

I see the remorse flash across Clint's face, but I doubt its sincerity. "It was awful. She...was awful. You know the saying that you don't know what you've got until it's gone? It's very true. Until you left, I had no idea what I was losing."

"Sorry to interrupt, but I have scrubs." I love Melissa. Her timing is perfect. Much longer and our new doctor would be dead on the floor, a coffee pot wedged in his handsome head.

I accept the scrubs with a forced smile, as I fight to maintain my composure. "Clint, I need some time to process this news. Until then, I ask that you keep a professional distance."

I turn on my heel, stomping into the locker room. I pull off the soiled clothes with such vehemence I'm shocked the seams don't rip.

"So, that's the infamous Clint."

I look up to see Melissa lounging on one of the benches. "That's Clint."

"I'm assuming this is not a happy accident."

My smirk screams volumes. "No. It's more like a seven car pile-up. That's how Clint is when he wants something. He pays no mind to obstacles, just bashes right through. I used to find it motivating. Now I find it aggravating as hell."

"What are you going to do?"

I release a huff of annoyance, pulling the braid from my hair. "I don't have a hell of a lot of choices. I'm locked into a contract. So, I'm going to work with him. Hopefully, as little as possible."

"I have an idea."

"Please don't tell me to screw Josh again. My head is beyond messed up at this point."

Melissa shakes her head, laughing. "I'm not, although I stand by my earlier directive. What you need is some time to chill out."

"Should we go to the bar after our shift?"

"Sure, but that's not what I mean. I go to yoga twice a week. Great place. Why don't you join me?"

I shrug because I doubt yoga will help my situation. A beer and a 2x4? Maybe. A mat and singing bowls? Likely not.

"You don't have to give me an answer now. Just think about it."

I hear my phone buzzing in my pile of discarded scrubs and grab it. "Knowing my luck, it's my mother," I mutter, but stop when I open the message, a slight smile finding its way across my face.

"That smile tells me it's not your mother."

She's right. It's not my mother. Instead, as if by magic, it's Josh. A video of the beach at sunset and five words.

I wish you were here.

I release a long exhalation, feeling the calm of the waves even inside the hospital. "It's from Josh."

Melissa sends a knowing smile. "I know. How is your buddy doing?"

"Fine, I guess. Did you know that he's a model? He works with a variety of surf companies, so he's up in Los Angeles for the next couple of days."

"I'm hardly surprised he's a model. In fact, that's why he looks so familiar. I've seen him in some ads for board shorts, or something of that nature. He looked like a golden god, surrounded by a harem of exotic looking women. The poor man."

I force a smile. Melissa doesn't mean anything bad by the statement, but I'm reminded—once again—of the sharp differences between my life and Josh's.

I work through the rest of my shift, with only minimal interaction from Clint. I catch him looking at me from across the floor, but he makes no move to speak to me outside of patient discussions.

I have to admit that he's a godsend to this emergency department. The man is a brilliant diagnostician with an affable bedside manner. Judging from the ogling of the nurses, he hasn't lost his touch there, either.

"Call me if you want to go to yoga," Melissa reminds me as I sign out.

I answer with a wave because I know where I'm headed. Home, to change into some comfy clothes and then to the beach with my camera. My appetite for photography is voracious now, and I find a great deal of peace just being near the sea.

"Are you headed home?"

I turn and look into Clint's face. He's as handsome as ever, bearing a strong resemblance to Clive Owen. His hair is shorter, and his tanned skin indicates he's been somewhere besides New York in late fall. Likely our Mediterranean vacation. With that realization, the anger resurges, and my resolve is resolute. "I am, but only for a minute."

"Where are you going?"

"I don't see how that's any of your business, Clint."

He leans against the doorway, sending me his best sultry look. It always worked in the past. With multiple women. It's not working now. "Can we at least play nice?"

I cross my arms over my chest and offer a shrug. "I hope so because our jobs are difficult enough without the addition of petty drama. I can be an adult if you can."

"Fair enough. I was hoping you might want to grab a cup of coffee. We could go watch the sunrise. Addy, you had to miss me a little bit."

Clint has never used that tone before. It's softer, uncertain. If he wasn't such a total wanker, it would be appealing as hell. "It's a bit of a shock, seeing you like this. I need some time to process that you're here in San Diego."

He cups my face—a bold and uninvited move—and I can't help but notice how cool his touch is, compared with Josh. Everything about Josh is warm like the sun. Clint is the dark side of the moon. But both men are equally mysterious. "I'm here because you're here."

Taking his hands from my face, I give them an awkward squeeze. "I need time."

"I really fucked up, didn't I?"

With a sad smile, I tell him what he already knows. "I think we both know the answer to that question."

CHAPTER TWELVE

ALCHEMY UNFOLDING

*I*t's uncanny how my heart rate and breathing slow the second my feet hit the sand. Maybe it's the cathartic crash of the waves or the cry of the sea birds overhead. It also might have something to do with the fact that I can see Josh's cottage from my car, even though I know he's a couple of hours north of here.

The waves are gigantic today. What did Sean call them? Bombs. Definitely bombs. I realize how little I know about surf culture and make a mental note to study up on the subject.

I plant myself on a boulder, shivering against the early morning chill. It might be southern California, but the air has a bite, especially by the water. I settle onto my stomach, snapping off a few photos of the surfers riding the waves.

They're good, but Josh is an entirely different species. He has a grace about him that defies logic. Through my camera lens, I see a figure riding the crest of one of the waves. His movements resemble Josh—what little I've seen of his surfing, anyway. I focus in closer and realize that it *is* Josh in the water.

He's supposed to be in Los Angeles. But he's here. My insecurities drop by for an early visit, bombarding my sleep-addled brain. *Maybe he only told you he was going to Los Angeles so that you wouldn't bother him.*

But the fact is, I don't think I am bothering him. I allow him to initiate almost all conversations, and aside from the drunken lip lock, I haven't made any forward moves.

My phone rings, startling me, and I drop my camera. "Damn it," I curse, checking it over for damage. Thankfully, it only dropped a few inches and seems to be intact. A broken lens is all I need.

I stare at the phone and roll my eyes skyward. Clint. Again. A month ago, I would be thrilled to hear from him. Now, he's an annoyance. When it rings again, I realize that he isn't going to let up. "What's up?"

"You still are, apparently."

"I'm taking photos at the beach." I balance the phone and camera, clicking off a few more rounds. God, Josh is magnificent to watch. A true water baby.

"What beach? I'll come join you."

"You never showed any interest in my photography before."

"And that's part of the problem. I didn't take your hobbies seriously. I'd like to change that, Addy."

I'll give it to him, the man certainly knows all the right things to say.

"Come on, I'll bring coffee."

"I'm actually leaving soon," I fib, although I do want to move on before Josh catches sight of me.

"Even better. I'll meet you at your apartment."

I throw the phone an exasperated look. I know most women think I'm insane for giving the cold shoulder to a handsome, successful doctor, but most women also didn't walk in on said doctor giving someone else a vaginal massage. "I told you, I need time. Please don't push me."

Clint releases a sigh—of exasperation, likely. I'm not falling into line. Mother would be so disappointed. "What about lunch?"

"Today?"

"Perfect. I'll pick you up."

"No, I wasn't saying yes—" The man is killing my vibe. I grab my camera and point it toward the ocean again, but Josh is gone from the waves. I guess he high-tailed it out of here faster than I could.

"Addy, would you please have lunch with me?"

I look up, forgetting Clint completely. Josh is headed in my direction, a warm smile coloring his features.

"Addy!" Clint's voice barks out through the phone.

"I have to go," I mumble, disconnecting the call. I know it's rude and likely uncalled for, but, in truth, Clint had it coming.

"Hey, beautiful."

I wave, feeling myself blush. I've been called beautiful before, but until Josh, the words never resonated. "Ignore me. Just pretend I'm not here."

"Well, that's damn near impossible, Addy. To what do I owe this pleasure?"

"I came to photograph the water. I thought you were in LA?" I'm trying to appear nonchalant. I pray it's working.

"I came back early." Those eyes. God was showing off when he created a man like Josh.

"Missed San Diego that much?" I tease, smiling up at him.

"I missed you. I knew you were off the next couple of days."

My entire body flashes at his statement. He can't be serious, can he? Because if he missed me and I missed him, then what does that mean?

It means, as far as your heart is concerned, you're a goner.

Shaking away my internal monologue, I hold up my camera. "When I realized it was you surfing, I tried to photograph you, but it's impossible."

"Why is that? Odd angle? I can take another run for you."

"It's not you. It's me. I'm not talented enough to capture you, Josh. You're exquisite out there. You're one with her. It's like alchemy unfolding."

The smile on his face radiates pure joy. "That may be the greatest compliment I've ever received."

"I doubt that," I reply with a nervous giggle.

"Don't."

"What?"

"Don't ever doubt the effect you have on me." He settles next to me on the rocks, and I feel my body flame. Any close proximity to this man is dangerous territory as far as my hormones are concerned.

His gaze is intent on the ocean, as if they're holding a conversation only the two of them can hear. "Surfing is like sex."

"Isn't everything in a man's world?" I tease as he stands up, positioning himself in front of me. Without a word, he gently pushes my thighs apart, stepping in between my legs.

Holy hell, the flame just surged into an inferno. His hands rest on either side of the boulder, just outside of my thighs and desperately close to where I've wanted his fingers to return since our hike.

His head is mere inches from mine, and I can't be sure if it's the wind or his breath tickling my skin. "Not all men think about sex 24/7."

I raise my brow. "What kind of crap line are you spouting?"

Josh laughs, his hands now cupping my thighs. Sneaky bastard. Maybe if I keep him laughing, he'll keep moving upwards. "Women think about sex quite often, too. Especially when they meet a man who knows how to touch them." The joking smile slides from his lips as his fingers squeeze my legs, pulling them closer around him. "What are you thinking about right now, Addy?"

I need to resist. I sure as hell don't want to, but we agreed to be friends. The friend-zone is safe. Boring as hell and not anywhere near what I want, but safe. Safe keeps my heart unbroken and head in control.

God, safe sucks.

Staying his hands, I offer a pointed smirk. "I think that you still haven't explained the correlation between sex and the sea."

"Ah, right. You distracted me." His hands grip me closer, but I'm not complaining. Any chill in the air is long forgotten with his hands on my body.

"How did I do that?"

Josh has a wide variety of smiles. The one spreading across his face is different than those I've seen before. It's smoldering, whispering of promises without saying a word. This smile is sex with the lights on and the world watching.

"You have to treat her with respect, firm but gentle strokes, waiting for her to let you in. If you're lucky—and she does—you worship every second of that connection."

I know damn well he isn't talking about the ocean. I also know that I don't discuss sex, love, or anything resembling intimacy. It's a topic that makes me uncomfortable, due in large part to my naivety in the area. But Josh doesn't ask permission to enter my innermost thoughts—it's as though he already has the key.

"She really captivates you, doesn't she?" I fight desperately to control my racing heart and the myriad of feelings stirring inside me.

Josh nods, his aqua eyes holding me rigid. His gaze tells me I'm going to have to do better than that. I need to dig deeper.

I search my soul for the feelings I never let escape, the ones bubbling to the surface every time I'm near this man. "You don't fully understand her, but somehow, that doesn't make her any less desirable."

"Quite the contrary. It arouses my curiosity. It makes me strive to discover what makes her tick."

"It's quite a powerful emotion between the two of you."

"I believe the term you're looking for is love."

My mouth turns to cotton as I hold his intense stare. *Please don't let me be reading him wrong. My heart can't handle it.* "Is that what you feel for her?"

"Without a doubt. From the second I saw her, I knew we were meant to be together."

My heart speaks before my brain can filter my response. "I'm sure she feels the same way." I jerk my head to the side as my cheeks flame from my unexpected and blatant admission.

Breathe, Addy. Breathe.

A small gasp escapes when Josh's hand moves across my back. "Sometimes, I'm not entirely sure what she feels with regards to me."

I can keep playing the verbal banter, but my heart tells me it's time to move on. Time to stop looking at the ocean and jump into the damn thing. I raise my chin to meet him full face, offering what I pray is a smile that's both seductive and reassuring. "You don't know?"

His arms wrap around my waist, pulling me forward those few precious inches until I'm pressed against him. "I see hints of her feelings, but she always slips away before I can grab her to me. I know she's scared, but she doesn't realize she has complete power over me."

"She doesn't want power over you."

"I'll give her anything she asks for. She only has to ask." His lips graze my hair, awakening an entirely new set of nerve endings.

"Don't make promises you won't want to keep later. You might live to regret them."

Josh tips my chin up, forcing me to meet his gaze. "We'll see about that. Maybe one day, she'll have as much faith in me as I do in her."

Enough of standing at arm's length. It's time to get up close and personal. "I think you're remarkable. Intoxicating. You remind me of all the glorious things I've been taking for granted." I run my fingers along his beard, tracing my thumb across his lips.

"You're intoxicating, Addy," Josh whispers, brushing his lips against mine and setting off a shower of sparks.

"Somebody, help! We need help down here!"

If there are any words in the English language that will squelch a moment in an instant, it's those words. Our kiss ends before it ever began, our lips breaking apart as our focus turns toward the ocean.

At first, I don't see anything, save for a few frantic surfers running along the water's edge. Then, something bobbing in the water. But it isn't a something. It's a *someone*.

Josh and I fly into action at the same time, running full force toward the sea. Without a moment's hesitation, Josh is in the water and swimming toward the distressed surfer.

I bite back a cry when I see who it is—the older gentleman who dropped by Josh's house the other day. I rush waist-deep into the ocean, helping Josh pull his lifeless body from the surf.

No pulse. No time to waste. "You, call 911," I bellow as I straddle the man's chest and begin compressions. He's blue, but the water is cold this time of year. "Come on. I know you miss your wife, but it isn't time to see her yet." With a mighty compression, water spurts from his lungs, and I help turn him onto his side.

He opens his eyes, coughing on saltwater and seaweed before offering me a crooked smile. "Thought I was a goner there for a while, didn't you?"

There is no emotion on this planet as good as the feeling of saving a life. I collapse back into the sand, laughing as the onlookers rush to cover him with towels.

I'm exhausted but sated. I hear the ambulance sirens and let my guard down enough to feel the cold of the gray day. After spending ten minutes speaking with the EMT, I'm positively frigid.

I look up and catch Josh's gaze, his mouth ajar as he makes his way to my side. "You were amazing, Addy. You just saved his life."

"It's my job." I hug myself in a futile attempt to get warm.

"Come on. Let's get some dry clothes on you."

"No need. I'm heading home."

"Absolutely not."

"You've loaned me enough clothing for one week."

"I won't take no for an answer. We get you warmed up, and then you can pass out because I know you worked all night. Then this evening, we're having a celebration."

"What are you celebrating?"

"At this point, I'm celebrating our resident heroine."

"What are you really celebrating?" I manage, my teeth chattering.

"It's Mariah's birthday."

My high vanishes like cotton candy in the rain. "You have fun, Josh. I'm not going to crash that party." I start the walk back to the boulder, praying no one stole my purse and camera during the melee.

But Josh isn't easily dissuaded. "She asked me to invite you."

I bark out a laugh. "I highly doubt that."

"She did. She felt terrible about her behavior the other day and wants you to know that not everyone is an asshole like Frank."

I need an excuse. One that will placate this maritime god. "Haven't I done enough celebrating lately?"

"This is a different kind. My California, remember? If you're not having fun, you can leave, but please, give it an hour."

I stare into those impossibly blue pools and realize I'd likely scale Everest or base jump if Josh asked me. "I reserve the right to change my mind after I'm not half-frozen and over-tired."

Josh grins, looping an arm around my shoulder. "Fair enough. We can renegotiate the terms later. But I plan on having something amazing in store for you when you wake up. If you leave, you'll miss it."

"I hate when people do that," I grumble, elbowing him in the ribs.

"But you don't hate me. Do you, Addy?"

I shoot him a fake glare, acutely aware that what I feel for this man is the complete opposite of hate.

MY TEETH ARE CHATTERING SO HARD that any plan to appear sexy is long forgotten by the time we reach his cottage. I might freeze first.

"Would you rather a bath or shower?"

"Shower is quicker," I mumble, noting that my always pale skin is now decidedly blue. I have one mission. Get warm. I strip off my clothes and step into the shower, the warm water peppering my skin like tiny bullets. Soon enough, it turns into a pleasant reprieve, and I'm feeling human once again.

I walk out of the bathroom, wrapped in only a towel and pad into the kitchen. "Josh? I was wondering if you have a t-shirt—"

The question dies in my throat as my chill returns. Frank is sitting at the breakfast bar next to Josh.

Wonderful.

I hate having pale skin. You can't hide embarrassment. It sticks out like a lobster at a rodeo, and I feel one hell of a flush happening. I offer a weak wave in Frank's direction. "Hi there."

Frank sends me a lopsided grin before taking a sip of his coffee. "Nice outfit."

Josh jumps to his feet, shooting Frank a scathing glare. "I'm so sorry, Addy. When Frank heard about Johnny, he stopped by to make sure he was okay."

Frank raises his mug in my direction. "That was one hell of a save, Addy. We're all grateful."

Did Frank compliment me? I think the world just tilted on its axis.

"Glad I could help," I mumble before following Josh back to his bedroom.

I notice him staring at my legs, so pasty white compared to his bronze skin. "I think I'm the palest woman in San Diego."

Josh grins. "Top five, anyway."

I force a smile, but his ready agreement stings. I know I shouldn't read too much into it. Besides, I'm sure I'm just exhausted and emotional. We'll go with exhausted.

"I like the Snow White look."

"Got a poison apple for me? Women want to look like Barbie, not Snow White."

"I think she's hot."

Thanks for that brutal honesty, Josh. I shake my head, sliding on my trusty emotional armor. "Everyone thinks Barbie is hot. Lucky for you, every woman out here, with the exception of me, looks like her carbon copy."

Josh hands me a pair of boxer shorts and a shirt. "I meant Snow White."

There go those sparks again.

Josh grabs my hand, pulling me next to him as we face the mirror. "Everywhere I'm light, you're dark. Everywhere I'm dark, you're light."

Yet another reminder of how different we are. "We're complete opposites."

"Opposites attract, Addy."

A series of muffled bangs sound from the other room, and Josh rolls his eyes. "I'll be right back."

My guess is that Frank is throwing a temper tantrum. It must be difficult to pretend to like me, even for a few minutes.

Time to get dressed and go home. I can only pray I'm not pulled over in Josh's clothes. How in the world will I explain that get up?

I pull off the towel and bend at the waist, drying off my hair.

The door opens, and I yelp with surprise, pulling the towel off my head to hide...everything.

But instead of apologizing, Josh stares. Openly stares, his eyes roving up and down my form. "I should probably avert my eyes, huh?"

I didn't think I could get any more embarrassed. I was wrong. "I guarantee you've seen a lot better. And younger."

"You want to know what I'm thinking right now?"

I turn to him, my eyes wide. Likely I don't. "What?"

"I wish I didn't have a lesson right now and could climb into that bed with you. Spend all day touching that gorgeous body of yours."

"I wish you could, too." Holy hell, where did that brazen statement come from? I'm never so forward.

ALCHEMY UNFOLDING | 105

A grunt sounds from Josh's chest. It's almost primal in nature. "You're even more beautiful than I thought possible."

"You've barely seen me."

"I'll see every inch of you, Addy. That's a promise." He glances at his phone as the alarm sounds. "Fucking bad timing."

I wave him off, offering a smile. "Go. I need to sleep, anyway."

He closes the distance between us, pressing a kiss to my lips. "Don't you dare leave this house. Promise me."

As the door shuts, I whisper, "Not even possible."

CHAPTER THIRTEEN

SEIZE THE MOMENT

*S*leeping is the most delicious activity. Correction. Sleeping in Josh's bed is delicious. I wake up, half expecting to find him naked next to me, fulfilling his promise from earlier. Sadly, I'm alone, but I won't hold it against him. I know he has obligations to his students and sponsors.

That fact doesn't keep me from fantasizing about his tongue skating along my sleeping body. Is there any better way to wake up?

I stretch and notice a note on top of my freshly laundered clothes. The man is a saint.

You are so beautiful when you sleep. I only stayed for a few minutes because otherwise, I'd never leave, and my students would have my head on a platter. I'll be done by two. Can't wait to spend the rest of the day with you.

I slip on my clothes, making a beeline for the kitchen as an idea hits me. He isn't here, so technically, I can discover the brand name of that magical coffee. What he doesn't know won't hurt him. Right? I open the cabinet, stretching on tiptoe as I slide boxes out of the way, searching for the metal tin. *Where the heck is the damn thing?*

"You wouldn't happen to be looking for the coffee, would you?"

I turn to face my golden god, a guilty expression on my face. "I would never do such a thing."

Josh laughs as he reaches past me, pulling out an unmarked tin. "I didn't think so. Have a seat. I'll make this for you. Just so you know, it's a blend. You're not going to find this in the store."

"That means I'll have to keep bothering you."

Josh winks at me. "That's the idea."

"I can make my own coffee. You don't have to wait on me."

"Shush and sit down. I like taking care of you."

I perch on a barstool, feeling completely out of my element. This man washes my laundry, cooks for me, saves me from sweaty nightclubs—where the hell did he come from? "How was surf school?"

"It was epic. Good waves today. I worked with the veterans." He hands me a cup of coffee, which I accept with a smile.

"They're very lucky to have an instructor like you."

"I'm the lucky one. They're heroes, each and every one. When they're out on the ocean, they're reminded of that fact."

Everything this man says and does is making me fall deeper and deeper for him. Soon, the bottom holding my heart from him will break loose, and I'll have no other option but to tumble head over heels in love. That bottom is crumbling fast.

"Are you done for the day or on a break?"

"I'm done." He goes into the living room and returns with a wetsuit. "After you eat, put this on."

The blood drains from my face. I remember the waves earlier this morning, and I know I'm not equipped to tackle them. "Josh, I don't—"

His hands cup my face, and once again, I'm reminded of the hot vs. cold of Josh and Clint. "She's calmed down. Do you trust me?"

"I do, but I've never surfed."

"Don't worry, beautiful. I'll take it easy on you. I want to show you something." He presses a kiss to my lips, and I'm damn sorry it's an abbreviated version.

My phone buzzes on the counter, and Josh glances at it; habit, I'm sure. Then his hands drop from my face, tapping the counter.

I glance at the caller ID. Of course, it's Clint. Who else would it be with such impeccable timing?

Josh, for his part, does not appear amused. "Why are you still talking to him? I know it's none of my business, but Addy, you told me the other day what he did to you."

"Trust me, I'm not speaking to him because I want to."

"What does that even mean? Why speak to him at all?"

Bombshell number one, dropping now. "He's working with me. Here, in San Diego."

Josh's eyes widen as a scoff slips from his mouth. "He followed you here?"

"I guess. That's what he tells me." I fiddle with the coffee spoon, hating every moment of this conversation.

"Are you getting back together with him?"

I shake my head vehemently. "No."

A muscle ticks in Josh's jaw. He's angry, and I'm not sure how to convince him that Clint isn't a threat. With a sigh, he tugs at his long locks, before grabbing a bottle of water. "You need to tell me if I'm in the way here."

For the first time, I see the uncertainty in Josh where I'm concerned. I hate seeing uncertainty in his face; it's far better suited for glorious smiles. I walk over to him and loop my arms around his waist, knowing that my intentions need to be made clear. Fast. "There has never been one moment where you have been in the way. You make me happy. You make me forget the damage Clint inflicted."

A smile tugs the corner of his lips as he pulls me closer. "This is the first time you've ever hugged me. Consider yourself lucky I enjoy it so damn much. Otherwise, I might not take you on our little excursion." He gives me a quick slap on the ass, motioning in the direction of the wet suit. "Go get changed."

I grab the garment, still unsure if this is a good idea. But one look at Josh's expectant face and I cave. He's worried about being in the way? He *is* the way. He's everywhere, in my every thought.

"Promise you'll keep me safe?"

"Cross my heart."

I CAN'T BELIEVE I'm on a surfboard. Granted, I'm sitting and not standing, but it's a start.

Josh paddled us out to a calm area to introduce me to his world. All I know is that my heart is in so much trouble.

The ocean is magnificent. It's familiar and yet strange, all in the same breath. "I understand why you love it out here. The world falls away."

Josh loops his arms around my waist, resting his head on my shoulder. I hate to admit how much I love the feel of him. "It quiets the din. There's so much noise in life that you can't hear anything beyond it."

"I've spent years hearing nothing but noise."

"You still do, Addy. I think you're afraid of the quiet. Scared of what you actually feel when the world isn't watching."

I don't know how the man does it, but he pegs me every time. His honesty is brutal but without a trace of the condescension always present in Clint. He's making observations without passing judgement, and I know he sees me more than anyone else ever has. "I've always felt lost, so I wore masks in an effort to look like I belonged. I dreamt of tearing off the mask and living my truth, but I'm not that brave. I've never been brave."

"I disagree. You rushed into the ocean without a second thought to save Johnny, a man you didn't know. How many people would do that?"

"It's what I'm trained to do."

"Training only takes a person so far. Instinct and the willingness to act on it is what gives you courage." His grip tightens, his warm breath tickling my ear. "Let the sea give you courage. She has plenty to spare."

I close my eyes, letting the waves work their magic. Everything falls away as I'm lulled by the gentle rocking and rhythmic sounds. What if Josh is right, and I do have more moxie than I give myself credit for? Why can't I embrace life on my terms, letting the opinions and doubts of others fall by the wayside?

I pull myself to a squatting position before standing—ever so slowly—on the board. I'm wobbly as a newborn colt, but I'm standing.

A wave nudges the board, and I stumble, but Josh steadies me, his strong hands wrapped around my thighs. "See? Way braver than you thought you were."

I know it isn't much, but this tiny victory flies in the face of all the things I've been told in my life. Be safe. Don't take chances. Don't make waves. Turns out, it was all a load of crap.

"Just feel her. Don't fight her. Her movements are no different than your heartbeat. Connect to your heartbeat, you'll connect to her."

With a slow exhalation, I close my eyes again and do the one thing my mother always warned me against. I feel, without care for the consequences. "It all seems so simple out here. Like anything is possible."

"Anything is possible, Addy."

I wobble again before taking a seat on the board, this time facing this delicious man.

"How did it feel?"

"Scary. Good. Scary and good," I reply with a laugh. "I know it's nothing to you, but—"

His finger presses against my lips. "Don't ever say that. Watching you move out of your comfort zone is highly impressive." His fingers drop to my thighs, moving with idle strokes. "Can I ask you something?"

My stomach flips. I hate that question. It's a segue into more difficult questions. "Sure."

"It's about your age."

Great. I did say the questions always became more brutal.

I rub my hand across my forehead, forcing a smile in his direction. "If you're lucky, you may get to be as old as me one day, too."

"That's not what I meant. I don't see the age. I see you."

"I don't hear a question, Josh."

He picks up my hand, interlacing our fingers. "Why are we pretending to be friends?"

My heart stops. This conversation can go one of two ways. "What do you mean?"

"Give me your reasons."

"For?"

"Why you're hesitant to move us out of the friend zone. Also, age can't be one of your reasons."

My eyes widen. "But it's a huge factor."

"That's a load of crap. The fact that you were born before me is a non-issue."

I wish that were the case, but I remember all too well Mariah and Frank's scathing glances. "You know that's not true. Age will always be a determining factor."

"For you, maybe."

"So, my age doesn't matter to you?"

Josh shakes his head, his lips pursed in a thin line. "Nope."

"Not at all?"

"Not even a thought, Addy. It's never been a factor in my feelings for you. So, tell me."

"Tell you what? You said I can't use the fact that I'm older as a reason!"

Josh grins at me, biting his lower lip in a move that is part adorable, part bad-boy, and all sex. "This is my game. We play by my rules. So, besides age, why are you and I a bad idea?"

I hesitate, chewing my bottom lip. The man is perfect in every way. Gorgeous, smart, sexy, funny, and kind. Throw out the age factor, and there's no reason in hell I shouldn't be jumping at the opportunity—and he knows it. "I hate this game."

"Let me help you find some reasons. Are you not attracted to me?"

I shoot him a look of utter exasperation. "You know that's not the reason."

A slow, lazy smile crosses his face. God, I hate him. Or really want to kiss him. I'm not entirely sure, but I'm leaning toward option number two. "Good to know you are attracted to me. Let's see. You don't enjoy hanging out with me."

"I love our time together."

"I do, too." He snaps his fingers. "I've got it."

I can't hold back the smile. "Do you? You've figured it out?"

"I have. It's so clear. I'm horrible in bed."

Now my laugh is full-blown. I can't help it. A sex discussion with this man turns me into a bundle of nerves and hormones. "I highly doubt it, but then again, how would I know?"

"Good point. We definitely need to address that issue. I mean, you can't give an honest opinion otherwise. But...I have touched you." His fingers trace my lower lip. "Did you enjoy it as much as I did, Addy?"

I'm out in the middle of nature, and yet I can't find enough air as his fingers drift across my skin. I grasp his hand, halting his movements. "Behave."

"Trust me, I am behaving. You have no idea what I'd really like to do to you right now."

He's right. I don't know, but I'm dying to find out. I inch toward him, closing the distance between up. "Then tell me."

Josh's expression changes, darkens. The desire is evident in his face, and for once, I'm not running from it. "I'd rather show you."

"Heads up!" A voice behind us shouts, and we look up in time to see a wave headed straight for us.

In my defense, I didn't freak out. Then again, I didn't have time. Within a second, I'm off the board and turning ass over teakettle in the water. I break the surface, sputtering and laughing.

Thanks for breaking that moment, Universe.

"Are you okay?" Poor man. My tumble into the sea has shaved years off Josh's life.

I raise a hand and laugh. "So much for being one with her. It's more like indigestion than a heartbeat."

Josh shakes his head, holding out his hand to pull me back onto the board. "I'm so sorry about that."

"It's fine. I'm swimming back. Go catch a wave, or whatever you call it."

"I'll come back with you."

"Josh, I may not be from this coast, but I did grow up on an island. I've got it. Promise."

He glances toward the horizon. Some beautiful waves are kicking up. He'd be a fool not to take advantage. "Are you sure?"

"Absolutely. Go have fun."

"Be careful, my Addy."

I don't know why the addition of a possessive pronoun sounds so good, but it does. So damn good. I want to be *his* Addy.

With a final smile, I swim the back to the shore. It's a bit further than I thought, but I reach the beach and take a seat on the sand, eager to watch Josh in his element again.

I'm not sure why I'm more comfortable watching him from afar. I've never experienced the feelings and emotions that swirl every time I'm near him. That plethora of emotions only showcase my lack of experience with matters of the heart, and it's such a turnoff to me that I'm sure he'll feel the same way.

"Hey there, Mrs. Robinson. You look like a regular surfer now."

I roll my eyes at Frank and offer a chuckle. "Hey yourself, kid."

I hope he'll continue walking or, better yet, join Josh in the surf. I'm wrong on both counts. Frank settles next to me, and he's not abiding my three-foot of personal space rule. "I'm thirty-one. So, if I'm a kid, what is Josh? A toddler?"

"All man. Age does not determine maturity."

"Is that a fact?"

"I'm sure it's a hard concept for you to grasp. Here's what I don't understand. If you hate me so much, why are you sitting with me?"

Frank shoots me a surprised look. "I don't hate you."

"Could have fooled me."

"Are you staying for Mariah's birthday party? She's turning the big two-five. I remember turning twenty-five. Seems like eons ago."

His words are innocent enough, but his meaning isn't lost on me. It's yet another reminder of how my age difference is a bigger issue than Josh wants to admit. It seems like every time I take one step out of my comfort zone, his friends are there to shove me back into my hole.

"Josh said that Mariah asked me to attend. I'm not sure I believe him."

"That would be a surprise. Mariah's had a thing for Josh for years. They used to date, but I guess they just fuck now. I can't be sure of the details." His gaze shifts to my face—a face that is swiftly draining of all color. "You know how it is."

I can play into Frank's hand and rip him apart verbally, but it's apparent he'll only be back for more. He knows my weak points and takes great delight hitting me there, again and again. "Can't say that I do."

"I just assumed you and Josh were also...intimate." He bumps his fists together, and I fight back the urge to take a swing at his jaw. What an absolute sleaze.

The worst part is the internal whisper that Josh is better suited to someone like Mariah. She's young, she lives the same lifestyle. Did I mention she's young?

I'm done with this conversation. Just a few minutes near Frank kills the buzz from the ocean and my time with Josh. I push myself to a standing position and jerk my thumb toward the water. "Can you tell Josh I had to leave?"

I swear, Frank seems giddy at my statement. "Leaving without saying goodbye?"

"I forgot, I have somewhere to be tonight." It's a terrible lie, and I'm a terrible liar, but I don't care at this point. I need to escape.

Frank stands and motions for me to turn around. My body tenses when he pulls down the zipper of the wetsuit a few inches. "You'd never get out of it by yourself. Go. I'll let him know."

I mumble some thanks and spare one more glance for the beautiful man riding the waves. Josh claims age doesn't matter, but he's wrong. In the eyes of everyone else, it's the only thing that does.

I SCURRY BACK to his cottage, stripping off the wetsuit and throwing on my clothes. Of course, since I'm trying to do everything in a hurry, it takes twice as long.

I contemplate leaving a note but don't want to take the time. I'll text him later to explain. I bolt out the door but stop dead at the familiar profile walking towards me. So much for a clean getaway.

"Where are you going?"

I toss my bag in the backseat, offering him a rueful smile. "I forgot I have somewhere to be."

His fingers tap the roof of my car, a perturbed look on his face. "All of a sudden, you have somewhere to be?"

"Yes."

"What did Frank say?" He grits out the question, his agitation evident.

"He just reminded me of my place."

"Your place?"

"With regards to you."

"Addy, you're not in a relationship with Frank. Why are you listening to him at all?"

"According to him, I'm not in a relationship with you, either. He told me about your history with Mariah."

Josh hits the roof of the car. "Damn it."

It's all the answer I need. I don't seek clarification. Why add salt to an already festering wound? "Thank you for today. I made your bed and I—"

His hands encircle my upper arms, and I struggle to contain my tears. What is wrong with me? I spent the first four decades of my life never shedding a tear. Was I saving them all for Josh? "Please don't go. Let me shower, and we'll go somewhere. Just you and I."

I want to be near him so badly, but my heart can't handle much more. "You have Mariah's party."

"I'll skip it."

I splay my fingers across his chest, feeling the thrum of his heartbeat against my hand. "I won't let you. Have fun tonight."

"Please stop running away from me."

I stand on tiptoe, brushing my lips against his. They're even softer than I remember, with a hint of salt from the ocean. I want to grab Josh to me, strip off his wetsuit, and kiss every inch of him. But I hold back. Frank's words are too raw in my head, and they're mixing with my own self-sabotage ingredients.

"Hey man, you taking the beer run with me?"

I glare at Frank, standing just past us with his own annoyed expression. If I didn't know better, I'd swear he has the hots for Josh, too. "I'll see you later."

I slide into the driver's seat, watching as Josh storms past Frank into the house. I know I didn't start this mess, but I still feel bad. Tonight is about Mariah, bitch though she may be. She deserves a happy birthday, with happy guests.

"Here goes nothing," I mutter as I step from the car, leaning against the door. "Josh," I call through the open screen.

He appears a moment later, his features terse. "Yeah?"

I look first at Frank and then back at my gorgeous surfer who's waiting for what I have to say. "I'm off tomorrow. Come by if you have a chance."

The corners of his mouth tug up as he nods. "I have students until two."

"Perfect." I smile at him, and for once, I couldn't care less who's watching.

Josh throws open the screen door and hops over the railing, striding to my car. My eyes widen at his acrobatics, but he doesn't want to talk. He cups my face and lowers his mouth to mine, his tongue sliding along the seam of my lips.

With a soft moan, I grant him entrance, my hands winding around his neck as he pushes my body against the car door.

Kissing is addictive. Correction. Kissing Josh is addictive. Some part of me realized it even during my drunken haze, but this time, when his lips claim mine, I feel it in every pore. His tongue coaxes me, sliding against mine as his hands slip under my shirt to caress my spine. This kiss is everything my body never knew it needed. It sets me on fire. It's hungry and possessive. Josh is staking his claim. And I'm staking mine.

I push my hips against him, a nonverbal plea for release. Josh changes the angle, his tongue sliding along the roof of my mouth and setting off a new shower of sparks. His mouth encloses my top lip—nipping, sucking—and driving me out of my mind. He wants control, and I let him take it.

"Damn, son. You two plan on coming up for air anytime soon?" The voice holds no animosity, only minor amusement at our overt sexual display. "But don't let us stop you."

Josh pulls back a touch, his mouth nuzzling mine. "Wasn't planning on it, Dad."

My eyes widen as my face lights up like a blowtorch. *Please, God in heaven, tell me Josh didn't just say Dad.*

Josh pushes himself off the car and grabs my hand, caressing it with his lips. It's both sweet and stimulating, but I'm a bit too freaked out to appreciate it.

I know I'm going to have to meet the eyes of the gentleman in front of me. I just don't know how. I can't believe that my first introduction to his father involves me playing tonsil hockey with his son. What a story for the grandchildren.

"Dad, this is my Addy. Addy, this is my father, Stephan Gibbs."

"I figured this had to be Addy. Who else would it be?"

My gaze flies up, shocked by the man's total lack of surprise. I see the resemblance between Josh and his father—although his father's coloring is several shades darker than his son. "It's nice to meet you, sir."

"We don't do sir, here. Just call me Dad."

My gaze volleys between Josh and his father. He's joking, right? I barely call my own mother by that moniker, and we have blood ties.

"I'm glad to finally meet you. My son won't shut up about you."

I shift my gaze back to Josh, expecting him to appear embarrassed. But he meets my gaze full-on, daring me to look away. It's intense and disconcerting, particularly since I'm still recovering from the most erotic kiss of my life.

A woman can only handle so much excitement in a five-minute period.

I have two choices. Honestly, I have more than two choices, but running away and hiding likely isn't a good option. So, I can fry under the weight of the embarrassment, or I can bask in it.

I'm in the mood for basking.

With a shake of my head, I send a fake glare in Josh's direction. "You told him about me falling over the guard rail, didn't you?"

Josh and his Dad exchange a glance before bursting into

laughter. Apparently, my drunken tumble is not classified information. "I didn't go into specifics, except to state that the guard rail obviously has a grudge against humans." At my questioning look, he adds, "Dad fell over the same guard rail."

"In the same damn spot," his father adds with a wide grin.

"We're both talented, then." I can't help but return his grin as he offers me a high-five. Mr. Gibbs, much like his son, is impossible to dislike.

"She's a keeper, Josh," Mr. Gibbs remarks, draping his arm around his son's shoulders.

"I think so, Dad."

My face flames again, even though it's thrilling to hear some positive accolades instead of biting criticism.

Mr. Gibbs picks up on my discomfort, offering me his elbow. "Let's go have a drink, and wait for the birthday girl to make an appearance."

"I was just leaving."

"You have somewhere else to be?" He studies my face, and I know he reads me as well as his offspring. "You have time. I'll make you a deal. Share one drink with me, and I'll let you escape these hooligans. Fair enough?"

I chuckle, looping my arm through his. With an offer—and smile—like that, how can I refuse?

CHAPTER FOURTEEN

FOURTEEN EROGENOUS ZONES

*I*t's fairly apparent by the leering looks coming from Frank's direction, that he's none too happy that I've changed my mind about attending the festivities.

Too bad, Frank. Too damn bad.

I steel myself when I see Mariah walk onto the back deck, but her expression remains guarded as she nods in my direction. Perhaps Josh did speak with her, or maybe she doesn't want to make waves tonight. Regardless, I'm not looking a gift horse in the mouth.

Stephan Gibbs leaves not long after Mariah's arrival, gifting her with a traction pad for her board. At least, that's what they call it. Either way, she's thrilled with the purchase, throwing her arms around him in a bear hug before he departs the party.

On his way out, Mr. Gibbs grins at me, hugging me around the shoulders. "Don't let them get to you, Addy. Remember, their opinions are not indicative of my son's opinions."

I nod and muster a smile, but the truth is that

opinions *do* matter, and Josh's friends are obviously important to him. I don't want to drive a wedge between them, if I even have the power to do such a thing.

I feel terrible that I don't have a gift, but remember a Visa gift card in my wallet. I pull it out and head into the kitchen, hoping to make peace with Mariah. "I didn't know it was your birthday, or I would have gotten you a card."

Mariah accepts the gift card and pulls me into an awkward embrace. Strange. "Thank you, Addy."

One of us has to dive into the deep end of the pool and address the elephant floating in it. I open my mouth to start, but Mariah beats me to it.

"There's a reason men like Josh are single."

I send her a questioning glance, urging her to finish that statement.

"They want to be. I know that isn't what you want to hear, Addy. It wasn't what I wanted to hear, either. Sometimes the truth hurts."

"Why are you telling me this?"

"You seem like a decent person. I didn't want to like you, but you're genuinely kind and hell, you saved Johnny."

"You know, people can change."

Mariah considers my words, tasting them in her mouth before turning her lips downward. "Maybe he has. I can't say for certain. But there's often more to a situation than meets the eye. If I were you—hell, if I were me—I'd keep a tight leash on my heart. You want a good lay? He's your man. But love?"

She doesn't elaborate, but my heart doesn't need to hear more. It's heard enough. Deep down, I knew. Josh was meant to be a casual flirtation, an epic lay to prove I wasn't broken. Turns out, my pleasure center wasn't the only thing Josh turned on. He flipped the switch for my heart as well.

Now I have to figure out how to turn it back off.

As I stroll back onto the deck, I overhear snippets of conversation. Ah, the alcohol has kicked in, and the discussion has segued to sex. I wonder who initiated the topic change. My money is on Frank, considering the speed with which he's downing his beers.

Great. This should be a fabulous time.

I spy Josh seated in a corner with a few beach bunnies surrounding him. Funny how natural they look together. I stick out like a sore thumb. His face lights up when he sees me, and he beckons me over, patting his lap. "Have a seat."

As much as I'd love to take him up on his offer, I opt for safety. And distance. "I was going to head home."

"You can't do that," Frank exclaims, tossing an arm around my shoulder. "The party is just warming up."

I turn to the drunken behemoth and force a smile. "You should be right in your element, then. Have fun."

Any other time, the man would be thrilled to see me hightail it home. Tonight, however, he's blocking my departure with the force of a linebacker. "You'll have fun, too. Pull up a chair. We're going to play a little game."

God in heaven, that doesn't sound promising at all. "A game?"

Frank holds up a small box, tossing it on the table.

Josh releases a groan when he reads the name. "No way. We are not playing that."

"It's Mariah's birthday. It's her choice. She wants to play, we play," Frank mutters, shooting me a wicked glance. "You're game, aren't you, Addy?"

I know a challenge when I see one. I can either scamper away from the party, proving that I can't hold my own with the younger crowd or risk utter embarrassment at the hands of a sex game. Decisions, decisions. With a shrug and swig of my beer, I return his glare. "Absolutely, Frank."

The rules of play are easy enough. Each person is asked a sexual question, and if you answer it, you gain a point. Each level gets progressively more carnal in nature until a winner is announced, although I'm not sure what the winner receives besides a raging case of blue balls. But I digress.

After a few innocuous rounds, the questions veer into racy territory. I'm only glad Josh's father isn't here to partake. That would be a level of weirdness I could never be comfortable with.

"So, Addy," Frank grabs a card, a smirk crossing his face. "If we were out to dinner and I said I wanted to have sex right now, what would you do?"

I roll my eyes at his sneer. The sleaze is taking great delight in making me uncomfortable. Only problem? It's not that bad a question. "I'd order another drink, Frank. In fact, I'd order an entire bottle. Although," I lean in his direction for effect, "I doubt there's enough alcohol in the world to make that offer appealing."

A bark of laughter floats up from the corner, and I turn to see Josh biting back a smile. If the titters of laughter around the circle are anything to go on, I'm not the only one who enjoys seeing Frank shot down every now and again.

"You think you're cute, don't you?" Frank grumbles, sliding the box of cards to Mariah. I know from his glare that I'll pay for my sharpened barb later, but right now, I'm basking in the glow of his silence.

Mariah rubs her hands together with devilish delight after reading the card. "This is a good one, and it's all for you, Josh. If you want to seduce a woman, how would you do it?"

"Pick up the check," Frank interjects, earning a few grunts of approval from the men seated around the deck.

"You're a Neanderthal," Mariah retorts, and I raise my beer in her direction. Solidarity is a beautiful thing. Especially when it's aimed at the man with the lowest IQ and biggest mouth in the place.

Josh meets my gaze and holds it, daring me to look anywhere but his face. "Do you know there are over fourteen erogenous zones on a woman? I visit every one, tempting her with my tongue, my teeth, my fingers. I bring her to orgasm time and again because there's nothing more beautiful than watching the woman you love receive pleasure. It's all about her. You take your time. You don't ever rush, even when she begs you to take her. You worship her, every single delectable inch of her."

He shifts forward, leaning across the table to grab my wrist. His fingers glide along my skin, and I bite back a moan as he brings it to his mouth, his tongue flitting over my pulse point. Dear Lord, I'm not going to survive this game.

"When you listen to her body, you'll know just where to touch her. She has a few weak spots, and your quest is to find them all." His tongue moves across the tips of my fingers, swirling each digit into his mouth, his teeth providing just enough friction.

I'm practically panting by the end of his description, my entire body flushed from the sensuality of his words. Not once did his eyes waver from my face.

"It's no wonder the women line up for you," Frank remarks, cracking open a beer.

His blunt observation snaps me from my erotic reverie, squashing the notion that Josh's words were directed at me.

I'm such a naive twit sometimes. It's no wonder Clint played me like a fiddle.

Sliding on my trusty emotional armor, I opt for a humorous comeback. Fanning myself, I release a heated sigh. "Well, I need to cool off after that. Then again, who wouldn't? Excuse me for a moment."

I hole myself up in the bathroom as Frank's comment plays on repeat in my head. Of course women line up for Josh; it's not exactly news. Why wouldn't they? He's the total package: gorgeous, sultry, kind, talented, and born thirteen years too late.

I need to go home and cool down properly with a vat of vodka and an ice bath.

"I was wondering when you were coming out of there."

I flash a smile at Josh as he leans against the hallway wall. "Were you waiting for me or the bathroom?"

"You. I apologize if I made you uncomfortable. It wasn't my intention. But most of all, I'm sorry, once again, about Frank."

I wave my hand, dismissing his apology. "It's fine. I think everyone knows that Frank is an asshole."

A smile lights up Josh's face. "Truer words were never spoken."

"You didn't make me uncomfortable, although that was some answer, Josh."

"I'm glad you approve."

I'm not sure approval is the right term. Bitter jealousy is a better fit for my emotions, but I'm not letting Josh know that. "Some lucky women. Like Frank said, it's no wonder they line up around the block."

"I've never done it."

"I know you're not a virgin."

Josh chuckles, running his hand over that glorious bearded jaw. "You got me there. I've had sex, Addy, but never with a woman I was in love with. That's an entirely different scenario."

"You don't do all that with every woman?"

Now his laughter borders on nervousness. "I ensure they have a good time. I'm not some love 'em and leave 'em type. But no, that level of intimacy is on reserve."

"Ever plan on taking it off the reserved list?" My breathing is becoming more and more difficult as Josh closes the gap between us.

"Yes. The woman I'm in love with will get every facet of me."

I realize my mouth is hanging open, my lips parted as I try to come up with a response. Any response that doesn't involve me throwing myself into Josh's arms and begging him to take me on the inaugural ride on that intimacy train.

But I don't have to say a word. Josh senses the change in energy. He has to. It's palpable.

I gasp when his hand encircles my waist. He removes the beer bottle from my hand and sets it on a shelf before backing me against the wall. I'm trapped between his broad body and the sheetrock, but I'm not looking to escape.

I meet his gaze as his fingers press against my lips. They continue their journey along my jaw, down the side of my neck and across the top of my breasts, before wrapping around my dress strap and sliding it from my shoulder. "Close your eyes."

My breathing sounds even louder as my eyes drift shut. A soft moan escapes when his lips brush against my collarbone, his tongue sliding along the curves of my skin.

"I told you before, Addy, that you need someone to take their time with you." His mouth travels up my neck, nipping at my pulse point.

I lift my arms in a bid to participate, but Josh encircles my wrists, holding them behind my back. "You remember when I said there were over fourteen erogenous zones on the body?" His tongue flits along the curve of my ear, nipping on my lobe. "I'm going to find every single one on you...and I hope it takes all night."

I open my eyes, my breathing shallow and rapid. My entire body is awash with feelings, sparks lighting off everywhere.

Tucking a strand of hair behind my ear, his mouth hovers against my lips. "Tell me, beautiful. Does it sound like something you would enjoy?"

"I'm broken, remember?"

Josh shakes his head as his fingers glide under my tank, tracing along my abdomen. "What I remember is how wet you were. I also remember telling you how much I want to taste you. Can I taste you now, Addy?"

"Yes," I manage to whisper, my heart pounding like a freight train.

Those talented hands skim along the hem of my dress, dancing up my thighs, his gaze locked on me. He doesn't say a word. He doesn't have to. Josh's eyes scream his intentions as he slides his fingers along my folds.

"What the hell are you doing, Josh? Are you brewing the beer? Oh shit, my bad." Frank peers down the hallway with a look that says he's anything *but* sorry that he broke up yet another intimate moment. In fact, the bastard looks right pleased with himself.

"You see the fridge. Get it yourself," Josh barks, a grimace crossing his features.

"Sorry. If you want to fuck her, just go fuck her."

I jump when Josh's fist makes contact with the wall. I know it's not at me, but I've never seen his anger riled. "I'm warning you, Frank."

"Fine. Jeez," Frank mutters, slamming the patio door with extra force.

Josh's face is rigid, his body coiled from Frank's pointed comment. I splay my fingers across his chest, pressing a tender kiss to his lips. "It's fine. Don't let him get to you."

"It *isn't* fine. Everything about Frank lately isn't fine."

"Shh," I whisper, running my hands along his beard. "But it doesn't matter."

"You matter, Addy. I need you to know something. I don't want to fuck you," Josh murmurs, nuzzling my mouth, his beard tickling my skin. "I want to worship you."

CHAPTER FIFTEEN

MOVING DAY...FOR THE LIVING ROOM

*M*oving furniture always sounds like a good idea until you're halfway in the middle of doing it. Then you realize two things—furniture is heavy and moving it alone is damn near impossible.

My buzz of energy is fading fast as I stare at the jumble of pieces now precariously arranged in my living room, but I need something to take my mind off Josh.

Between that kiss in front of his Dad and our almost make-out session in his hallway, my hormones are in an upheaval. My God, that man can kiss. It's unlike anything I've ever experienced before. It didn't just light up my lips, I felt it in every cell of my body. They need to pull boys aside in high school and give them lessons because kissing is not something that comes naturally. At least that's been my experience.

Until now.

I skate my finger along my lips. They still tingle at the memory. Josh did promise to kiss me when I wasn't expecting it. He certainly made good on his word.

I open my eyes, sliding back into reality. A reality that involves relocating a boatload of furniture. Ugh.

"Enough stalling, Perkins. Get moving," I grumble, gearing up like a football player in the hopes of pushing the loveseat to the other side of the room. My first attempt moves it approximately six inches. At this rate, I'll only need another three days to finish. Wonderful.

My doorbell rings, making me jump. Visitors are a rare occurrence out here, especially considering I know less than a dozen people.

I pull open the door, sweating and huffing like Puff the Magic Dragon.

Josh, looking cool as a cucumber, stands on the opposite side of the vestibule. His eyes widen when he takes note of my reddened face, messy top knot, and sweaty brow. "What in the world are you doing?"

"Yoga?" I lie, smirking in his direction.

"That's some pretty intense yoga."

"Actually, I'm going to yoga later with Melissa. Some studio on Park Boulevard." I offer up a cheeky grin. "You should tag along. I'll wager you do yoga, since you're Buddhist and vegan and perfect."

Josh returns the smile, tweaking my nose. "I do practice yoga, and maybe I will. But that still doesn't answer my original question. What are you doing right now?" His face pales. "Please tell me you're not having sex."

"Fully clothed?" I counter.

"Wrong way to answer that question."

I giggle, feeling a sense of satisfaction that he seems so upended at the idea of me fornicating. "Definitely not having sex. I am engaged in something *far* more entertaining. I'm rearranging my living room."

"Thank Christ about the sex part, but you're moving furniture? By yourself? Addy, you shouldn't be doing that. You could get hurt." He brushes past me into the apartment, assessing the damage. "You're far too tiny to be shoving couches around the living room."

"I'm not that tiny." I stretch to my full height, which is still significantly shorter than his six-foot frame.

Josh tips my chin up, swooping in to steal a kiss. It's certainly not like yesterday's 'bowl me over' kiss, but it will do. For now. "Where do you want things?"

"You don't have to help me, Josh. You keep doing me favors. It isn't right."

"Then make it up to me."

That sounds interesting. *Okay, mind, time to vacate the gutter.* "Name it."

His eyes widen as that sex-on-a-stick smirk crosses his face. "Really?"

I plant my hands on my hips and wait for his request. My guess? He's going to demand oral gratification, not that I'd mind. With Josh, I'd relish the task. "You've saved my ass on numerous occasions. It's time for me to pay up."

Josh considers my words, as a cheeky grin crosses his face. "I'll have to consider all my options. But first, let's get this mess sorted for you."

The independent side of my nature wants to argue that I can handle the situation. Still, the rational side of my being knows that Josh is far stronger, and his help will move this process along light years faster. Thank God for rationality.

Within twenty minutes, all the furniture sits in new locations, and Josh hasn't even broken a sweat.

"What do you think? Better?" Josh gazes around the room. "I

don't know what it looked like before, but I know it's better than the leaning tower of furniture you had earlier."

"Definite improvement, but it's not my furniture. I rented the apartment furnished."

"Really. Where's your stuff?"

"I left it in New York when I accepted the travel nursing gig."

His brow furrows. "Wait a second. You're not here permanently?"

I shake my head, certain that we've discussed this at some point. "My contract is for twelve weeks. Fairly standard. After it runs out, I can opt to stay here, or I can go elsewhere."

"You can go anywhere? Even Hawaii?"

I nod, tossing him a water bottle from the fridge. "If they have a nursing need. Never thought about Hawaii, though. I hear it's paradise."

I realize this conversation is heading down a dangerous path— one I don't have answers for at the moment. The truth is, I have no clue where I'll wind up once my contract runs out. I do know that San Diego looks better and better every day. "Regardless, I'm not going anywhere for the next couple of months, so you'll have to put up with me until then." I survey the living room, arching my brow in his direction. "Have you decided what your payment will be for all this assistance?"

Josh pulls me to him, locking me in his embrace. "First, I want to take you to dinner."

"How is that repayment for you?"

"I thought it was obvious. I get to spend time with you."

I've never, not once in my life, met a man who always said the right things. Until Josh. He's either the smoothest player the world has ever known, or he's perfect. My money is on perfection.

"I won't turn down dinner. What's the second thing?"

"Kiss me, and you'd better make it good. None of that platonic crap from earlier."

"You kissed me this morning. Remember? So, it's your crap style, buddy," I scoff, biting back a laugh.

Josh shrugs, leaning against the arm of the couch, those eyes smoldering in my direction. "Teach me, then."

I know damn well the man knows how to kiss. He showed me —and all the party guests—just how talented he is in that arena. But if he's laying down a challenge, who am I to decline?

I put on my best strut, messy bun and all, and close the distance between us. With a gentle push onto the sofa, I've got Josh just where I want him—on his back and waiting for me. I straddle him, taking my time to skate my entire body along his as I slide my way up to his mouth. When his body hitches, I know I'm doing something right.

I glide my tongue along the side of his neck as my hands move along the planes of his chest, his low groan spurring me on.

His thumb sweeps across my lips, and I bite the tip, swirling my tongue along the length. Oh yes, I want him to know exactly what I have in store for him later. Tongue, teeth, lips, I use them all.

Josh knits his free hand into my hair, holding my gaze for one more intense moment before claiming my mouth. I savor every second, tasting him, sliding my tongue against his, nibbling those full lips that make me forget my own name. The kisses are harder now, as Josh commands my tongue to do his bidding. He's taking back the control he gave earlier, and I'm only too happy to submit to his whims.

I pull back, my breathing harried and panting. "I think the pupil has outshone the teacher." I press my hips against him, feeling his erection grind against me.

"She's a hell of a teacher," Josh responds, holding my body to him and sending a delicious shudder through my body.

"Come with me." I crook my finger at him, sending Josh a naughty grin as I climb off him. Offering him a hand, I ignore his wide-eyed expression as I lead him to the bedroom. "Don't get too excited. It's not what you think."

"Dammit," Josh groans. "A guy can dream."

So can a girl, Josh. So can a girl.

I motion to the bed. "A little-known fact about me. I took several classes in massage. I'm pretty damn handy with these bad boys." I hold up my hands, a seductive pout on my lips. "I think it's the least I can do after all the help you've given me. That, and touching your body, is a definite perk."

I'm not sure where my sex-kitten persona came from, but I'm hoping like hell that it makes Josh as hot as I am. I expect him to leap onto the bed, ready and waiting for a massage, complete with a happy ending.

Instead, he hesitates. Every second he dallies, his eyes shifting between the bed and my face, shoves my confidence down another notch.

Did I read him wrong? Again? There's no way he didn't want that kiss. Hell, he asked for the damn thing!

Time for damage control. Ego, please return to your seat. You are not moving to the head of the class. "It was just an idea. I thought you'd enjoy it. Sorry, I...sorry." Now I'm babbling. Even better.

His hands frame my face, forcing me to meet his gaze. That intoxicating sea-green gaze. "Addy, I want to strip down and lay on that bed more than anything. But I guarantee that I won't be able to keep my hands to myself once you touch me." He pulls his hands through his golden hair, giving the long locks a tug. "I need to know you want that as much as I do."

I don't know if it's the tremble in his voice or the earnestness emanating from his statement. All I know is the idea of his hands touching my body sounds like an amazing plan.

I trail my fingers along the waistband of his jeans, my fingers grasping the button-fly. "I'm willing to risk it. The question is, are you?"

The words barely leave my mouth before his mouth crushes mine, his body backing me toward the bed. We tumble onto the mattress, our hands a flurry of activity as we strip off our shirts, desperate for skin-to-skin contact. He unclasps my bra, the hunger rising in his eyes as my breasts spill out into his hands. His tongue flicks my nipple, and I arch against his mouth, desperate for more.

So much more.

"Addy? I know you're here. The door is wide open."

Holy shit. Clint. Is. Here.

I bolt to a sitting position, noting Josh's curious and unamused gaze. Can't blame him. Five minutes more, and we both would have been naked. "What are you doing here, Clint?" I volley back as I grab my bra and toss it on, fumbling with the clasp.

"Clint is here? Your ex? Why the fuck is Clint here?" Josh hisses, his eyes shooting daggers in my direction.

Now I know what Josh looks like when he's pissed. It's not pretty. He's still pretty, but he's also really angry, and understandably so. It looks bad, and we both know it.

I was about to get the first amazing sex of my life, and my adulterous lech of an ex bumbles into the moment. Way to kill my vibe, Clint.

"I don't know," I whisper as I pull my shirt over my head. "I'll be right back."

I storm into the living room, wearing my best 'are you fucking kidding me right now' glare. "What are you doing here, Clint?"

"Good morning to you, too. The door was open."

"So? That's not an excuse to walk into my house."

"Why? Are you entertaining someone, Addy?" He gazes around the apartment, obviously unimpressed. "Why are you staying here? Your mother said she would send you money."

"I don't need her money. Or yours. I work for a living, remember?"

"How am I supposed to tell her you're living in a one-bedroom shack?"

"First, it's hardly a shack, and second, don't tell her anything. Is that why you came here? To check up on me?"

Clint paces the living room, projecting his 'I know best' routine. I've seen it a million times when he speaks to patients. It works on them. Me? Not so much. "I wanted to take you to breakfast."

"She's busy."

Oh, lovely. Another addition to the party. I turn to see Josh emerge from the bedroom, wearing only jeans and a disgruntled expression.

Clint glares at me. "Who's he? The pool boy?" It's one of the many traits I dislike about my ex-boyfriend. When he deigns someone as beneath him, he doesn't speak to them directly. Instead, he speaks around them.

"Jesus, don't be such an asshole, Clint." I rub my brow. A migraine is imminent. "This is Josh. He's my friend."

Now I'm getting glares from both men. Even better. No matter how much Josh may hate that introduction, it's the truth. I'd love to say that I'm dating Josh, but I'm not. That status of our relationship has never been discussed in any way, shape, or form. I'd be a fool to presume otherwise.

Clint shoots Josh a look, dismissing him out of hat. "Right. Hey guy, can you give us a few minutes? I need to speak with Addy."

I exchange a glance with Josh. His jaw is clenched so tightly I fear he might crack a tooth. He hates this situation. Come to think of it, so do I.

"Clint, why don't you come back later? Better yet, call me to discuss whatever it is that is so urgent."

Clint plants his hands on his hips, and I wait for smoke to come out of his ears. I've rarely seen him this riled. "I tried that. You didn't pick up your phone. Look, it's about your mother, but if you're too busy..."

What an asshole. Figures he'd play that card; he knows I'll cave.

I return my focus to Josh, but his jaw has softened, replaced by a look of concern. I grasp his hand, giving it a squeeze. "I'm so sorry. Can I give you a call later?"

Josh gives a tight nod, his fingers tickling my palm. Even now, his caress is reassuring. "Sure. I hope everything is okay."

God, I love this man. "Thank you."

Josh ducks into the bedroom to retrieve his shirt and shoes. On his return, he walks up behind me and loops his arm around my neck, hugging me to him as he presses a kiss to my temple. It's a move that is both sweet and territorial. He's letting Clint know where he stands, and I'd be lying if I said I didn't love it. "I'll pick you up tomorrow for dinner. Six o'clock."

I pivot, the confusion evident in my face. But it's the expression on Josh's that stops any further questioning. He needs some reassurance, and I have no issues giving it to him. "Six o'clock."

He's halfway to the door when he turns, his gaze locked on me. "Actually, I'll see you this evening. I've decided to take that yoga class." He drops a kiss on my mouth and walks out, sending Clint a scathing scowl.

As soon as Josh leaves, the air changes. It's just Clint and me. Alone. It's funny. I spent four years with the man, but I never knew him. After only a month around Josh, I feel like I know every facet of him. Well, almost every facet, and I'm blaming Clint for delaying that delectable journey.

Clint clears his throat, bringing me back to the moment. "You're going out with *him*?"

My back goes up at his tone. Who is he to judge? "Yes, I am. Do you have a problem with that?"

"Is he even legal?"

"Are you asking if he's a citizen?"

Clint's eyes narrow. He is not amused. Come to think of it, neither am I. "I know he's a damn citizen. How old is he?"

"Oh, *that* legal. He's most definitely all man."

He scoffs at my reply, only making me more heated. "You're not seriously dating him."

"What if I am?" I'm tired of all these people thinking that Josh and I are such a bad idea. It's ludicrous. "What's so wrong with that?"

He throws up his hands before planting himself on the couch. "Go ahead. Make a spectacle of yourself."

He's cutting chinks into my armor, and I'm fairly certain he knows it. Time to put on a brave face and get Clint the hell out of here. Fast. "What's the matter with my mother?"

Clint shrugs, studying his fingernails. "Nothing that I know of. I had to say something to get him to leave."

And just that quick, Clint wears out his welcome. I scan the room for something heavy to throw at the imbecile's head. "Get out," I grit through clenched teeth.

"What?"

"Don't what me! You claimed there was something wrong with my mother. You lied and insulted both me and Josh. Do you get your kicks making people feel bad?"

"I'm sorry. But when that kid touched you—"

"He's not a kid. He's twenty-six years old."

"Jesus Christ. What's happened to you, Addy? You do realize how it looks for you to be seen with him. Right? You're almost forty."

It's funny. Before San Diego, people assumed I was in my early thirties. Now, after meeting Josh, I feel like an old, shriveled up hag, thanks in part to my ill-intentioned ex-boyfriend. My nostrils flare as I bite my tongue so hard, I taste blood. "I told you to leave."

Clint stands, his face purposefully neutral. He walks over to me, pulling his fingers through a few strands of my hair. "Lunch. Tomorrow."

"Are you deaf? Did you hear what I said?"

"Give me one lunch to plead my case. After that, I'll leave you alone."

I know he's lying. I also know if I don't appease him, he might never leave, and I won't be responsible for what I do to his corpse if he doesn't. "Fine."

"Don't sound so enthused."

"I'm not," I grit out, pointing in the direction of the door. "If you know what's good for you..."

I don't have to say anything further. With a mock salute and a wink, he walks out of the apartment.

With a sigh, I sink into a chair. Clint might be gone, but his words remain.

Am I making a spectacle of myself? Is the age difference that obvious? Is everyone laughing at us?

I grab my phone and dial Josh. I need time. Time to think. Time to reflect. Time to get good and stinking drunk.

He picks up on the second ring. "How's your mother?"

"She's fine. Clint lied. There's nothing wrong with her."

Josh guffaws into my ear, but I can't blame him. Clint's behavior is borderline psychotic. "He's a piece of work, Addy."

I pull at a thread on the chair, my thoughts jumbled. "That's an understatement. I've been thinking—"

"No. You aren't canceling dinner." Does the man own a crystal ball for his daily scrying?

"But—"

"What did that asshole say?"

I sigh, flopping back against the cushion. "What do you think he said? He brought up the obviousness of our age difference."

"He would."

I expect him to negate Clint's statement, argue that the difference isn't that apparent. When he doesn't, I feel even more trepidation about dating a younger man. "I don't want you to be embarrassed by going out with me. What if people talk?"

"If they talk, it will be because you're gorgeous. And I will never be embarrassed to be by your side. The question is, Addy, are you embarrassed to be seen with me?"

His words give me pause. I never thought of it in that manner, how my insecurities could be read as embarrassment on my part. "Never."

"Then there's no problem. Go rest, and I'll see you this evening."

"Are you really coming to yoga class?"

I can feel his smile through the phone. "If it means I get to spend time with you, absolutely."

We end the call, but the battle between my emotions and my brain rages on.

Josh is cathartic for my soul and my body. But will the opinions of others destroy us before there even *is* an us? I don't know how many more wars I can wage with friends and family members who only see numbers. I also don't know if I can get past the numbers. I'm a scientist, and facts always win.

In this case, the facts aren't looking too good. All signs point to heartache. Namely, mine.

CHAPTER SIXTEEN

YOGA CLASS

I know tons of people who adore yoga. They live for their time at the studio. All I can say is good for them because I am not one of those people. I'm not saying it doesn't have its benefits, but I can think of about a million easier ways to find inner calm than twisting myself into a human pretzel.

It might also have something to do with the fact that I suck at yoga, but I digress.

Regardless, here I am, fully prepared to lose my equilibrium as I attempt to balance on one leg while holding a plate of flaming bananas foster on my head. Or something to that effect.

"I'm so glad you came," Melissa comments from her mat as she moves effortlessly through the movements. My friend is a yoga addict—a 'yoddict', per her own description.

She claims that yoga saved her sanity, and if I would just cave to the quiet, the calm will follow. My friend has never been inside my brain. It's chaos personified. I don't have a hamster on a wheel. I own a damn zoo, and they're all hopped up on speed. Calm isn't happening anytime soon.

"It should be interesting."

"Addy, you don't need to know all the poses. Just flow."

"I'm flowing, I'm flowing," I mutter. Just flow. What does that even mean?

"Well, well, I didn't know you were joining us. Aren't you a welcome and handsome surprise?" Melissa's nudges me as her grin widens.

He came. I don't know why I'm surprised. Josh is always good to his word, but his appearance is an embarrassing reminder of the Clint fiasco earlier today. I swivel on my mat, sending him a shy wave. "Hey. I didn't know if you were going to come."

Josh unrolls his mat, ignoring the drooling looks of the women around him. He's wound his hair up into a man bun, and although I usually hate that look, it's sexy as hell on him. Who am I kidding? Everything is sexy as hell on Josh.

"I told you'd I'd be here." He leans forward, giving my braid a small tug. "I hope you're feeling better. Did you get some rest?"

"I did." I want to apologize to him. Even though I technically didn't do anything wrong, I need him to know where I stand. Rising up on my knees, I cross over to his mat, wrapping my arms around his neck. "I'm sorry," I whisper into his ear.

His arms encircle me, but I feel a hesitancy. I hope it isn't because of what happened earlier. When I pull away, I notice he's focused on the front of the studio and the petite redheaded instructor who just walked in the door.

Feeling silly about my public display, I make haste back to my mat, exchanging a look with Melissa. She shrugs it off, and any further conversation is shelved as our instructor begins the class.

She introduces herself as Chantelle, her voice soft and gentle. Everything about her is fluid, graceful, and hypnotic. She moves on land the way Josh moves in the ocean.

I sneak a peek over at Josh and realize he's tenser than I am. I thought he loved yoga? His jaw is set, and he keeps his eyes downcast except for the glances he's stealing at our lovely instructor.

Addy, you're an idiot. He has to look at her if he's supposed to follow her lead. Stop inventing problems where there are none.

With a deep exhalation, I shake away any off-putting feelings and focus on the flow. My stilted, erratic flow. Hey, I don't claim to be any good at this sort of thing.

Chantelle winds her way around the room, gently guiding the participants into the correct position. Her hands wrap around my hips, pulling them back. "There you go. Breathe in through the nose and out through the mouth. Relax into it."

I know she's trying to be helpful, but I've been breathing for thirty-nine years. I think I've got it down.

Then she moves to Josh. I don't need to see them to feel the energy change.

Then I hear her speak. Her voice remains soft, but there is an excited edge to it now. A familiarity. "Josh! I can't believe you're here. Wait for me after class. I'm so excited to see you."

There goes any chance in hell I have at finding zen today.

I spend the rest of the class wondering how they know each other, how well they know each other, and what—if anything—it actually means. In other words, my zoo just received a new shipment of speed. My brain is on overload.

When the class ends, Melissa tugs my elbow, leading me to a quiet corner of the changing area. Apparently, she heard Chantelle, too. "How does Josh know Chantelle? I've never seen him here before." Her senses are heightened, like a bloodhound that has caught a scent.

I shrug, offering my best nonchalant expression. "I'm not sure. They look about the same age. Maybe they went to school together."

Melissa clicks her tongue against her teeth, unconvinced. "Maybe. Shall we go? Let's grab your man and have a drink."

"Is that standard practice after yoga?" I joke, throwing my clothes into a duffel bag. "I dressed for comfort, not commingling." I stare down at my ripped jeans and t-shirt, the niggling of self-doubt creeping in.

"It is for me."

We walk out of the changing room, and time stops.

You know that feeling that washes over you right before your life shifts drastically? I've only felt this way once before in my life —when I walked in on Clint and Debra riding the hobby horse. I didn't like the feeling then, and now, as I watch Chantelle and Josh converse, I despise it even more.

It's not like they're making out against the studio wall, but there is something cozy about their body language. They know each other—intimately—and I'm not sure I want any further details.

Melissa follows my gauge, clearing her throat to gain my attention. "Go grab your man and let's get out of here."

There's one problem with her demand. Josh is not my man. And looking at the smile on his face as he talks to Chantelle, I'm not sure he ever will be.

"Addy," Melissa hisses. "Come on. We've spent enough time here."

"I don't even know if he wants to join us."

"Only one way to find out." My friend is through waiting around. Looping arms, she half-drags, half-walks me over to the corner where Josh and Chantelle are speaking.

Right before I open my mouth to say something, I see it happen. Their phones come out, and numbers are exchanged.

Melissa sees it too, and it's enough to halt her forward progression.

"Can we just go?" I'm fighting back the tears. Again. I swear, Josh is terrible for my emotional health.

"Sure."

We aren't halfway across the studio floor when I feel a hand on my shoulder. "Hey, I was just coming to look for you."

Sliding on my emotional battle gear, I turn to face Josh, noting that Chantelle is watching us with a great deal of interest. "You found me."

One thing about Josh—he's excellent at reading people. One thing Josh may not know about me is that I'm also no slouch in that arena. It comes with the nursing territory.

He jerks his thumb over his shoulder. "I didn't know Chantelle was the instructor here."

"Small world." What else can I say?

He lets out an embarrassed chuckle, shifting his weight from one foot to the other. "I haven't seen her in years."

I know that laugh. I know that stance. But most of all, my gut is screaming that whatever connection these two had years earlier, is still present today.

"How nice for you." I hope I sound civil, but I'm pretty sure he might catch a cold from the frost in my tone. Summoning all my courage before I devolve into a puddle of tears, I offer a wave. "It was good seeing you. Have a nice evening."

I don't make it two steps before Josh grabs my hand, pulling me outside onto a small balcony. "What the hell, Addy?"

"What the hell is right, Josh." I cross my arms across my chest. It's my best attempt to appear fierce, but let's face it, I'm hardly intimidating.

My attempt fails miserably. The corners of Josh's mouth quirk as he tugs my braid again. One more time and I'm decking him. "You're jealous that I'm talking to Chantelle."

Fuck him for being right. "It's not my business who you speak to. She's a beautiful woman, Josh. She's perfect for you."

The teasing smile slides from his face, replaced by a grimace of distaste. "What is that supposed to mean?"

"It means exactly what I said."

"You want me to go on a date with her?"

I shrug, throwing my hands up. At this point, I just want a drink. Or ten. "That's entirely up to you." I've had enough of this discussion. I turn the door handle, but Josh's arms encircle my waist, pulling me against him. "Let me go, Josh."

"No way." His voice is heated at my ear, his hands within centimeters of areas he shouldn't be touching in public.

"What do you want?"

He nuzzles my hair. "I want you to admit you're jealous of Chantelle. Then I can admit I'm jealous of Clint." His grip tightens as his fingers slide under my t-shirt, all the way up to the edge of my bra. "Then, we can admit that we actually really care about each other."

I turn in his arms, my best stern expression at the ready. But it fades when I meet his gaze. It's hard to remain icy next to a man whose core temperature is hotter than the sun. I don't stand a chance of not melting. "You go first."

"I figured that would be your terms."

I rub my brow, allowing some of the anger to leave my body. "I'm sorry I'm jealous. I don't have any right to be, but I can tell there's something between you."

Josh straightens, clearing his throat. Here is comes. "There was something between us, but that ended years ago. Now she's only looking for surf lessons."

My back stiffens. I call bullshit on that statement. "You and I both know that's a lie."

His rueful expression admits that I'm right. "I'll tell Chantelle that I can't do it. She'll need to find someone else."

I release a sigh, not sure if I'll end up hating myself for saying this later. "That isn't fair either. I mean, I work with *my* ex—"

"Yeah, the one who moved across the country to be with you." He sends me a knowing look. "The one you kicked *me* out of your house to talk to."

Wait a second, did I do that? "I didn't—" I stop myself, the words faltering when I realize that's exactly what I did. "I'm sorry. I should never have asked you to leave. I didn't figure you'd want to stay with Clint around."

"I'd much rather be around when that asshat is near you. So, what do we do, Addy?"

"Tell them both to go pound salt?" I reply with a smirk. "Is that an option?"

Josh smiles, pressing his lips against mine. The kiss might be a PG version of the earlier ones, but it's filled with emotion, his fingers stroking along my neck. "I didn't mean with them, beautiful."

The balcony door opens, and I know who it is without turning around. Josh stiffens in my arms, a muscle ticking in his jaw. "What's up, Chantelle?"

"Sorry to disturb you, but I have another class now." What a load of crap. She's likely been watching this whole time, just waiting to jump in and smash the moment.

"Not a problem." Josh offers her a bland smile before stepping back into the studio.

I turn to squeeze past the tiny redhead. Not so fast.

"Thank you for joining us. Will I see you again?" Her light green eyes hold mine, but I can't read the emotion behind them. Her armor is as thick as my own.

"Quite possibly. Thank you. The class was lovely."

"I'm so glad you enjoyed it. Many thanks for bringing Josh back into my life." Now her face lights up as her gaze floats over to Josh.

I'm tempted to claw her eyes out, but I'm not sure I want to spend a night in jail for pummeling granola girl. "I hear you two have a history."

Her eyes widen with surprise. Apparently, she wasn't expecting Josh to be so forthcoming. "We certainly do. You know what they say about history. It has a tendency to repeat itself."

And there it is. A veiled warning that she is set to make her move, and I'd do well to get the hell out of the way.

She really does deserve a good mauling, or at least some hair pulled from that pretty little head. "They also say that those who don't learn from history are doomed to repeat it. Thankfully, Josh is a quick study."

I don't wait for a reaction or response. All I know is that this is no longer a yoga studio. It's a lion's den.

"Wow, who knew Chantelle was such a bitch?" Melissa flags the server, ordering another round. At this point, she could order three. I need all the alcohol they can give me.

"She knows what she wants, and she wants Josh. Apparently, every woman does." I maintain my gaze on the swirling contents of my glass as I stir the drink into oblivion.

"I think it's mixed, Addy."

I bang the table with my fist. "What do I do, Melissa? I've never felt this way before."

"Clint's a catch, too, you know. At least to the outsider. He's extremely good-looking, a doctor, personable—"

"When he isn't shagging his secretary," I remind her.

ALCHEMY UNFOLDING | 151

"I said to the outsider. My point is that you must have dealt with catty women before now."

I nod, taking another sip of my drink. "They were lined up. The difference was that I didn't really care. Not until Josh, anyway. I was never afraid of losing Clint, but I'm terrified of losing Josh. Worst part? He isn't even mine." With a groan, I bury my head in my hands. "What's wrong with me?"

"You're in love. Isn't it a blast?"

I send her a scathing glare, but my gut knows the truth. I am in love with Josh. I'll likely never tell him, but it's a fact, regardless.

"I have a crazy idea."

I finish off my drink before meeting her gaze. I need liquid courage. "What's that?"

"Why don't you tell Josh how you feel?"

"Hard pass. I am not up for being made a fool of again."

"When did Josh make you feel like a fool?"

"He didn't. Clint did."

"Might I suggest you stop holding Josh accountable for the crap your ex put you through?"

She has a point. A good point. It still doesn't mean I'll listen. "I'm having lunch with Clint tomorrow."

A frown of puzzlement creases her brow. "Why? Does Josh know?"

"Clint made me a deal. I have one lunch with him, and he'll leave me alone."

"I repeat, does Josh know?"

I wince at her pointed question. "No, I haven't said anything to Josh."

"Addy, please get your head out of your ass."

"What is that supposed to mean?"

"Just what I said. You're angry that Josh ran into an ex-girlfriend and exchanged numbers. I get it. I'd be mad, too. But you forget to mention the lunch date you're having with your ex. See the hypocrisy there?"

"Josh and I aren't dating, Melissa."

"Well, you're certainly more than friends."

My head returns to my hands with another groan. It's the safest place, really. "I don't know what we are."

Melissa gives my arm a reassuring pat. "Then there's a good chance that Josh is as confused as you are. All I can say is don't fuck up a future reminiscing with the past."

CHAPTER SEVENTEEN

NOT TAKING NO FOR AN ANSWER

*C*lint is not a man who's easily dissuaded. Even though I canceled our lunch date the night before, here he stands on my doorstep, a bouquet of roses in his hands.

The roses are beautiful, but I know he put little to no thought into the purchase, considering my favorite roses are pink and not red. Still, it's an effort. Too little, too late, but there's no need for me to be a bitch.

Until he opens his mouth.

"Are you still going to dinner with that kid?" he demands, thrusting the flowers into my hand.

"Good morning to you, too." I close the door behind him, steeling myself for this conversation.

"Answer the question."

"I don't have to answer any question that you pose, if I don't feel like it. But yes, I am having dinner with Josh. I assume you have an issue with that."

Clint hesitates, and I see him playing an internal monologue about what he needs to say to keep me away from Josh. It's a perk of knowing someone for so many years. "I don't like it, Addy."

"Thank you for your unsolicited opinion. Anything else?"

"I know I don't have a right to say anything, and I also realize that I'm the last person to give out relationship advice. I had a great woman, and I fucked it up completely."

It's the closest thing I've ever heard to an apology from Clint. It's a welcome shock, and I feel some of the resentment ease with his earnest statement. I didn't realize how much angst I'd been holding over his betrayal. "Thank you. I needed to hear that."

"I don't deserve a second chance, but I'm asking for one."

I release a low groan. "Clint, I can't even—"

"I just want you to consider it. Let me do it right this time."

"What does that mean? Do what right?"

"Love you. Take care of you. Spoil you. All the things I didn't do the first time."

"Why didn't you do those things, Clint? Why did it take me leaving for you to even consider wanting to include those ideals in our relationship? You did them for Debra," my voice cracks at the last statement, but it's more mortification than heartbreak. "You didn't think I knew, but I did. I knew about the jewelry, the expensive dinners, the flowers." I motion to the roses in the vase. "Red roses are Debra's favorite. Not mine."

Clint frowns, gazing out the window instead of my face. "I'm trying."

"No, you're putting in as little effort as you believe is necessary. Why do you want me back? We weren't happy."

His eyes blaze with sudden, unleashed anger. "Does the kid make you happy?"

"He has a name."

"I don't give a shit what his name is, Adelaide." And there it is, the condescending tone I'd grown to know and loathe with Clint. "Have you done any research on your boy toy? Because I have."

"Why am I not surprised," I grumble, pacing lines into the carpet. "Pray tell, what did you find out? Is he a felon? Murderer? Leper? What heinous crime is Josh guilty of?"

"He's the quintessential party boy. You really should examine his social media accounts and those of his closest friends. It's interesting how...popular Josh is with the ladies."

I've heard enough. I'm not sure where the line between truth and bullshit lies, but Clint crossed it the moment he stepped over my threshold. I pick up the flowers and hand them to him. "It's time for you to leave. Don't forget your roses."

"Addy, I'm trying to protect you."

"Right," I guffaw, a headache brewing behind my eyes. It's become a daily occurrence lately. "When did that happen? When you were screwing another woman?"

"I know I messed up, but this guy isn't as perfect as you might think. He's playing a game. He's typical. A typical, young playboy. I just thought you should know."

"He's not the social butterfly he once was. That's not his life anymore." I don't know why I'm telling Clint anything about Josh. It's not his business, but I feel obligated to defend myself and my relationship with Josh. Whatever that relationship may be.

"That's what he's telling you."

"What are you implying?"

"The photos are fairly recent, yet you're not in any of them. I find it odd that he's dating you, and yet, there's no sign of you on his social media feeds."

I scoff at the ludicrous statement. "That's ridiculous. We haven't taken any photos together, and we haven't known each other that long."

"Perhaps I'm mistaken. I do know that when I was seeing

Debra, I never took her to any public location. All events were reserved for you."

"What a guy," I mutter, tempted to pitch something at his head.

"My point is that Debra was someone I kept very private. I hid away our relationship—apparently not that well, but I wasn't showing her off. Everything was on the down-low."

"What is your point?" I seethe, my foot tapping with wild abandon on the floor.

"Just be careful he isn't hiding you away. If you're that special —which you are—he should want to show you off." He casts a withering glance at the roses. "Keep the flowers. Give them away if you don't want them."

I spend the next thirty minutes considering all aspects of my discussion with Clint. I know he hates the idea of Josh and is trying to undermine our fledgling relationship, but his statements echo with truth. When you're embarrassed by someone, you don't take them places. You squirrel them—and your relationship— away. Clint is right on one count. I don't want to be played for a fool again.

In his defense, Josh hasn't had much opportunity to take me anywhere, and he's taking me to dinner tonight. Clint's theory? Disproven.

I can't believe Clint researched Josh on social media. I guess that's the norm these days. Even more strange, that I never bothered to check out his profiles. But now, it's an itch begging to be scratched.

With a sigh, I flip open my laptop and search for Josh's accounts. They're easy to find. Front and center. I skim the photos, most of them surfing or sponsor related.

Then I see a folder marked 'Good Times'. This has to be what Clint was talking about. I click into the file, and there are so many photos. The locations are scattered along the southern California coast, shot mostly in restaurants and nightclubs. There's a similar vibe pervading the pictures—gorgeous men with equally beautiful women draped over them. I think one woman is wearing a bandana in lieu of a skirt. How cute.

Still, they're innocuous, and all were taken before I met Josh.

Clint, you're such an asshole.

Then I see it. Scrolling almost to the bottom, I find a photo of Josh and Chantelle, aka Little Red Yoga Hood. I'm aware it's a petty nickname for the auburn beauty, but I'm in a petty mood.

They're sitting on a boat, his arms and legs wrapped around her lithe form. But it's the smile on their faces that stops me. He looks so happy. They both do.

Why is her photo still on his accounts? I thought they were ancient history. Apparently, he and I have different definitions of ancient.

With a grunt, I shut the laptop case.

What am I supposed to do? I can't unsee the photos, and now the seed that Clint so meticulously planted has taken hold. Granted, he was hoping the club photos would send me over the edge, but it's the personal photo of the woman who's now back in possession of Josh's phone number that's really the doozy.

Maybe it's better if I walk away now and cut all ties.

Maybe I pretend I never saw the photos—let Clint's opinion be damned.

Or maybe I play it safe and keep Josh in the friend zone.

Friends don't get hurt when someone falls in love and that someone isn't them. Friends is the only box I feel safe in, and it's where my heart will have to stay.

CHAPTER EIGHTEEN

FIRST DATE JITTERS

I'm shocked I haven't paced a hole in the carpet. I've never been so nervous on a date before, and this isn't even a date. After seeing that photo of Josh with Chantelle, I know I'm safe, but only in the friend zone.

Still, I'm not sure where we're going for dinner, so I opt for a dark pink sundress and strappy sandals. I'm also wearing a black lace g-string and matching bra, even though I have no intention of shedding my clothes in front of Josh. Again. But considering how often it seems to happen, I want to be prepared.

That and I look hot as hell in the damn lingerie. *Eat your heart out, Josh.*

Inwardly, I'm shaken. The knowledge that Josh still carries a torch for Chantelle and the woman is once again in his life, deflates the balloon of my self-confidence.

That, and Clint has totally screwed with my brain—again. The bastard.

I have a plan all set for tonight. We enjoy a pleasant dinner and split the bill. Then, I let him know that I want to remain friends. Since his ex has shown up back in his life, Josh will likely be relieved. He's one of the sweetest men I know, and I think the idea of hurting anyone guts him.

Granted, the idea of him with another woman guts me, but c'est la vie.

The doorbell rings, and I take a few deep breaths, praying I don't pass out before I open the door. This pretending not to be emotionally invested is exhausting.

Josh stands on the other side of the door, a bouquet in his hands. White daisies and dark pink roses tied with a taffeta ribbon. I can tell from the wrapping that he actually stopped by a florist to pick out the flowers. Two seconds in and I'm already in trouble.

"Hi," I manage, letting him into the apartment. "You look wonderful."

He really does. He always looks good, but tonight he is spectacular. A black button-down hugs his pecs, his blonde hair pulled back to showcase the most gorgeous face I've ever seen on a man, complete with a sensual smile that echoes in his eyes. "Wow. You are stunning, Addy."

If I didn't know better, I'd swear he's nervous. "Thank you. I wasn't sure where we were going tonight, so I figured this would cover most of the bases."

He glances at the flowers and then at my dress. "I'm glad I went with the pink. You didn't seem like a red roses type of girl."

I'm not sure why the statement makes me tear up. I'm just an emotional wreck lately. I bury my face in the flowers, noting the heady scent. The flowers from Clint lacked any smell at all. "They're beautiful. You didn't have to get me flowers."

His gaze moves to the counter, where the other bouquet sits in a vase. "I see I'm not the only one." A muscle jumps in his jaw as he lets out a loud sigh.

I wince at the faux pas. I meant to move the damn things. "I tried to give them back, but Clint told me to keep them. If they bother you, I'll throw them away. Yours are so much prettier."

His smile is part bemused, part hesitant. It seems we're both on our guard now. "You don't have to throw out the flowers. They didn't do anything wrong."

"Good point. Let me put these in water, and I'll be ready to go. Where are we headed?" I want to keep the conversation light while trying to force my heart to still when I'm within ten feet of him.

"We're going back to my house. I wanted to cook for us tonight."

My eyes widen as Clint's warning reverberates in my brain. Is Josh hiding me? Is he keeping our relations quiet so that no one is the wiser?

It doesn't matter. You're friends, remember?

"Oh, okay. I guess I could have worn yoga pants." I squeeze my eyes closed. First, I hate appearing ungrateful, and second, I don't want to remind him of Little Red Yoga Hood. Not that Josh needs any reminding. A woman like that is hard to forget.

"We can go out, Addy. Anywhere you want. I just...I thought it would be more romantic at home. No strangers around us. Just you and me. Finally."

If Clint hadn't dropped by with his verbal bombshell, Josh's words would bowl me over. But that snake of an ex has planted a tenacious seed, and all I can think is that Josh doesn't want to be seen in public with me.

Plastering on a brave smile that I pray reaches my eyes, I grab my purse and squeeze his forearm. "I think it's a terrific idea. No one's ever cooked for me before. I'm guessing there's still no side of bacon, though."

My light banter is contagious as Josh links his fingers through mine. "Still no bacon, but I promise, you won't miss it."

HE'S RIGHT about the bacon. I forget about it as soon as I step through Josh's front door. Clint's accusatory statements also take a backseat as I gaze around the living room. The bouquet at home was just a preview. Six more vases of flowers decorate the living space, and candles are everywhere. The smell of incense wafts through the house, and from this vantage point, I can see he continued the decorations into the backyard. "You did all this for me?"

His hands frame my face, his thumbs brushing across my skin. "Only for you, Addy."

That does it. I try holding back the tears, but it's a futile attempt. I wipe them away, praying that Josh doesn't see me crying.

I forget that Josh sees everything. "Not the reaction I hoped for. I certainly didn't want to make you cry. I just want tonight to be special. I want you to know how much you mean to me."

"They're happy tears. No one has ever done anything like this for me before. It's gorgeous."

"You're gorgeous."

And with those two words, I realize being friends with this man will be damn near impossible.

Josh strolls into the kitchen. "Everything is cooked, I'm just letting it simmer."

I peek over the breakfast bar. The man doesn't do anything by halves. I see four different pots on the stove, but he manages them with the same grace he handles the ocean. "Can I help?"

Josh smiles at me as he stirs one of the dishes. "You can open the wine. It's chilling in the fridge."

"I thought you didn't drink."

"I drink on special occasions." He offers me a taste of one of the courses. It's an eggplant dish that melts in my mouth. "And you are a very special occasion."

ON TOP of being a world-renowned surfer with fashion model looks, Josh is also a gourmet chef. His middle eastern style feast tastes so damn good, I want to lick my plate clean.

After dinner, we settle into the giant lounger on the patio. It's literally a bed outside, and far too comfortable, especially with Josh's proximity.

"It's a beautiful night," I murmur, gazing at the stars. It is a perfect night, cloudless and bright, with a slight breeze that carries the scent of the ocean. "I want to thank you for the wonderful meal. For the decorations. For...everything."

"You want to thank me? Kiss me, Addy. I've been waiting all night."

"Have you?"

His fingers trace along my jaw, sparks shooting through my body. "You know I have."

With a sigh, I roll onto my back. "I wish you were older. Or I was younger."

My words surprise me. I'm shocked I actually voiced it.

"Why is the age difference such a big deal for you?"

My eyes widen at his blatant question. I guess he's diving right in. "Josh, you know why."

"No, I don't. Is it your personal preference or based on the assumptions of others?"

I turn back onto my side, propping my head on my hand. "People talk, Josh. And they're not kind, particularly when the woman is older. Your friends are among that group. When they thought there was something happening between us—"

"Something is happening between us."

"You know what I mean. Your friend calls me Mrs. Robinson. Mariah has flat out told me that I should stick with a man my own age, and we've never even slept together."

"See? We should sleep together since they're already talking."

I know he's joking, but his words enflame my core. If our previous intimate encounters are a sample of the total package— holy hell, what an exquisitely talented man.

"Don't you care what people say?"

"Nope, and you shouldn't either. Addy, there will always be people who have something negative to say, particularly when they're jealous."

"Jealous? I doubt either of them are jealous."

"They are. Mariah wants me, and Frank wants you."

"Frank hates me!"

"He wants you, and he covers it by acting like he hates you. Trust me, he and I almost came to blows the other night."

"Over me?" I find that scenario impossible to imagine.

"Let's just say he made his feelings known, and I asserted my...authority."

"Huh." Josh, a gentle pacifist, almost got into a knock-down drag-out fight. Over me. "I'm not going to lie. That's pretty hot, Josh."

His eyes widen at my statement. "That I almost got into a fight?"

"No, that you were willing to go that route to assert your dominance. But don't put that pretty face in harm's way again. I'm not worth it. I'm not even yours."

"Only because you don't want to be. And Addy, you are always worth it."

I turn away from his gaze, that paralyzing, mesmerizing gaze that feels like drowning in a warm blue ocean.

"My point," Josh continues, "is that some people will always find fault with the person you're with. If it's not our age difference, it's because I'm a surfer. Or from California. The reasons are endless, but they're all bullshit. It doesn't matter what other people think."

"Oh, no?"

"Not at all. It only matters what you think. What you want." He leans back on his elbows, studying me. "What do *you* want, Addy?"

"In a relationship?"

He nods. "What characteristics? Do you even know the answer to that question? If no one else has a say—which they shouldn't by the way—what kind of man do you want by your side?"

I suck in air slowly, but it never seems to reach my lungs. How is this man able to lay out my issues with such clarity?

I know what kind of man I want, and he's sitting next to me. I'm never forward, but if he's granting me such honesty, I need to return the favor. "I never dreamt someone like you existed. I feel my best around you, Josh. Actually, I feel like an upgraded version of myself. I'm happy, peaceful. I'm not angry anymore. And calm. Very calm."

The corners of his mouth quirk as his fingers trail along my arm. "Is that so?"

"Except when you're touching me."

His brows raise as his fingers stop moving, but he doesn't retract his hand.

"I can't stay calm when you're touching me."

Another smile as the gentle caress resumes. "How do you feel when I touch you?"

"Like I'm a firework with a lit fuse, about to explode into a million tiny pieces."

His fingers move to my thigh, sliding under the hem of my dress. "What about now?"

"Josh— "

"Tell me."

"Like the fuse is getting shorter."

His mouth nuzzles my neck as his tongue slides along my skin. "Let me make you explode, Addy."

I should stop him. I open my mouth to stop him, but the only sound from my lips is a low moan, followed by a ragged breath when his fingers slide past my underwear and stroke along my folds.

His kiss deepens as his fingers slip inside me. "You're so soft, Addy. Soft and wet."

Another moan. It's all I can manage.

Josh moves over top of me, lowering my back to the lounger. His hand cups the back of my head as his tongue laves against mine. His other hand? All kinds of busy as his fingers pump in and out of me. First one. Then two. When a third finger joins the party, I moan into his mouth.

Holy shit, I don't think I can handle this.

His thumb circles my clit, effectively driving me out of my mind as his tongue massages every corner of my mouth.

When he moves his hand away, I whimper with surprise. I was so close. Why would he stop? But one look into his hooded gaze tells me he's far from finished.

I gasp when his hands hook under the edge of my thong. "Lift up."

"What are you doing?"

"What does it look like? Now lift up."

Josh holds my gaze as he tosses my underwear over his shoulder. He then pushes my skirt up to my waist, leaving me fully exposed.

"Get up here," I beseech. "I want to kiss you."

"And I want to kiss you." But instead of moving up my body, he's traveling south. His tongue traces a line between my collarbone and cleavage, leaving a trail of sparks in his wake.

"Wrong way, buddy." I try to keep my voice light, but my heart is pounding like a freight train.

"Oh no, I'm definitely moving in the right direction." He suckles my nipple through the dress, soaking the fabric. "I'm dying to taste you."

His words send a spark of apprehension through me. Clint hates oral sex. And foreplay. To be fair, the selfish bastard has no problem being on the receiving end, but his stingy sexual appetite left me with a huge issue surrounding the act.

"You don't have to do that."

"Are you kidding? Since that hike, it's pretty much all I can think about."

"No, Josh. I-I'm not any good at that."

His turquoise eyes widen, and he chuckles. "Beautiful, I think what you mean is that they weren't any good at it."

"No, they—"

His fingers press to my lips, ending any further discussion as he tongues along the curve of my hip. "Addy, I want to taste you. You smell amazing, and I know you're going to taste even better."

"But—"

"Shh. Relax. You might just enjoy it." His mouth hovers over my pussy as his tongue swipes along the seam.

It's incredible. In just that second, he surpasses every oral experience I've ever had.

Josh growls low in his chest, spreading my lips and running his tongue along each edge. "You're delicious."

His tongue sinks into me, and for a moment, time ceases to

exist. I can't hear or see, all I can do is grab hold of his long hair and press him closer.

His hands band around my thighs, locking my legs open, granting him access. He's insatiable as he feasts on me, and unless Josh is one hell of an actor, he's enjoying this as much as I am.

Long, talented fingers slide deep inside me, curling around to hit a spot I never knew existed on the human body. My hips buck involuntarily. I'm going to explode just like that firework. They'll never find all the shards.

"Josh, please," I beg for the release I know he can bring me.

He pulls back an inch, but I remain pinned by that velvet stare. "Come for me, Addy. Come all over my tongue. I can't get enough of your taste."

When his tongue slides deep inside me again, my body hurls itself off the cliff and into oblivion.

I'm not sure how long it is before I regain any sense of time or place. I gaze over at Josh, catching the satisfied smirk on his face. Hell, he should be proud of himself. Talk about a life-changing experience.

"Wow. I just...wow. I've never—"

"I know. And I'm damn sorry."

"You're sorry?" I steel myself. Great. Here it comes.

"Yes. A pussy as delicious as yours needs to be licked daily."

I flounder to find words, but I needn't bother.

Josh winks at me, pressing a kiss to my inner thigh. "I know just the man for the job."

His flirtation makes me smile. "Do you? Maybe I should ask him if he's interested."

"No need to inquire. I assure you that he's definitely interested."

He wants to be playful, I can play. "Josh?"

"Hmm?" His fingers run along my side, stirring my insides

back into a frenzy. My body is already geared up and begging for more. "What can I do for you, beautiful? Just name it."

I consider asking him, but showing is far more fun. Climbing on top of him, I offer him a sultry smile as my fingers fumble with his zipper.

"What are you doing, Addy?" His words are more curiosity than inquiry, and if his seductive gaze is anything to go by, he sure as hell doesn't want me to stop.

"Returning the favor."

"Is that so?" His voice is low, heated, much like his delicious skin.

"It's my turn." Pressing kisses along his washboard stomach, I tongue his navel, feeling his body clench. "I've wanted to touch you as much as you wanted to touch me."

"One condition."

Condition? That doesn't sound promising. "What?" I continue my oral exploration, pressing kisses along his hip.

"I come deep inside you."

My gaze shoots upwards, meeting his. My head screams to back away slowly, but my body is too far gone. I want him. No, I'm so far beyond wanting at this point. I crave him.

"Can I, Addy?"

I don't answer with words. Instead, I slide down his pants, freeing him from his boxers. I slide my hand along his shaft. I never thought I would find a cock so attractive, but he's long, thick, and beautiful. I bend my head and let my tongue circle the tip, his hips bucking against me. "Anything you want, Josh."

A low groan escapes Josh's mouth. "You," he grunts. "I want you, Addy. I want all of you."

"Then, I'll give you all of me." I grasp his length and lower my mouth around him. I flatten my tongue and run it from base to tip, scratching my nails along his hair roughened thigh. His grunt of satisfaction spurs me on, and when his hand wraps in my hair, I lose my last vestige of control.

"Take your dress off. I need to see this incredible body."

I slip the straps off and shimmy out of the dress. I am so glad I opted for the fancy lingerie. Judging by Josh's heated expression, so is he.

"Fuck, just look at you, Addy. I want you so bad. Get back over here."

I don't waste a second getting back to his side, my body aching to feel him inside me. Josh pulls me against him, his hands sliding along my ass as his lips seize mine in a scintillating kiss.

"Josh," I murmur as his expert tongue flicks against my pulse point, my nails raking across his skin.

We jerk from our hormone infused haze at the sound of shattering glass at the front of Josh's house.

"Stay here," Josh warns, throwing on his pants to go investigate.

I scramble into my clothes, figuring it would be par for the course to be killed by a psycho killer only moments after the most explosive orgasm of my life.

Universe, what a cryptic sense of humor you have.

"Don't worry, Dad. It's not a big deal." Josh is speaking louder than necessary, likely to warn me that we have company. At least it's company that isn't planning on slitting our throats.

"I broke the damn flowerpot. I'll replace it."

The patio door opens, and Josh walks out, wearing a rueful smile. "It's my Dad. He's had a bit too much to drink."

My heart is still in my throat, thinking my corpse was going to decorate tomorrow's newspaper. "Is he okay?"

"It's hard for him this time of year. The anniversary of my mother's death is tomorrow. This was their final night together."

I run to Josh, throwing my arms around his waist. "I'm so sorry for both of you. I'll get out of here." I blush, turning my head away. "Sorry I got so carried away before."

He grasps my chin, forcing my gaze upward. "You need to get carried away like that every single day." His fingers tuck a piece of hair behind her ear, tracing along the length of my neck. "What you do to me, Addy. I've never felt this way before."

I know I've never felt it before, either. But I can't risk saying it, putting it out there. Making it real. "I'm going to call a cab."

"Please stay."

"I don't want to intrude. You need to spend time with your father."

"You aren't intruding. My dad knows how important you are to me."

"He does?"

"Yes," he laughs, his fingers curling around my hip. "It's not exactly a secret."

The door swings open as his father lumbers onto the deck. "Josh, I can't get the damn coffee machine to work." Mr. Gibbs stops when he catches sight of me, a sheepish expression crossing his face. "Shit. I *am* interrupting."

I force a smile for the man. He looks so lost. "You're not interrupting. I'll go make the coffee."

His father offers a sad grin and a wave of his flask. "You're a bad liar. Both of you, bad liars. But an old man appreciates it."

I squeeze his arm as I walk past. If the pain is this acute all these years later, he must have adored his wife.

Stephan spends the majority of the next hour reminiscing about Lisa, regaling us both with stories of their courtship. It's like a fairytale, only without the happy ending.

"To have a love like that," I murmur.

His father's gaze darts between Josh and me. "I believe you do.

The way you two look at each other." With that final remark, his head lolls to the side, and he's out for the count.

Josh repositions him, covering him with a blanket. I hope he isn't too mortified by his father's words. They don't seem to upend him in any way. He turns to me, offering me a hand up. "Let's go to bed. I want to hold you in my arms."

God, I want that so much. "I don't know—"

"Yes, you do. You know what your heart wants. It's what my heart wants too." He leads me into the bedroom, closing the door behind us.

"Josh, we don't make sense. You're gorgeous and brilliant and talented—"

"I thought those were good qualities?" He unzips my dress, pushing the straps off my shoulder.

"They are. But you're also so very young. I know you claim not to care about the age difference, but there's no future here. There can't be."

"Why not?"

I turn to face him, holding the dress up with my hand. "What happens when you get tired of this? Of me? When you miss the club scene and late-night parties and nameless lays?"

"Addy, I don't do any of that now. I can't stand the club scene. I don't party, and the only person I want to be inside is you."

He might be lying. But he might also be telling the truth, and right now, truth wins. He's right. I want him, and he claims to want me. The other issues will sort themselves.

With a smile, I release both the dress and my inhibitions. No, we won't have sex with his father in the next room, but I can at least show off my fancy lingerie with the lights on. Josh's eyes widen as he lets out a grunt of approval.

"Goddamn, you're beautiful."

I pivot, sending him a cheeky grin. "You think so?"

"I know so. I also know it's taking everything in me not to rip that gorgeous lingerie off your sexy body." His hands glide along my curves, his eyes alight with desire. "I'm hungry again."

"So am I, but it looks like we're on a diet for the rest of the night."

Josh groans, tossing his head back. "Ugh. I love you, Dad, but your timing sucks." His eyes glow with mischief. "We could be quiet."

"I don't think that's possible. You heard me earlier."

"Fuck, now I'm hard as a rock thinking about it."

I crook my finger at him, beckoning him to the bed. "I know *I'm* not good at staying quiet, but do you think you could? I have some unfinished business I'd like to settle."

Josh wastes no time stripping down to his naked glory. "I'm all yours, Addy."

Not yet, Josh. But soon. Very soon.

CHAPTER NINETEEN

THE MAN IS PERFECT

*W*aking up in Josh's arms is a luxury I want every day of my life. He held me the entire night, my head cushioned against his chest, and my leg thrown over him in a possessive gesture.

I trace the line of his pecs, loving the feel of the hair under my fingers. Then, before my head can say otherwise, I press a kiss to his heart. His grip tightens around me as his mouth nuzzles my hair.

"I love waking up to you."

I meet his gaze, resting my chin on his chest. "Me, too."

He draws closer, cupping my jaw and pulling me into a slow, sensuous kiss. I stretch up as the kiss deepens, my fingers scratching along his chest, demanding more. Josh meets me more than halfway, rolling me onto my back, his teeth scraping along my neck.

Our movements are heated, growing hotter, and more frenzied by the second. His hands cup my breasts as his tongue skates down my body. He teases my nipples, rolling them between his thumb and forefinger, and I arch up against his hands. I release a moan as his mouth claims me again, his hips grinding against me.

"I want to be inside you, Addy," Josh huffs against my neck.

"I want that, too." My body doesn't care to think about the consequences. I need him. I wrap my legs around his waist, pulling him against me.

I feel his erection pressing against my stomach. He's so close, but it's not nearly close enough. I know once we cross this line, we can't ever go back. My hand closes around his shaft as he bucks against my palm. "Addy." His voice is a strangled moan, thick with desire. He needs me as much as I need him. It's been building since that first day, and now, it's at boiling point. He ducks his head into the crook of my neck, his breathing heavy and panting.

"If you want me, take me."

"I've never wanted anyone this much in my life. But I refuse to rush this moment. I need to be inside you all day, feeling you come around me, again and again."

"You don't want me now?"

Josh releases a strangled chuckle. "More than oxygen. But my father is in the next room, and I want you to be anything but quiet."

I groan with the realization that his dad is literally on the other side of the wall. How in the hell did I forget? Oh yes, I'm laying here next to Neptune, and that's enough to make me forget my own name. "Shit, I'm sorry."

"Stop apologizing. It took everything I had not to slide inside you just now. But we'll have our time, and I'm going to make it so spectacular that you'll never leave my side."

My lips part in a saucy grin. "Careful what you wish for. You might end up stuck with me."

"That's the plan, Addy."

I let out a sated groan as Josh rolls off me, pushing himself off the bed.

I pop up, picking up my scattered clothing from around the room and pulling it on. I'm so out of sorts that I'm shocked my dress isn't inside out.

I hear movement on the other side of the wall. It looks like his dad is up.

With a final grin, we walk into the living room. His father is awake, but not yet upwardly mobile. "My head is blasting."

"I can make you some coffee," I offer.

"Thank you, dear. I am so sorry I ruined your night."

I smile and shake my head. "You didn't ruin anything. Last night was perfect."

Mr. Gibbs looks at his son. "Grab this one up before someone else does. She's a rare one."

"I'm working on it, Dad."

Josh's words simultaneously soothe and enflame my soul. There's no way what I feel—what *we* feel—is wrong.

"Are you coming with me to visit Mom?" Mr. Gibbs questions, rubbing his hand across his brow.

I nod at Josh. I know he feels like he's abandoning me, but I won't have it any other way. "He is." I select the largest of the bouquets and hand it to Mr. Gibbs. "He picked up flowers for her, too."

"They're beautiful," Mr. Gibbs murmurs, thanking me as I press a mug of coffee into his hand.

Josh pulls me against him, nuzzling my neck. "You know, I was wrong."

My eyes widen. Did I overstep my bounds? "About what?"

"When I woke up next to you, I couldn't imagine loving you more. But then you go and up the ante once again, and I know that I couldn't love you more than I do in this moment."

✸

MY HIGH CONTINUES straight through my shift, and I manage to aggravate everyone with my cheerfulness. Okay, Melissa is highly amused. Clint, however, is less than thrilled. He barks orders in my direction, and I piss him off further by responding with a smile.

Fuck him. He should have realized what he had *before* he tossed it out the window.

My phone buzzes, and I glance at the text, a grin painting my face.

"I know who that's from," Melissa says with a knowing wink.

"I hate that we work opposite schedules, but I plan on making the most of our time together."

"Listen to you. What changed?"

I shrug, biting my lower lip. "I guess I did. I finally realized Josh was serious. I thought I was just a member of his harem, but it looks like I was mistaken."

"I told you he wasn't like that. You need to listen to me more often." She glances at the clock. "Why don't you go take a break?"

"I'm fine."

"Okay, I'm telling you to take a break."

I offer a salute and smirk at my boss. "Yes ma'am. I'll be back."

Tonight is too pretty to spend indoors. I'll eat while basking in the moonlight. Maybe sneak in a talk with Mr. Wonderful.

"Addy."

I jump at the unexpected voice, breaking into a smile when I see Josh leaning against the outside wall. "What are you doing here?"

"I came to surprise you. I wanted to see you."

Not caring who sees, I run over to him and pull him into a

deep kiss. He's always so warm, and those lips of his are more addictive than any drug.

"Hello, beautiful." His smile assures me that he's more than pleased with my overt display of affection. "Come on. I prepared a late dinner for us."

We stroll to his truck, and he pulls out a collection of tins. I swear the man is spoiling the hell out of me, and I love every second. "A girl could get used to this kind of treatment, Josh."

"That's the idea." He leans over, stealing a quick kiss before offering me a plate of food. "I figured it might be better than hospital food."

"Is there anything you can't do?" I tease, digging into the delicious vegetable pasta dish.

I expect lighthearted banter in return, but Josh turns serious. "I can't walk away from you."

"I don't want you going anywhere. I want you right here. With me."

His fingers caress my jaw, a strange look in his eyes. He's silent for a few beats, and I wonder if I've said too much. Perhaps my forward declarations came on too strong. Finally, with a small smile, he says one word. "Okay."

My brain starts whirring with all the possible meanings behind that two-syllable word, but my heart intercedes.

Stop it. Just go with it.

I smile up at him as I finish off my meal, breathing in the cool night air. "How was your day? How's your Dad?"

He taps the steering wheel with his water bottle, and I see him searching for the right words. Sometimes, there aren't any. "He's doing better, and it's thanks to you."

"Me? I didn't do anything."

"It makes him happy to see me care about someone like I care about you. And...to see that person return the affection."

His statement gives me pause. I highly doubt that someone like Josh has had to deal with many broken hearts, but perhaps I'm mistaken. "I'm crazy about you."

I want to scream that I'm in love with him, but I don't want him leaving tire marks as he screeches out of the parking lot. Men are strange when it comes to the 'L' word, at least the men I've been around. Even Clint rarely used the term, and it was never backed by any affection.

Josh smiles at me as he strokes his hand along his beard. "Not quite the declaration I was hoping for, but I'll take it."

Wait a second. Does Josh want me to tell him I love him? Should I say it? I feel my body tremble with the idea, but my alarm breaks into the moment. Saved by the bell. Literally. "It's time for me to get back. Thank you so much for doing this."

"I'm glad I got to spend a few minutes with you."

"How did you know when I was going on a break?"

Josh lets out a laugh. "You caught me. I called and spoke with Melissa. She helped to set it up."

"No wonder she insisted I take my break now." I lean over the console, capturing that gorgeous mouth in another kiss. "Thank you, handsome. When can I see you again?"

"Tomorrow? I have some stuff to do during the day, but my evening is free."

"Sounds perfect." After a final kiss, I pop out of the truck and head back to work, realizing that everything about Josh is perfect, including the way he makes me feel.

CHAPTER TWENTY

HOW FOOLISH CAN ONE WOMAN BE?

For a brief moment, I contemplate wearing some sexy lingerie with only a raincoat thrown over the top. Very va-va-voom and leaving no doubt what my mind—and body —wanted.

I'm so damn glad I didn't go with that option.

"Mrs. Robinson, what a surprise," Frank leers at me as he opens the door.

"I could say the same thing," I respond through gritted teeth. Sad part? I'm not even surprised that the man is at Josh's house. I wonder if he actually has a home of his own. I am, however, getting a bit tired of the frat house mentality that seems to pervade Josh's residence.

I want to get laid, damn it, and I don't want to do it with a bunch of drunken hoodlums on the back patio.

I walk into the house and find Josh in the kitchen with Mariah and a few nameless beach bunnies. I swear, the term is appropriate. They seem to multiply like rabbits, and none of them are ever fully clothed. It's as if their uniform is a bikini top and shorts.

To say I'm less than thrilled is an understatement.

"Hey Josh, look who's here," Frank comments, stealing a beer from the fridge.

At least my man has the decency to look sheepish. The bastard. "Hey, beautiful. Give me one minute, okay?"

I shrug, because what other choice do I have? Storming out and nursing a bottle of vodka and an unsatiated sex drive? The options are plentiful.

Instead, I take the beer that Frank offers and stalk into the living room, settling in a sunbeam drenched chair. I don't know how Josh does it with people always milling around. I would lose my damn mind. Then again, I'm also thirteen years older. The concept of community living went out of fashion years ago.

"Hey," Josh steps in front of me, blocking the sun. "Come with me." He leads me into the bedroom and locks the door. At least now, his cronies will have to knock before barging into our private moment.

I glare at the door with a pointed stare. "Do you need to lock me in?"

"No, I need to lock them out. I'm so sorry. This was supposed to be done by now."

"What is *this* exactly? It looks like a bunch of people hanging out and drinking."

"We had a photoshoot earlier in the day, a bunch of local business people who are living the quintessential San Diego life."

"Right," I mutter.

"Instead of going home afterward, everyone came here. It was Frank's idea. It was a bad idea."

I bite my lip to avoid the rant playing in my head. Frank isn't worth my energy. But I'm so aggravated at this point, I'm beginning to wonder if Josh is worth my energy, either.

"Please don't be mad." His hands wind around my shoulders, rubbing my skin.

I shrug off his touch. I'm far too annoyed at the moment. "I'm not mad."

"Yes, you are. You have a right to be."

"Why couldn't you call me and tell me plans changed?"

"I lost track of time."

It's an innocent response, but it hits with the weight of a bulldozer. Josh forgot to call me and cancel. I wasn't important enough to remember. I let out a slow exhalation and a defeated shake of my head. Vodka bottle, here I come. "I won't keep you."

"Addy, no, please don't go."

"Josh, I'm really not up for another night with your friends. They all hate me, remember?"

"That's not true."

"It's true enough. For me, at least." I pull out my phone, flipping through my messages. "Besides, Sean mentioned a concert downtown. I told him I had plans, but it looks like I don't. What the hell, I'm dressed for it." I hate that I spent two hours getting ready for Josh, but at least I know I look good.

Damn good.

Josh's fingers wrap around my arm. "Who the hell is Sean?"

"A friend."

"Is he?"

"You're joking, right? You're giving me shit about seeing a band with a work buddy when there's a handful of half-naked women in your kitchen?" I'm so over this situation. I should have known happiness was a drug with a short half-life. "I'm out of here."

His arms wrap around me, preventing any forward movement.

"I'm sorry." His mouth nuzzles my neck, and I hate how intoxicating it feels. I want to be unaffected by his demonstrations, but my body has a mind of her own. "Please don't leave. I'll kick everyone out right now."

I turn in his arms, glaring up at him. "You know all those bonus points you earned for being so amazing? You just lost half of them because you're a real shit for this, Josh." I rub my hand over my eyes. "I just...I had plans for us tonight."

His fingers tip my chin up to meet his gaze. "You think I didn't? There are satin sheets on the bed, massage oil on the nightstand, candles everywhere, wine in the fridge." His lips brush against mine, beckoning me to play. "I had plans, too."

"I guess plans change."

"They don't have to change. Let me get rid of everyone, and then you and I—*just* you and I—can spend the evening together. And the morning. And all of tomorrow." His hands skate to the hem of my dress, his fingers sliding against the back of my thighs to cup my ass. Presumptuous bastard.

He's lucky I crave the feel of his hands on my body.

But he's not getting off that easily.

I step out of the circle of his arms, crossing my own across my chest. "Don't bother. They're already drinking. Besides, I'm not in the mood now, anyway."

Josh's foot taps the floor, and I see the agitation building. Good. Give him a taste of his own medicine for once. "Are you going out with Sean?" He bites out the name with distaste.

It's ironic. The fact that Josh is jealous actually makes me feel a bit better. At least I'm not alone in that emotion. "Are you hanging out with the beach bunnies?" I glare back at him, but instead of feeling rising ire, I'm now feeling amusement.

It doesn't help that Josh is also biting back a smile.

"We suck, don't we?" Josh asks, the grin breaking free of its restraints.

"You suck," I remind him, skewing my mouth to keep from returning the smile.

"As I recall, you're amazing in that department."

My eyes widen at the obvious sexual statement. Brazen ass. Two can play that game. I can torture him all night with a body he's not allowed to touch. And with that, my decision to hang out with Josh and his pack of beach pals is decided. "Too bad you *forgot* our plans. You would have had another chance to experience it. Right now."

I turn away at the expression on his face. My words have completely undone him.

This round goes to me.

ALCOHOL BRINGS out everyone's inner artist. Sometimes, it's a good thing. In the case of Josh's friends, it's a recipe for disaster. Good for a laugh, though.

A couple of the beach bunnies have decided to host an impromptu talent show as the sun dips below the horizon, although I know it's just code for wanting to strip down in front of the guys. If they whip out a guitar and start singing Kumbaya, I'm out the door.

I'm enjoying the scene from the safety of the patio railing. The few beers I've consumed are loosening me up, and I'm taking full advantage of my toned legs and the high cut of my dress. Hey, my legs may be pale, but I work out five times per week. They're shapely as hell. I know it, and judging by the looks the men keep shooting in my direction, they know it as well.

One thing these young girls fail to realize is that eating a cheeseburger—or black bean burger—isn't a bad thing. Those calories help you gain two very attractive assets, namely, boobs and an ass. I may have a decade and a half on these women, but I'm pretty damn sure I'm holding my own.

Josh's hands rest on my knees, pushing my legs apart. His lips flit by my ear as his beard sends minor shockwaves down my spine. "You need to stop."

I send him an innocent look. "Stop what?"

"You know what. You're headed for that spanking I promised earlier."

I press my cleavage together, leaning in toward him. "I do apologize. I'll try to behave for the rest of the evening."

His lips nuzzle my neck while his hands—those tricky, tricky hands—slide further under my dress to knead my ass. "Fuck behaving. Let's go."

"Go where?"

"Anywhere."

My fingers trace the line of his lips as I shake my head. "You can't leave your own party."

"Yes, yes I can."

"Josh, come play a song with me." Ah, I knew it had been too peaceful and quiet.

I look over Josh's shoulder at Frank, holding two guitars. I have to admit, my curiosity is piqued. "You play guitar?"

Josh groans against my shoulder, giving my skin a soft nip. "Not well."

"I want to hear you play."

He raises his head, and I hold that unwavering turquoise gaze. "What do you want me to sing?"

"You sing, too? I'm impressed."

"Don't be. I haven't performed yet."

The beach bunnies are clapping and looking with expectant

hope in my man's direction. Time for him to give the crowd what they came for.

"Get to it, then. I want to see if you're as musically talented as you are everywhere else." My hands drift down, my fingers brushing against the bulge in his jeans.

Josh moans against my skin. "Little vixen. We leave as soon as I'm done. I won't make it to my truck before I rip this dress off your body."

"Go play, then we'll see."

With a final groan, Josh pushes off the railing, settling into a chair next to Frank.

One of the beach bunnies yells out a request for a song I've never heard, and I grab a fresh beer and adjust my position so that I can drink him in while I drink up.

I figure he'll be decent, but I'm wrong. He's magic. Those long fingers strum the guitar, and his deep voice rocks with a gravelly sound that evokes a smoky blues bar.

The entire world falls away as he plays. It's just him and me. The song ends with squeals and applause and even a whoop of appreciation from the neighbor's yard.

"Play another one, Josh," Beach Bunny #3 coos. I could learn their names, but to be honest, they're not that important in my life.

Josh nods, tuning the guitar. "This one's for you, Adelaide."

Every head turns in my direction, so I raise my beer in response. I expect a cheeky, flirty song. I'm wrong.

Instead, that gravelly voice croons *"When You Love Someone,"* by Bryan Adams. I love the song. Always have. I always wondered what it felt like to love on that level. Watching him watch me, I no longer have to guess.

When the song ends, Josh strips off the guitar and walks into my waiting arms. I'm fairly positive the beach bunnies want to murder me, but one look at his smiling face, and I could care less.

Frank, ever the gracious host, breaks into the moment. "Ladies, it's your turn. Josh and Addy, you won't want to miss this."

"Want to make a bet?" Josh murmurs into my neck. His lips have been attached to some part of my body since he finished his song, and I'm in no hurry to make him leave.

"You've got to watch us, Josh," Beach Bunny #1 beseeches.

With an aggravated groan, Josh turns around, popping onto the railing next to me. "I'm watching."

"They're your fan club," I remind him.

"I suppose so."

"Should I be worried?"

Josh stares straight ahead, but I see the smile tugging up his mouth. "They're not wearing a hickey I gave them, beautiful. You are."

I'm thankful for the darkness. It covers the hickey I didn't realize I had and also the flush flooding my body. "Thanks a lot!"

His response? A nip to my shoulder and a non-verbal promise that I'll have many more by the end of the night.

With a squeal, the music starts, and the beach bunnies begin their performance. They bump and grind against each other, shaking their hips and thrusting out their tits. It doesn't matter that they lack any real rhythm; they're beautiful women wearing hardly any clothing. I'm fairly certain all the men are carrying hard-ons right now.

I sneak a peek at Josh, expecting to see a trail of drool from his lip. Instead, I meet his gaze. He's been watching me, not them, and that knowledge further stokes the flame in my body.

Their dance finishes, and I pray they'll disperse soon for parts unknown.

"Alright, Addy. Your turn." Frank says, motioning to the front of the room.

I send the ogre a surprised look. "I don't sing. Or play guitar. Trust me, the dogs in the neighborhood will thank you."

"You don't have to sing. How about you dance for us?"

"You don't have to do it, Addy." Josh squeezes my thigh.

I hate Frank, but I'm never one to turn down a direct challenge. "Do I get to choose the song?"

"Of course."

I shrug and hop off the railing, kicking off my shoes. "Fine. Josh, will you sit up here while I dance?"

Josh nods and plops down in one of the deck chairs. He's likely gearing up for his role as bodyguard, concerned I'll make a total ass of myself.

But I have a little surprise up my sleeve, too. I was always a clumsy child, so my parents enrolled me in dance. When I turned twelve, I enrolled myself in belly dancing. My hip shake can put Shakira to shame.

The music starts, and I lose myself to the rhythm. I move without thinking, my hips swaying as I entrance the hell out of everyone there. I don't feel sexy when I'm dancing. I am sex. I meet Josh's gaze, and it's just as I hope. His jaw is on the ground, his eyes focused on my undulating hips.

I move closer, and his hands wrap around my thighs, his fingers dimpling my skin. I see the desire burning hot in his face, but I want to stoke the flames higher. I want him insatiable for me.

I straddle his lap, moving my ass against him with seductive strokes.

The music stops, and the men let out catcalls of appreciation. But Josh drops his hands, not meeting my gaze. Odd. He propels himself off the chair and into the house.

Definitely not the reaction I was hoping for.

Beach Bunny #2, my least favorite, sends me a smug smile. "Maybe he's not a fan of that type of dancing."

And just like that, every ounce of sexiness oozes from my body like water through a sieve.

I scurry back to the deck corner. My plan? Shoes, purse, keys, gone.

My phone buzzes. Seriously, people? I ignore it, but it buzzes again. And again. With an exasperated huff, I grab the stupid thing.

It's Josh.

Come inside. NOW.

Well, shit. That doesn't sound promising.

The entire house is dark when I enter. Where the heck is he? I glance down the hallway, wondering where he's hiding and how mad he is at this moment. "Josh? Are you okay?"

Without warning, Josh steps from the shadow, grabbing my wrists and pushing me against the wall.

A surprised whimper escapes my lips as he holds my hands above my head, his muscular frame pressing against me.

He slides his free hand down the length of my arm, curving it around my jaw. The moonlight glints in his eyes, and I see the same emotions churning as when I danced for him.

"Josh—"

His mouth crushes against mine, our tongues tangling as he presses himself closer. I arch my back, my trapped hands preventing much forward movement. He tastes so good, and I want more of him. All of him.

I moan into his mouth as his free hand travels along my side and slips under the hem of my dress. He isn't playing around. His fingers slide inside me, and I tighten around him.

When his other hand releases me, my hands immediately wrap around his neck, tangling in his long hair. For every stroke of his tongue, I'm there. I'm ready. I've been waiting for this moment.

Strong hands cup my ass, hoisting me up as I instinctively wrap my legs around his waist.

It's his turn to groan as we grind against each other. The energy surrounding us crackles with electricity.

A low moan shudders from his body as his mouth delivers a series of nips along my neck. "I need you, Addy. I'm going crazy over here."

"I thought you were angry at the way I danced."

"I am angry. I want this house empty, so I can take you in every single room." He thrusts forward, and I feel his cock grind against me with the most delicious friction. "I can't wait any longer. It's consuming me. Every time I see you, every time I smell you, every time our bodies touch"—another thrust, this one making us both moan— "I want to own every part of you. I don't want there to be an inch on this body that I haven't explored."

My hands glide their way down the muscled lines of his back, my nails scratching against the soft cotton T-shirt. "You want me now?"

"Right here. Right now." Josh's lips nip my shoulder. "Tell me I can, Addy."

"Sorry to interrupt the love fest—"

"What the fuck do you want, Frank?" Josh bellows, his anger shocking even to me.

"Sorry, man. But Chantelle is here, and considering *you* invited her, I thought you might like to know." Frank turns and walks out, muttering about thankless assholes under his breath.

The glow that I was basking in only a second early? Oh yeah, it's gone. "Chantelle is here? Chantelle from the yoga studio?"

Josh clears his throat, his gaze focused on the wall. Funny. For the first time, he won't make eye contact. "Yeah."

"Your ex-girlfriend, Chantelle?"

"Yes, but it's not what it looks like—"

No. He doesn't get to do this. Clint did this, and I looked like a fool for years. "Put me down."

"Addy, stop struggling. Please listen—"

"Put. Me. Down. *Now.*"

Josh lowers me to the ground, his fist tapping against the sheetrock. "Will you give me two minutes to explain?"

"I have one question. Did you invite her tonight?" I pray that it's another of Frank's gimmicks, designed to drive me out of my mind.

But this time, Frank isn't to blame. The asshole award goes to Josh. "I did, but—"

"No, I'm done listening. You forget our plans, but you remember to invite your ex-girlfriend to your party? Fuck you. I'm out of here."

"Addy, stop." Josh attempts to wrap his arms around me, but this time, I'm faster. I duck under his grip and dash to the kitchen to grab my stuff.

"Hello. I didn't expect to see you here." Little Red Yoga Hood, for her part, looks perfect. Of course, she does. She's even wearing her best fake smile, which she flashes in my direction.

"Ditto, sweetheart," I mumble. I'm past being nice. I don't care what his ex thinks about me. In fact, I want her afraid of me. She should be afraid of me. My blood is boiling lava at this point.

"Addy, please wait." Josh storms into the kitchen, stopping dead when he sees Chantelle.

"Hi, Josh. Is this a bad time?" She motions to the patio. "Should I wait outside?"

"No," I answer for him, "it's a perfect time for you both. I'm sure you have tons of reminiscing to do." I grab my stuff and make a beeline for the door.

Fuck him. Thank God I *didn't* fuck him. That's the only saving grace. He'll have to get his old lady kicks somewhere else.

Josh jogs after me, grabbing my arm. "Addy, will you stop and listen?" His eyes are ablaze with emotion, but this time, I'm too far gone.

I jerk my arm away, my body flooding with anger. "No, you listen. I won't let anyone make a fool of me again. Not Clint and certainly not some twenty-six-year-old kid. Goodbye, Josh. Have fun with your little friends."

CHAPTER TWENTY-ONE

WHAT DO YOU WANT, ADDY?

"*H*e did what?" Melissa screeches, likely waking up the neighbors—in China.

I admit that I'm glad she's having this reaction. I always worry when I have an emotionally volatile blow-up that I'm the one in the wrong. Emotions are a bad thing, at least according to my mother. So I'm validated that my friends are equally pissed by the situation.

I raise my glass of vodka in Sean and Melissa's direction. "I sure can pick them, can't I?"

Sean pats my knee, sucking back his own drink. "It's not your fault that Josh and Clint are assholes. That's on them."

"But that's just it. It *isn't* on them. Clint fucked his secretary for months, and when he's caught, he doesn't even apologize. It took him a cross-country plane ride to work up the guts to muster a half-assed apology. And Josh," I spit out his name, "is likely banging Little Red Yoga Hood as we speak."

"Little Red Yoga Hood? That's inventive, Addy." Melissa and

Sean try to stifle their laughter, but it's a moot point. Hey, I get points for originality with the bitch's nickname.

"I don't think Josh is screwing anyone," Melissa states, staring pointedly at my phone. The damn thing won't shut up. He keeps calling. Again and again and again.

"You think he'd get the hint that I'm not answering it."

"So, what was his reason for inviting his ex-girlfriend to his house? I don't get that." Sean shoots us a confused look. "Why would he purposely fuck himself over?"

"He *forgot* he made plans with me. Remember?"

"I don't know. That man has been on point the entire time. You need him, and he's there. Immediately. Why, when he's so close, would he screw up in such a major way?"

I shrug. My head doesn't know, and my heart doesn't have the strength to consider possibilities. "Maybe he felt bad about screwing me? And screwing me over?"

"You said you two were moments away from having sex. I highly doubt he had a sudden change of heart in the heat of the moment. Sorry, Addy, men don't think like that. It's full-on cock talk at that point," Sean adds, shaking his head as my phone lights up. Again. "You want me to talk to him and tell him to leave you alone?"

I shake my head. What I want is to go to bed and throw the covers over my head. For at least a month. "Thanks, but I'm good. I need to get rid of this blasted headache."

Melissa squeezes my shoulders on her way inside. "Vodka is generally a bad idea for headaches, sweetie."

"Great idea for heartaches, though."

Sean sends me another sympathetic look. "I'm sorry, Addy. I really thought he was a good guy."

"Me too. But I apparently have no radar for assholes. None."

Another swig of vodka. Ah, there's nothing like the cool burn. "How's your dating life?"

"Crap, but relatively good compared to yours. Actually, I've been talking with Amy."

My eyes widen. "Your ex? Wow. How's that going?"

Sean shrugs. "She's sorry. She misses me. I don't know what to believe. Same shit as with you and Clint."

Melissa clears her throat, and I swing my head up. "Addy, there's someone here to see you."

"Oh, for fuck's sake. Can you get him out of here?" I demand, putting my glass down with such force the ice cubes jump. At this point, I'm not even sure if it's Josh or Clint, but I don't want to see either of them.

Melissa sends Sean a look. I know that look. They're abandoning ship. Leaving me to sink with Mr. Wonderful Asshole. "Actually, we're going to get going."

"Why? I don't want you to leave."

Melissa leans in close, her hands framing my face. "Just hear him out, okay? He said he'll go after you hear him out...if you still want him to leave."

"I don't want him here at all," I mutter, as tears back up in my eyes.

"Yes, you do." She presses a kiss to my forehead, and then she and Sean desert me. Bunch of jerks.

I take another swallow of vodka, hoping that the teaspoon in my glass will be enough to get me totally snookered.

"Hey."

I know I should be the adult in the situation, but I'm not feeling it at the moment. Petulant brat suits me much better. That and I'm a toxic combination of heartsick, mortified and angry. Either way, I hope Josh wore his battle gear.

"Where's Chantelle? Waiting in the truck?"

"No. I sent everyone home. I'm barely speaking to any of them."

"Why break up a perfectly good party? I was the cog in the wheel, but I left. Should have been smooth sailing after that."

Josh plops into the seat next to me with a sigh. "Will you stop for one minute?"

"Stop what?"

"Acting like you hate me. I'm trying to apologize and explain."

"Does it matter *why* you did it?"

"It matters a whole hell of a lot to me. It pushed away the woman I love." He leans forward, grabbing my hands. "I'm in love with you, Addy. I didn't want to tell you like this. I wanted to tell you while I was holding you, not during a fight, but you need to know how I feel."

I'm sure he hears my heart hammering against my rib cage and the blood roaring in my ears. His words aren't soothing. They only confuse me further. Besides, words don't mean much anymore. "You can't say things like that. It messes with my heart."

Josh's eyes widen, his hands tightening around mine. "It was aimed for your heart. I would do anything for you."

"Then why lie to me?"

"Can I explain?"

I wish I could kick him out and forgo the explanation. But my feelings for him and a morbid curiosity convince me to let him stay. "Fine. I need to get more vodka first, and I *don't* want you to give me any shit about it. It's because of you that I'm drinking right now."

At least the man is smart enough not to pass judgement. "I'll get it for you."

He returns with the glass, extending his other hand in my direction.

I send his hand a pointed look. "What?" I know what he

wants. The temperature is dropping, but I'm as stubborn as a mountain goat. I'll freeze to death first.

With an exasperated sigh, he sets my glass on the table before scooping me into his arms.

I tense immediately. I may adore the feeling of his arms around my body, but there's no way I'm letting him know that piece of information. "Put me down."

"Relax. I'm bringing you inside."

"I don't want to go inside."

"You're half frozen. Grab your glass. You can hit me with it if you want."

"Tempting offer," I grumble, snatching the glass from the table.

Without warning, he presses a kiss against my forehead. "I just told you I love you. Stop pretending you hate me."

"Maybe I'm not pretending."

He presses his forehead to mine, and I inhale the minty flavor of his breath. Being this close to Josh sends my emotions into a tailspin. "I really hope that's not the case."

Good to his word, he deposits me on the couch, although his fingers graze my breast, and judging from the slight smirk on his face, it wasn't an accident.

Thankfully, body tingles aren't overtly apparent, or I would be beyond screwed. With my jaw set and my best glare at the ready, I shoot daggers at him. "Talk."

Josh settles next to me, his foot tapping with nervous energy. Good. You should be scared. "Chantelle and I met years ago on location. We were modeling for the same company."

"Of course she's a model. How original."

He pins me with one of his laser stares. I'll admit I'm saucy as hell right now. "Yes. She was. Anyway, we met on location and started dating. She was my first love, or what I thought was my first love."

I nod, unsurprised by his revelation.

"Then, my mother got sick. Well, Chantelle couldn't handle it."

"Were they close?"

"No. My mother hated her. But Mom's cancer took time away from Chantelle, and she didn't like that."

My eyes widen at his admission. "You're joking."

"Afraid not. So, she started spending more time with Frank. Made a move on him a few times, and he finally let me know."

"Wow. Sounds like a winner."

"I dumped her, and she begged me back. All the normal shit. But I was focused on family and surfing. I didn't need someone like that in my life. Then she moved, and I had no idea she was back in San Diego until that yoga class."

"And it was love at first sight again. Am I right?"

Josh's eyes bulge with surprise. "Absolutely not."

"I assumed when she showed up at your house that you two were on the path to reconciliation."

"Addy, I was seconds away from making love to you."

"You mean, screwing me."

Josh falls to his knees in front of me, forcing me to look at him. "No. I was going to make love to you. You really have no clue what you mean to me. Do you?"

"No, Josh. I have no idea." I return my focus to the glass of alcohol in my hand, but it's lost its appeal, both as a numbing agent or a weapon.

"Do you love me, Adelaide?"

My heart thumps against my ribs. "How am I supposed to answer that?"

"Honestly."

"After what happened tonight? Why was Chantelle there? After what she did, why would you want her around?"

"I didn't. But she was one of the models at the shoot today, and when Frank so graciously invited everyone else, I felt like I had to invite her along, too."

"Yet, you forgot about me." I want to appear indifferent, but damn it, he hurt my heart. That and the vodka has put my filter to sleep.

"I *never* forgot about you. I kept hoping I could get rid of them before you arrived."

Now the tears threaten to make an encore. "I guess the only good thing to come out of tonight was that we didn't have sex. I'm glad of that, at least."

"I humbly disagree."

"I guess you would."

"What? Want to make you mine? Addy, I'm not apologizing for that."

"Would it have meant anything beyond a notch on your belt?"

"Is that what you think? You're a conquest?"

"Hardly. I don't know what I am."

"You're the woman I love. I'm in love with you, Addy. You think I would be here right now if I didn't love you?" Josh runs his hands along my calves, giving them gentle squeezes.

"I don't know."

"Yes, you do. But the idea that I love you scares the hell out of you."

"I think we should call it friends. It's safer, protects my heart."

He can't hide the pain washing over his features. "I don't want to be your friend, beautiful. I do, but I want to be so much more than that. I'm not with her. I'm with you. I'm here."

I want to take the wall down. With Josh, it would be so easy. But I can't allow that to happen. Instead, I have to remember the pain I felt when his ex was standing in his kitchen, mocking everything I thought I meant to Josh.

But I also don't want to continue fighting. Or pretend that I hate him. With a sigh, I set down the untouched vodka and fall back against the couch cushion. "What do we do now?"

"If I had my way, I'd be carrying you into the bedroom and making love to you for the rest of the night."

I wish his words didn't light the flame inside me. I wish I could act like they meant nothing. I'm not that talented.

He sits next to me on the couch. "But I'm happy just being next to you. You want to watch a movie? Your choice."

I nod and begin flipping channels. I'm acutely aware of his turquoise gaze homed in on my face, but I force myself to ignore it. "Anything I want?"

"Anything you want."

I mean the movie. By the look on his face, he means something else. I flip through countless titles, finally settling on a romantic comedy. It's innocent, and we might even garner a few laughs. Heaven knows we could use them tonight.

I settle into the cushions, pulling the blanket over me and wondering how I ever wound up in this predicament.

I jump when his hand closes around my foot. "Sorry. I'll give you more room."

"I don't want more room, Addy. If anything, I want less." His hands curl around my foot, hitting every pressure point. "You're so tense. Even when you sleep, you're tense. It's like you're always waiting for something bad to happen."

"Too many years of emergency nursing," I mumble, but I know it's a load of shit.

So does Josh.

"Too many years of being treated shabbily by people who should have known better. People who should have done better. Move up a tiny bit."

"Why?"

Josh squeezes in behind me, wrapping his arm around my waist. "So I can lay here."

"Josh, friends don't cuddle like this." There. Nothing like using his own line against him.

His hand slides under my shirt as his tongue trails along the top of my shoulder. "We are so much more than friends, Addy. Here's the deal. You can continue to be mad at me, and I'll"—his fingers slip into my panties, circling my clit—"keep apologizing."

"Is this about sex? Are you mad because we didn't have sex earlier?"

Josh rests his head on my shoulder with a resigned sigh. "Addy, if this was about sex, we would have had it already."

I hate that he's right. If I was only meant to be a quick lay, it certainly wasn't working out that way for him. "I suppose you have a good point."

"Do I want you? Every second. But I'll wait as long as you want."

I turn in his arms, finally ready to face that unnerving gaze. "Why are you doing this? Why are you still here?" My words aren't angry, but they're painfully honest.

He leans in, dropping a kiss on the tip of my nose. "I told you. I'm in love with you."

I shake my head, unable to wrap my head around his words. "Josh, we can't be in love."

"That's the most ridiculous thing I've ever heard."

"It's not, actually. This is a train racing towards a brick wall."

"How do you figure?"

"We don't want the same things, Josh."

He adjusts on the couch, pulling me on top of him. Well, this is a dangerous position. "I assume you're referring to the future?"

"Yes, I am." I don't want to delve into it. I really don't. He's far too young to want the same things from life that I do.

"Addy, you've never—not once—told me what you want. How can you assume I don't want the same things when you haven't disclosed what those things are?"

"You're thirteen years younger. It's not a big leap."

A provocative smile stretches across Josh's face. "I think it's time that you tell me what you want."

"I don't—no, that's a bad idea." I don't need to feel any more awkward than I already do.

Josh, for his part, isn't letting it go. His stubborn streak runs as deep as mine. "It's a great idea." His fingers trace the planes of my face, that sexy smirk widening by the second. "Let me guess. You want to get married and have a baby."

I feel my face flush. I'm not even sure *why* I'm so damn embarrassed. "I don't want to discuss it."

"Well, too bad. Stop glaring at me. I know you're self-conscious, and I'm not sure why. You're hardly the first woman to want marriage and a child."

I hate him and his dead-on accuracy. "I never claimed to be original," I mutter, focusing my gaze on his shirt.

"There's nothing wrong with that dream. It's a good plan."

At least he hasn't run screaming from the room yet. Granted, I do still have the leaded glass I could chuck in his direction, should the need arise. I shrug, my finger messing with one of his buttons. "I'm not so sure about the marriage part, but I would love to have a child. I'm running out of time, though. I'd basically have to get started now." I offer a small laugh, trying to lighten the mood.

Josh cocks his head in the direction of the bedroom. "Let's go."

It's a joke, ovaries. Calm the hell down.

"How many kids do you want?"

"One is fine." I'm a bit shocked we are still having this discussion, but Josh is an inquisitive soul. I'm sure it's just harmless talk, a way to calm me down from the earlier situation.

"No. You have to have more than one. Three."

"Three, huh?"

"Yeah. I've always wanted three kids."

"Good to know," I squeak, feeling my face flush again. What the hell is wrong with me?

"I want them before I'm thirty, too."

I offer a nonchalant hug. "A child before you're thirty is plausible."

Josh smiles at me, and I'm reminded that he has a myriad of smiles, all of them exquisite. "I'd like all of them before I'm thirty."

My jaw slackens with surprise. "That's in four years."

"Better get started, huh?" He bites his lip, holding back a grin. I know he's messing with me, but my hormones are starting to believe this maniac's assertions.

"You're insane."

"I'm perfectly sane. And it's three years, by the way. My birthday is in two weeks."

Our birthdays are only a month or so apart. We're probably the same sign. Funny, I thought we were polar opposites, but astrologically, we're mighty similar. "Happy early birthday. So, three children in three years?"

I expect him to laugh, fess up that he was only messing around, but I'm met with the burn of his stare. "Yep."

"You are aware that a woman carries a child for nine months?"

"I took health class," Josh retorts.

"Interesting."

I feel the energy change. It shifts from light and joking to something heavier. More serious. More real. His fingers glide along my sides as Josh presses my body closer to his. "If I had my way, we'd have a baby next year, which means I have to get you pregnant now."

I swear this man needs to stop saying these things. My ovaries are in an absolute uproar. They don't know the difference between banter and serious conversation. To be honest, neither do I at this point. "You want kids so young. It's surprising."

"Why is it surprising? I'm not that young, and I've always wanted kids."

"How are you so certain of everything?"

"I've always known what I wanted from life—to surf, to find the woman of my dreams, and have a family. I just didn't know who I wanted to share that life with...until recently."

Dear God, it's a million degrees in here. I run my fingers along his chin, loving the scruff of his beard. "Do you always know the right thing to say?"

"No," Josh chortles. "I'm always in trouble with you. Remember?"

"Why are we having this conversation?" I'm meeting his gaze now. I'm present, and I need to know the answer.

"Why wouldn't we be? Addy, I think you're more comfortable with the idea of me being a prick than you are with the idea that I would gladly give you what you want. But—"

"There's always a but," I interject.

"Yes, there is. In this case, the but is you. You have to let me give you those things. You have to let me in."

"You say all the right things, but if I took you up on your offer, right now, you'd be out the door so fast you'd leave skid marks."

I've never felt such a power emanating from him as he tips up my chin. "Try me."

I'm shaking, and I know he can feel it.

Josh lets out a small sigh, pressing another kiss to my forehead. "Turn around and watch the movie. I'll leave it alone. For *now*."

I VAGUELY RECALL Josh carrying me to the bed and him curling up next to me. But when I awaken, he's gone.

I lounge against the pillows, mulling over our discussion from the night before. His discussion, really, since I didn't add anything of value to the conversation.

Am I crazy to believe him? Is it nuts to be so sure of someone after only a month? What if I had taken him up on his offer?

I pad into the kitchen. Josh must have cleaned up everything before he left. Either he's a closet neat freak, or he really is husband material.

Then I see it.

There, in his almost illegible scrawl, is a note.

Addy,

I meant every word.

I love you.

My foot taps restlessly against the floor as I read the note over and over again. He loves me. He wants to give me whatever I want.

That's when I realize. I love Josh, and I want to give him whatever he wants.

I glance at the clock. It's early, but there's no time to waste. Time to make that man mine.

I GROAN when I see Frank on Josh's front porch, a cup of coffee in his hand. "Just great."

"Hey, Addy, how are you doing this morning?" Frank, for his part, is unusually sedate. Almost friendly. I don't trust it one bit.

"I'm fine. How are you?"

"Looking for Josh. I figured he was with you, actually."

I wait for the sarcastic smirk, but instead, his face is openly questioning.

"He's not here?" I motion to a small convertible parked by the curb. "Whose car is that?"

For the first time since I met him, Frank looks uncomfortable.

"Frank, whose car is that?"

"It's Chantelle's. It was here when I arrived."

With his words, my heart smashes onto the pavement. "Are they"—I hold back a wave of nausea—"in the bedroom?"

"They're not in the house."

I glance toward the ocean, then at Frank. "Did you check the beach?"

Frank shakes his head but falls into step behind me. I stride across the sand, praying that I don't find him. Find *them*.

Universe, you are a sick bitch sometimes.

There, not fifty yards from me sits Josh, with Chantelle close at his side.

"Shit," Frank huffs as he catches sight of them. "I'm sorry, Addy. I didn't know."

He's likely lying and probably thrilled at my distress. "Right," I mutter.

"I swear. I didn't know."

I hold back the tears because that bastard, Josh, doesn't deserve them. It was all lies. Every look, every word, every touch. Lies. "Better to find out now, right?"

"Are you going down there?"

"Oh yes, I'm giving that asshole a piece of my mind."

Frank grasps my arm. "I wouldn't, Addy. I think it's fairly apparent what's happening. They had a real bond, back in the day. She hurt Josh, but she's grown up in the last several years. Just look at them. You can see the connection."

I force my gaze back to the beautiful duo. Frank's right.

There's something brewing between them. "So, he gets away scot-free?"

"He'll get away one way or another. It's your decision. Go down there if you think it will help the situation."

I shake my head, turning in the direction of my car. "No need. I've seen everything I need to see."

CHAPTER TWENTY-TWO

I CAN'T DO THIS ANYMORE

I now understand why I didn't cry when I discovered Clint screwing another woman. I was saving those tears for Josh.

I scramble past Frank and into my car, even managing to back out of the driveway before the floodgates open. Fifteen minutes later, I'm home, tears in tow.

It's a sad truth that when you bottle up your emotions for decades, they don't go away. They sit on a shelf in your heart, waiting for the door to crack open enough so they can pour out. Once that door is open, good luck shutting it again.

I have shelves worth of hurt in my heart, and my body is tired of holding onto them.

I bawl for an hour until the tears give way to sniffling and huffing. I know it's only intermission between sets. The second round of tears will arrive soon.

My head throbs, but it doesn't stop me from contemplating an early morning cocktail. When I say cocktail, I mean a bottle of vodka. Ice optional.

Snap out of it, Addy. If Clint wasn't worth the tears after giving him four years, Josh certainly isn't worth it after a month.

I repeat this internal monologue, over and over again, hoping that one time I might actually believe it.

I return the vodka bottle to the freezer and drag myself into the shower. Maybe the warm water will wash away my feelings for Josh, sweeping them down the drain and out of my life.

Yeah, that was a pipe dream. Literally.

My soul needs a recharge. I need the ocean. Josh isn't the only one who derives his sense of calm near the water. Besides, the bastard doesn't own the beaches. I'll just avoid the ones he frequents. No harm, no foul.

I grab my camera and water bottle, my eyes falling on the note still laying on the table. The note of sweetly elocuted lies. With a grunt, I ball it up and toss it in the direction of the garbage. It misses. Figures.

One of the many perks of San Diego is the miles of pristine coastline. I'm sure to find a beach without a single soul that knows Josh. That is my mission for the morning.

The fog is burning off, and it's going to be another splendid southern California day. I'm not worried. I have my own personal cloud to drag with me everywhere. Screw you, sunshine. I'm the queen of doom and gloom today.

I drive north out of the city, heading for parts unknown. Fletcher Cove sounds promising, so I park the car, gulping in a lungful of sea air as I exit the vehicle.

Peace.

Finally.

I turn off my mobile and leave it in the car. There's no one I care to speak to right now. I'll call Melissa later and share the news, but I'm done dumping my troubles on my beautiful friend. She has her own life, complete with issues I don't even know about. It's time to pay more attention to the people who matter and cut out those who don't.

I stroll along the shoreline, enjoying the warmth of the sun on my face and the coolness of the water beneath my toes. The Pacific is far wilder than my home ocean, but that's part of her appeal. I stare at the waves, wondering if Josh is somewhere along this same coastline, surfboard in hand.

I try to keep Josh from my thoughts, but it's a battle I stand no chance of winning.

I want to despise him. My brain screams that I'm justified in that approach, but my heart knows it's impossible. I can't hate Josh. I love him.

Above all, I want to know why. Why did he say those things? Why go to such lengths to spin a falsehood? What's the point?

All Josh did through his words and actions, is prove that he's a liar.

A thief of hearts.

I thought Frank's behavior was cruel, but Josh is the devil in disguise.

"Addy."

I whirl around, moving my hand over my eyes to make out the figure standing to my left. "Clint? What in the world are you doing here?"

He hands me a cup of coffee, before turning his gaze to the ocean. "I thought you might need it."

"I'm grateful for the coffee, but this can't be a coincidence. How did you know I was here?"

Clint chuckles, but it's tinged with embarrassment. "I was waiting for you at your apartment. When you pulled in, hysterically crying, it wasn't hard to put the pieces together."

"You were at my apartment?"

He chooses to ignore my questions, his sights locked on the

waves. "I know you, Addy, and I know I've never seen you cry like that before. I was concerned, especially when you drove off again. I had to ensure you were safe. So, I followed you. If you want me to leave, I will."

Some might find it creepy that Clint followed me, but I'm touched by his concern. A bonus is that he comes bearing coffee. "Thank you. I appreciate that."

"Getting any good photos?"

"Not really," I admit.

Clint motions behind him. "There's a bluff over there. I bet there are some beautiful views from the top."

It's ironic. Clint never showed the slightest interest in my hobby. Yet when the chips are down, he's there holding out an olive branch.

I notice the bandage wrapped around his bicep and send him an inquiring glance. "What happened? Did you get hurt?"

Clint chuckles. "No. Remember I talked about getting a tattoo? I finally did."

My jaw slackens. The man is one surprise after another. The man I first met, four years ago, talked about dreams and motorcycles and tattoos. I thought that man was long gone. Perhaps I'm mistaken.

"What did you get?"

"A dragon. I'd unwrap it, but I'm a bit worried about getting sand in it. I can show you at the car."

"Yes, please. I'd like to see it." And in that instant, I realize that I mean those words. "Do you want to take the hike up the bluff with me?"

He nods, and we begin our ascent. Clint is right, yet again. The view from the shore is beautiful, but the view up here is breathtaking. I feel a bit of my photo mojo flowing and lose myself to the surrounding nature, snapping off at least a hundred frames.

"These are pretty," Clint remarks, his fingers brushing along some pink petaled flowers.

"Those are clarkia. They're the unofficial flower of this area."

It's a benign statement, but I remember who told me that snippet of information. The same man who ripped my heart apart for kicks. I turn away from Clint, biting my lip and trying to hold in the tears brimming behind my lids.

I was doing so well.

"Do you want me to kick his ass? I have no problem beating the shit out of him."

I manage a laugh, wiping my eyes with the heel of my hand. "That's a generous offer, Clint, but don't bother. He's not worth it."

"If he's making you cry, he must be worth it. You never cried with me."

His words aren't accusatory. They're fact. I turn back toward him as his statement hits home. "You're right. I wasn't emotionally open with you. I can blame a thousand things—my upbringing, my Mother, my job—but it's all excuses. I'm sorry."

Clint ruffles my hair, offering a rueful smile. "Please don't apologize. Any damage in our relationship was my fault. My ego grew larger than my morals. I thought I could have it all."

I chew my bottom lip, finally feeling brave enough to ask Clint the hard questions. The questions to which I wasn't sure I wanted the answers. "Did you love Debra?"

Clint barks out a laugh. "No. Definitely not. How do I say this without sounding like an even bigger asshole?"

"Wow, this is going to be a good answer."

"She was...uncomplicated. No offense to Debra, but her needs were transparent. She was easy to read. Easy overall, I guess." He quirks his brow, and I bite back a laugh.

What a strange lady you are, Universe. Never in a million years

did I think I'd be sharing a laughter-filled conversation with the
man who cheated on me. But here we are.

"Did you ever love me?" I blurt out. I'm not sure I want the
answer, but for closure's sake, I need the truth.

"Very much, Addy. But I couldn't love you the way you
needed to be loved. I wasn't any good at it. The truth is, I didn't try
hard enough."

I stand beside him, focusing my gaze on the waves below. "I
think we both stopped trying. We became comfortable.
Complacent."

"I'm sorry that kid broke your heart."

I nod, tears rolling down my cheeks. "Josh didn't break my
heart," I lie. "He came close, but I escaped in time."

Clint turns to face me, a small smile playing on his handsome
features. "I'm still here if you ever think you can forgive me. There
were a lot of good times in our years together."

He's right, but I know moving backward is the wrong
direction. "I'll keep that in mind. Right now, I want a bubble bath,
some wine, and my bed."

"Care for some company?" Clint asks with a flirtatious wink.

I laugh off his statement. "Unless your name is Pinot Grigio,
you're not invited."

I LEAVE the beach an hour later, embracing Clint for what seems
like the first time in years. It's a real hug, and I feel reassured that
some part of the man I once loved is still alive under all the societal
pleasantries.

I'm calmer now. Not calm, but calmer. My heartache is gut-
wrenching, but it will fade. Eventually, the pain always fades. I

learned that when my Dad died. I'll always miss him, but the exquisite edge of loss has dulled over the years.

Time for some self-care. Solitary self-care.

I climb the stairs to my apartment, stopping dead in my tracks. Josh sits propped against my door, his head in his hands.

So much for staying calm. My body shakes as the coffee threatens to make a reappearance. "What—what are you doing here?" I eke out.

Josh's head flies up at the sound of my voice, and he rushes toward me, pulling me into his arms. "Addy, where the fuck have you been? I've been calling you all day."

I tense immediately, pushing out of his embrace. I have to remain stoic, but to do that, I need to get the hell away from Josh. Fast. I don't stand a chance when he's close to me. "What can I do for you, Josh?"

He pulls the hat from my head, brushing my hair from my face. "What's wrong with you? Beautiful, what happened?"

My eyes widen. He's really going to try to play this off. What a bastard. "I think, no, I'm certain that you know exactly what happened."

His eyes narrow in confusion. "Addy, I don't know what you're talking about."

I sigh as aggravation overtakes the heartache. "You're quite the actor, Josh. Something to pursue if the surfing doesn't work out."

I pull out my keys. I need to get inside. Now.

He grabs my arm, turning me to face him. "What the hell does that mean? All I know is I come back here, and you're gone. I've been calling for hours, but you don't answer. So I wait here, and now, you don't want to speak to me. Forgive me if I'm not following your path of anger, Addy."

My eyes flash with fury. I've had enough of little surfer boy.

"Why don't you ask Frank, since you're in the dark about this situation?"

A groan of frustration rises from Josh's chest. "Christ, what did he do now?"

I guffaw at the man's brashness. "*He* didn't do anything. You, on the other hand...it's not even worth it."

"It's not worth it? What isn't worth it, Addy? Me? Us? You're the most important thing in my world, so I think it's very much worth it."

I bury my face in my hands. "Stop lying. Please."

"What am I lying about?"

"Everything," I grit out, my blood boiling in my veins. "I hope you had a nice breakfast."

The color drains from Josh's face. "Oh, Jesus. Addy, it isn't what you think. I stopped home to grab something, and Chantelle was there."

"How convenient."

"Ask Frank. They arrived together."

My head spins at his words. I can't sort through the lies anymore. I'm beginning to feel like a pawn in some twisted, childish game. "When I arrived, Frank said he was waiting for you. He claimed to have no idea where you were."

"Are you surprised he lied to you? He doesn't want us together, beautiful. I realize that he will say just about anything at this point."

I know Frank is a liar and a meddler. I know this because I've seen him in action. Frank is an asshole, through and through. But his words and his actions are consistent. But Josh? His words and actions are polar opposites, and that is one hell of a red flag.

"You have interesting taste in friends." I insert the key in the lock and open the door. I need wine immediately. Besides, I can use the bottle as a projectile, if needed. "I want to be alone."

But Josh isn't heeding my warning. He follows me into the apartment, trailing me to the kitchen as I pour a huge glass of wine. "Will you just hear me out?"

"I'm so tired of hearing you out, letting you explain. Here's an idea. Stop doing things that hurt me. How's that for a public service announcement?" The tears spill down my cheeks, much to my chagrin. So much for a strong facade.

Josh closes the gap between us, wiping the tears with his thumbs. "Beautiful, don't cry."

"*You* make me cry, Josh. This," I motion to myself, "is because of you. Your actions."

He recoils from my words, pain flashing across his face. "Addy, I never want to make you cry. All I want is to make you smile. You have the most beautiful smile, and you don't even know it."

"Please go," I reiterate, the wine washing down my throat as I try to curb my emotions.

"I need you to listen to me."

"I think she's listened enough."

Our heads turn in the direction of the open door. Clint stands there, a threatening expression gracing his features.

I scrunch my face in confusion. "Clint, what are you doing here?"

He holds up the backpack, but his glare focuses on Josh. "You forgot this. Is everything okay here, Addy?"

Josh's eyes blaze with anger at Clint's words. "You were with *him*? Please tell me you didn't spend the day with this asshole."

"Watch your mouth, kid," Clint warns, taking a predatory step forward.

"Stop it. Both of you. I can't handle anymore." I take the bag from Clint, giving his arm an awkward pat. "Thank you for dropping this off. I'm fine."

Clint's gaze remains locked on Josh. "I think I should stay."

"No, you need to go," Josh counters, his words falling from his lips like ice shards.

"I'm fine, Clint. I promise."

He finally tears his gaze from Josh, focusing his attention on me. "Call me if you need me, Addy. I'll always protect you."

I nod, forcing a smile as he leaves the apartment. The tension in the apartment thickens, pervading every corner.

Josh turns to me, his jaw twitching. "Were you with him today?"

With that heated question, my anger flares. Finally. "What if I was? What does it matter? You have *nothing* to say after I caught you and your little girlfriend on the beach this morning."

"I was telling Chantelle about you. Damn it, Addy! Why didn't you say something when you saw us? I would have cleared it up then. But once again, you don't even give me a chance to defend myself. Instead, you run back to your ex. What the fuck is that?"

What Josh fails to realize is that I played this sick game with Clint. For four years. I'm expert level. "Don't you dare turn this around on me. I'm not the one who did anything wrong. Do you know why I went to your house this morning?"

Josh crosses his arms over his chest, his lips pursed. "Please, enlighten me."

"I found your note, and I wanted you to know how I felt. I didn't want to wait until the next time I saw you, so I drove to your house. Imagine my surprise when I find you camped on the beach with your ex-girlfriend. So I left."

"And went straight to your ex?"

I chuckle, but it lacks any mirth. It's sad and defeated, much like me. "No. I went to Fletcher's Cove. Clint followed me."

Now Josh is really pissed. "He followed you? This man is a stalker, Addy."

"He was concerned."

"How kind."

I'm done with this conversation. It's a merry-go-round from hell. "This isn't about Clint. It's about you and the lies you keep telling me."

"I've never lied to you, Addy."

The tears stream down my face as I strike the death blow. "You never tell the full truth either. It's always some version that will suit your needs and hopefully appease me. Regardless, I can't see you anymore."

The anger drains from his face. "Addy, don't say that."

"I'm serious. It was always a foolish idea. We are so different, and you are so young."

His fist makes contact with the wall. Lovely. I can't wait to pay for that repair. "You're back to the age crap again. I told you last night—"

"You told me what I wanted to hear. You're really good at that, Josh. But I don't care to hear anymore. I'm tired of people who say all the right things but don't mean them."

"What *do* you want, Addy?"

"I'm not having this discussion."

"You've never actually told me. In fact, you rarely tell me anything about you. It's one big guessing game. Meanwhile, I've been an open book since the day we met. So, please just answer the question, and I'll go."

"I want the love that only exists in fairytales. I want to meet someone who loves me, just for being me. But after recent events, I realize I'm not meant to have that love."

The agitation rolls off Josh as he paces the floor. "You claim you're searching for this great love. Well, here I am, Addy. I'm right here. All you had to do is let me in."

I shake my head. I can't hear this. "Josh—"

He grabs me to him, and that's when I see it. His eyes, those beautiful sea-colored eyes, are bright with unshed tears. "But you won't let me in, because the fact that I'm thirteen years younger overrules any other feeling. Overrules the fact that I'm in love with you." He draws his face close to mine. "Or that you're in love with me."

"This isn't about age. It's about honesty." To be fair, it's about my sanity at this point. What little remains of it after being emotionally pummeled by Clint and Josh.

"Bullshit, Addy. You spent four years with Clint, eating his lies because he fit the mold you created for your life. Four years of being unhappy. Unfulfilled. Unloved. You won't even give me a chance to love you. I understand how bad it looks with my asshole friends, but I'm not lying to you. I've never lied to you. But it doesn't matter. You see what you want to see."

"The truth is fairly apparent."

"Obviously not. My truth—*my truth*, Addy—is that I want to spend my life loving you. But you can't see that, and I don't know how to make you see it. I've tried everything I know." He runs his hands through his hair, letting out a strangled groan.

I really want to believe him. His words are everything I've ever wanted to hear. But his words and his actions don't align, and if I've learned anything from my years on this planet, it's that words can be falsified, but actions scream the truth.

Josh's actions today paint a vivid, terrible truth. He left my arms and my bed to return to the embrace of his first love. I don't need his explanation. The truth was apparent, and he can't color it any other way.

He sees it in the set of my jaw. I'm not yielding this time. I can't. Self-preservation has kicked in; my heart is on lockdown.

Josh huffs out a few breaths, shaking his head as if searching for something more to say. Realizing that there isn't any way to salvage this situation, he pulls me close, pressing his lips to mine. "I hope you see the truth. I hope you realize how much I adore you."

He leaves, the slamming of the door a physical reminder to the closing of my heart.

CHAPTER TWENTY-THREE

JUST KEEP SWIMMING

*T*hey say if you keep busy enough after a breakup, it holds the pain at bay. *They* are liars.

I work an extra shift and hit the gym every single day, but Josh is no further from my brain than he was the second he stormed out my door.

It was radio silence for the first two days. I thought that was painful.

Then he started texting, and I learned what pain really felt like.

I scroll through the messages, all from Josh, and contemplate what the hell I'm supposed to do.

Message #1: I know I said I wouldn't call, but I miss you, Addy. I can't stand this silence between us. I know I got angry at your apartment, but your ex was there—with you—when it should have been me. I sat outside your door waiting for you when you were spending time with a man who ripped your heart apart.

Message #2: I'm finally hearing all sides of this mess. You think something happened with Chantelle. Nothing happened. I heard

*her running her mouth the other night. I put her in her place.
Christ, what you must think.*

*Message #3: I meant every word I said. I wish you believed me.
I don't know what I'm supposed to say, Addy. Tell me what to do to
make this better. I miss you.*

I wipe away a few stray tears. I miss him so much it hurts to
breathe. Christ, love sucks.

Clint thinks I should lose his number. Melissa thinks Clint
should shut his mouth. Sean believes Josh for some unknown
reason. Me? I'm stuck in the middle, with no idea which way to
turn.

"How are you holding up?" Sean inquires, giving me a gentle
nudge.

"I'm grand," I lie, forcing a smile for my friend.

"Have you two spoken?"

I shake my head, focusing on the doctor's note in front of me.
"Better that way."

"That's a load of shit. If you love Josh and he loves you, not
talking is the worst thing you can do."

"He lied to me, Sean."

"Are you certain? Seriously, I know how it looks, but for some
reason, I believe him."

"Yeah, because you both have penises. Bros before hoes, or
something like that."

Sean chuckles at my pun. "It isn't that, although there is an
unwritten law somewhere. It's the way he acted that night at your
apartment. He was desperate to speak to you."

"Because he knows he fucked up, and he kept fucking up."

"It wasn't that. If Josh didn't care, he wouldn't have been there.
He certainly wouldn't have kicked everyone out of his house to
come and speak with you. There's another thing."

"What's that?"

"He introduced you to his dad. Guys don't do that unless they're serious about the woman."

"His dad hangs out all the time."

"So, how did Josh introduce you? As a friend?"

I recall my first introduction to Mr. Gibbs. My embarrassment that I was lip-locked with his son while he stood there, a look of amusement on his face. "No. He said this is my Addy."

"My Addy?" Sean sends me a searching look. "That speaks volumes."

"I caught him on the beach with Chantelle."

"Why didn't you speak to him right then and there?"

"Frank told me not to."

"Frank has been a constant in every negative scenario between you and Josh. Maybe you need to listen to Josh the way you listen to Frank."

"I know what I saw," I counter, trying to maintain a strong facade.

"Addy, you think you know what you saw. He wasn't naked and humping her. You also have to realize that Frank and Clint don't have your best interests at heart. Clint wants you back and Frank...well...I think Frank has a thing for you."

"Josh said the same thing. I highly doubt it."

"Don't. Men can be real morons when they have a crush. Especially if that crush is their friend's girlfriend." Sean pulls me in for a quick hug. "Sometimes, the truth is the least believable option."

THE REMAINDER of the shift flies by, thanks in part to a couple call-ins that reduce staff numbers. In other words? A crap shift. I clock out, thankful for the next few days off.

"Addy."

I turn, surprised to see Mariah standing there. I haven't seen the woman since that last party at Josh's house. "Mariah, hi. What are you doing here?"

"You didn't hear?"

I shake my head, hating the cold clamp of fear that comes with those words. "Hear what?"

"Mr. Gibbs is in the hospital. He had a heart attack."

My hand flies to my mouth. "Oh no! I didn't hear that. Is he okay?"

"He had to have stents, but they say he'll be okay. He's in room 405, if you wanted to say hello."

I actually want to run up there, but it's not my place to intrude. "I don't want to disturb him."

"It would do him some good. Josh isn't there, if you're wondering."

I nod, trying to appear unaffected, but I'm actually saddened that he's not there. Even though I know seeing him will only increase the pain in my heart. "Maybe I'll stop by, then."

Mariah takes a few steps before turning around. "I don't know what happened with you two, but I love my friend very much."

I turn back to face her, certain I'm about to get an earful. "I know you do."

"I was wrong for saying what I did on the day of my birthday party. I wanted you to be careful, but the truth is that Josh has loved you since practically the moment he met you."

I blink back tears, biting my lip. "He's back with Chantelle."

"No, he's not. He never was."

"But Frank intimated—"

"I told you when we first met that Frank is an asshole. I'll see you later, Addy."

I watch her depart, wondering more and more if I let Clint and

Frank color my version of the truth. More importantly, if their version was keeping me from the man I love.

I take the elevator to the fourth floor and knock gently before pushing open the door to 405. Mr. Gibbs is sitting in bed, reading the newspaper. "Hey there, bruiser."

"Addy. Come here. You're a sight for sore eyes." Mr. Gibbs pulls me into a hug, and I sink into it. I know where Josh gets his amazing hugging skills from now.

"How are you feeling?"

"Better now. It was a hell of a night." He leans forward as if telling a secret. "They say I have to quit drinking."

"It's a good idea. We want you around for a long time."

Mr. Gibbs leans against the pillows, his eyes a different color but possessing the same watchfulness as his son. "Where have you been, Addy? Josh told me he messed up."

I focus my gaze out the window, searching for words. "I'm not sure which of us messed up. It's so hard with the age difference."

"Why?"

"People talk. Most of his friends don't think we're a good idea."

"I wouldn't listen to them, unless what they're saying echoes what you feel. What do you feel for my son?"

"I'm in love with him." It's the truth, and I'm tired of hiding it.

Mr. Gibbs smiles, a broad smile that reaches from ear to ear. "I'm glad to hear that. He's in love with you."

I shake my head. "I don't think so."

"I know so. Last week he came by my house and asked for his mother's ring."

My head shoots up as I wipe my eyes. "What for?"

"What do you think? He knew it was soon, but he knew you were the woman for him."

"What day was this?"

"Last Thursday. He came by real early, too. Said he left you sleeping and had to hurry back, but he wanted the ring first. I don't know. Maybe I shouldn't tell you all this."

"I'm glad you did. I woke up, and Josh wasn't there. I went to his house to tell him that I wanted to be with him. I found Frank, and he led me to Chantelle and your son sharing breakfast on the beach."

"Ah, Christ. Josh told me about that. I've known Frank since he was about ten years old. He was never good at sharing, and he always wanted what Josh had. To be honest, I'm not sure what Josh saw in him after all those years, but my son is loyal to a fault."

"You think Frank set me up?"

Mr. Gibbs shrugs. "All I know is that my son came to get a ring for the woman he loves that same morning. I don't think he would have done that if the woman in question wasn't very important to him."

A cold wave washes through me. "Maybe the ring was for Chantelle."

Mr. Gibbs chuckles. "Trust me, it wasn't."

"His birthday is coming up, isn't it?"

"It's today."

"What?"

"I had hoped to be released, but my blood level—IN—whatever it is, isn't high enough. So, I'm stuck here for another day."

I jump to my feet, giving his father another hug. "Don't worry. I'll go celebrate his birthday with him. That is, if you think he wants to see me."

"Why are you still standing here? Go get him, Addy."

I RUSH to a bakery and buy a huge assortment of vegan snacks and a cheesecake that promises to taste like cheesecake. Without cheese or gluten or any of the usual cheesecake ingredients, we shall see.

I jump into the shower and spend a few minutes deciding between sexy underwear or sweet. I go with sexy because if Josh still wants me, I'm not letting him go this time. Frank and Chantelle be damned. A slip dress, cardigan sweater, and boots complete the outfit.

Now comes the hard part. My hands shake as I turn over the ignition. I pray Mr. Gibbs and Sean are right. My heart can't handle finding him in bed with another woman. But my heart also can't handle being away from him any longer.

CHAPTER TWENTY-FOUR

HAPPY BIRTHDAY, BABY

*M*r. Gibbs told me where Josh hides his key, but I worry that an unexpected visitor might earn me a trip to the precinct instead of a reunion kiss.

Baby steps, Addy. Let's start off slow.

I grab the bags of goodies from the car, leaving my overnight bag alone—for now. Hopefully, I *will* need it later.

My hand trembles as I ring the bell, and the seconds tick by like hours. What if he isn't here? Worse, what if he isn't alone?

The door swings open and I'm pinned by that stare I love so much. "Addy."

I'm overcome with emotion. I feel like I can breathe again, but terrified that he might steal the oxygen away at any moment. With a tearful smile, I hold up the bags. "A little bird told me it's your birthday. I saw your Dad. He's doing really well, but they're keeping him another day."

Josh only nods, his hand running over his bare chest, so I plunge forward.

I grab out the cheesecake. "It's vegan, and they swear that it tastes good, too. But if you don't like that, I picked up all kinds of goodies."

"Thank you. That was really nice of you."

I feel the apprehension wafting off him, but I'm not certain if it's because he doesn't know my motive or because there's a hot redhead in his bed.

Time to sink or swim, Addy.

"I miss you—"

I don't get to finish my statement. Josh pulls me against his chest, and I collapse into him, breathing in the only scent that's ever felt like home. We don't say anything for the next minute. We simply exist, our arms wrapped around each other, our hearts falling into sync once again.

Josh takes my hand, leading me into the cottage. "I'm so sorry, Addy. I had no idea what you saw that morning. What you *thought* you saw."

"Shh." I place my fingers against his lips, smiling when he offers them a soft kiss. "You didn't do anything wrong. I'm sorry that I believed Frank. You would think I would be wise to him at this point."

"I've never seen him like this before. I know he's jealous, but this is out of hand. I thought once Chantelle came back, that Frank would calm down."

"Why?"

"They started screwing again. I figured they would leave us the hell alone."

My eyes widen at the revelation. "Wait...Frank and Chantelle?"

"Yeah."

"I got that so wrong." I close my eyes, letting relief wash over me.

"It doesn't matter. You're here now." He smiles, pressing a kiss to my forehead.

Keep moving down, mister.

But he pulls away, heading into the kitchen. "Coffee?"

"You know me. Do I ever turn down coffee?" I unpack the goodies and spread them on the table. I'm so glad I'm here with him. "Hey, you know you're only twelve years younger than me now."

"Fixed everything, didn't it?" Josh grins over the breakfast bar, sending me a wink.

"How does it feel to be twenty-seven?"

"The same as twenty-six, honestly."

I know he's on his guard right now. I am as well. We've both been through the wringer where Frank is concerned. I can't tell if Josh has an interest in me beyond friendship at this point. There might be too much damage. But I'm not complaining. Having him in my life is *way* better than not having him at all.

I gaze into the corner, and my heart starts pounding in my chest. An easel is set up with a half-finished canvas. It's of a dark-haired woman staring out to sea, her dark eyes in silent conversation with the waves.

I didn't know Josh could paint.

I certainly didn't know he would paint me.

I move closer, transfixed by the portrait. "Is this how you see me?"

I jump when his hand moves along my shoulder, pushing my hair to one side. "No. I don't have nearly the talent to capture the exquisiteness that is you."

He offers me a mug of coffee, which I accept with a smile, my eyes volleying between him and the painting. "I swear, there's nothing you can't do."

"I don't know about that, Addy." Josh settles onto a chair on one side of the living room, coffee mug in hand. He's trying to appear relaxed, but I detect a nervous energy about him. I'm certain it matches my own.

"Do you prefer painting people?"

"I love painting women, not that I do it very often. But there are so many magnificent curves on the female body. Women are a living, breathing, work of art."

"Some women more than most," I murmur, not entirely sure into which category I fit.

"Some women fail to realize the power they wield. They're the most mysterious but also the most dangerous. They steal your heart, and you won't even feel them take it. But you'll never be the same afterwards."

Those blue-green eyes focus on me with such gravity. There's no mistaking his meaning.

This sexually laden conversation is only stoking my body into more of a frenzy. How am I supposed to act relaxed with this discussion?

The answer? I don't. I dive deep. With both feet.

I sprawl across the couch, cupping my head in my hand. "Tell me, what's your favorite part of a woman?"

"To paint or in general?"

"Whichever question you prefer answering."

His eyes regard me. Testing me. Trying to gauge where my head is at. "Every woman is different."

"So the whole boobs, legs, and ass thing doesn't hold true? I figured those were always the top choices amongst body parts."

Josh smiles. "I am a guy, Addy."

"Is that a yes?"

"That's a yes. I am a fan of the big three. But there are so many other areas that are just as sexy. Even more so."

"But," I coach, "every woman is different."

He nods, a bemused smile on his face. He knows I want more information, but he's got me cornered. To obtain it, I'll have to ask the question.

Swiping my tongue across my lip, I focus my gaze on the fringe of the pillow. "What about me?"

Josh strolls over to the couch, planting himself on the heavy oak coffee table. "You want to know what I think is sexy about you?"

Normally, my eyes would avoid his after such a forward question. But I'm done avoiding Josh. I fix his turquoise stare with my dark one. "Yes. What parts of me do you think are sexy?"

"Where do I begin?" His fingers trail along my hip, darts of sensation shooting through my body. I swear, every place this man touches turns into an overactive erogenous zone. "I love this area right here, where your hips flare out from your waist. You have this tiny waist and yet your hips"—he clears his throat, but it sounds more like a primal growl—"they curve outwards. It makes me want to wrap my hands around them. Pull you to me."

I'm shaking. Quivering under Josh's erotic words and tender exploration.

"And here, the line of your collarbone. The way your chest heaves when you're tired." His eyes meet mine. "Or excited."

"Like now?" I whisper.

"Like now," he repeats, his fingers tightening around the curve of my hip.

I inch my mouth closer to his, knowing full well that it's up to me to make a move. He's laid all his cards on the table. I just have to sit down at the table to play. "Do you want me, Josh?" My question is a heated whisper, spoken against his lips.

"So much, Addy." There's that growl again. A low rumbling in his chest that fires up my every nerve cell.

"I want you. I need you." My lips brush against his, the

electricity between us threatening to consume us both. I splay my hand across his chest, feeling the beating of his heart. "Take me."

It's all the encouragement Josh needs as his hands frame my face, and his mouth claims me. His tongue slides against mine, and I moan from the intense passion. A thousand fireworks are lighting off everywhere in my body as I tangle my fingers in his blonde hair and pull myself against his chest.

He stands, taking me with him. "Wrap your legs around my waist." It's an order but one I'm all too happy to oblige.

"Where are we going?" I purr, dropping kisses along the side of his neck.

"Bedroom," Josh grunts, pressing my body against him.

"Are you going to have your way with me?"

He pulls back to gaze in my eyes. "I'm going to love you, Addy. I'm going to love you the way you're supposed to be loved."

CHAPTER TWENTY-FIVE

ONLY YOU

We fall into Josh's bed, pawing and pressing each other closer.

I break the kiss to pull off my dress, watching Josh's gaze alight. I reach behind me to unclasp my bra, but his hand covers mine as his lips claim me again.

"I want to undress you."

My hooded gaze drinks in his sleek muscle as he kicks off his jeans. Rising to my knees, I trail my fingers along the lines of his abdomen as my tongue glides along his collarbone. Dipping further, I wrap my hand around his shaft, feeling him strain towards me. "Lay down," I whisper, taking his lobe in my mouth.

"Not yet." Josh opens the clasp on my bra, letting it slide from my body before lowering me gently to the mattress. His tongue circles my clit, sucking it through my underwear, and I moan at the sheer pleasure. He removes my underwear with one deft movement, as his fingers slide inside me, teasing me. He looks up, meeting my hungry gaze. "Tell me what you want, Addy."

I lace my fingers into his hair, bringing his face down to my sex. "Everything. I want everything."

Josh growls as the tip of his tongue expertly flicks my clit, his fingers stroking along my wetness. "More?"

He's not going to make this easy. But I'm all for begging if it means he'll continue. "So much more. Don't stop. Don't ever stop."

I lose track of time as his mouth and fingers bring me to one orgasm after another, turning me into a bowl of trembling, twitching nerves.

The man is insatiable, but I crave more. I crave him. But Josh isn't stopping. He's on a personal quest to give me all the orgasms I've missed in my life.

He's succeeding.

My back arches at his oral invasion while my hands fist the sheets.

"Josh," I breathe, gasping for air. "It's your birthday. I want to take care of you. I need to touch you."

His lips press against the apex of my thighs, his beard offering the most wonderful erotic friction. "Since it's my birthday, I get to do whatever I want. And licking you,"—he adds as he drags his tongue along my folds—"hearing you scream my name,"—his tongue sinks inside me—"is exactly how I want to spend my day. I have a half a mind to tie you up and really have my way with you."

I hold out my wrists with a playful wink. "Go ahead. I'm yours to do with as you please."

He grabs my wrists and lifts them over my head as his big body descends on mine. His free hand roams along my side, tracing from my breast to my hip. "Oh, Addy, the things I'm going to do to you."

I pull my wrists free to scratch my nails along his shoulders, pulling his mouth to me. "Care to share?"

"I'd rather show than tell," he murmurs, as our mouths meld.

This man's kisses—I've never experienced anything like it. There's urgency, but he never rushes. He drags out each motion as if savoring my taste for future memory. It also keeps me out of my head, forcing me to remain in the moment of bliss. Right here, right now.

I push him onto his back, straddling his narrow waist. "It's my turn."

The pounding at his front door makes us both jump. "Hey, birthday boy. Your ass had better be awake."

"Fuck." Josh jolts his head up.

"You did have plans." I can't believe how disappointed I sound. And feel.

"I totally forgot. When I opened the door and saw you there, nothing else existed."

My entire body thrums from his statement. If that's not love, I don't know what is.

"Let me go get rid of them."

That niggling of self-doubt creeps into the moment. "Are you sure? I can come back later. Or tomorrow."

Josh's eyes widen as he tickles my ribs. "Are you crazy? No way in hell. I don't even want to leave this bed."

I love him. God, I love him. I wish I had the guts to say it out loud because this man embodies love with every fiber of his being. Because of him, I now understand loving on such a level.

"Be right back." With a kiss to my stomach, he shoves himself off the bed and throws on a pair of jeans.

I lay there for a few minutes, basking in the glow of more orgasms than I thought possible in a lifetime when it hits me.

I want the world—and his friends—to know I'm here, and I'm here to stay. I grab my dress and toss it over my body before heading for the front door.

As expected, Frank is on the front porch with Mariah and a

couple surfers I've never met. At least I assume they're surfers. I don't really care. I just want them gone. Then I spot Chantelle at the back of the group.

Sorry, sweetie. You're going to be very disappointed, indeed.

Mariah smiles when she sees me. "Hey, Addy."

"Hey, Mariah," I wave, looping my arms around Josh's waist and laying my head on his chest. I'm never this bold. Ever. It feels fabulous. My gaze travels first to Frank and then to Chantelle. "Hello, Frank. Chantelle."

"Now, you're not coming today?" Frank inquires, his glare narrowing in my direction.

"No. I'm spending the day with Addy."

"She can come," Frank offers, and I swear he's biting his tongue to keep from saying anything more.

"I'm sure you're disappointed because who wouldn't want to spend time with this amazing man. But today, he's mine." I smile sweetly in Frank's direction, watching his core temperature increase with my statement.

"We planned this a while ago," Frank continues, ignoring Mariah's laugh.

"Frank, leave them alone. They want some alone time together."

"Yeah, Frank," I reply, squeezing Josh a bit tighter, "leave us alone."

"So, what? You're together again?"

I plant my chin on Josh's chest, meeting his gaze and offering a smile before turning back to Frank. "We are, Frank. You see, I'm in love with this man, and I've never been in love before, so I want to spend every second I can with Josh. I'm sure you understand."

I'm not sure where I suddenly procured such a set of brass balls, but the group's slackened jaws speak volumes.

Shaking it off, Frank barks out a laugh. "Whatever. See you later, Mrs. Robinson."

I turn and plant my hand on my hip. "You're just jealous it isn't you that I'm trying to seduce."

He laughs again, but it's tinged with uncertainty. He also doesn't negate my statement. Suddenly it's clear. Frank is jealous, jealous of the attention Josh pays me, and I reciprocate. "You think so, huh?"

I send him a wink and a playful pout as I grab Josh's hands, pulling him back inside. "I know so. But if you're nice, I may have a friend..."

With a final wave, I close and lock the door. Alone at long, long last.

"So, where were we?" I twirl to face Josh, expecting our usual, playful banter. Instead, I'm seized by the searching, desperate look on his face.

His hands wind in my hair, drawing me to him. I feel the heat of his breath as his intense stare makes me lose my own. "Do you mean it, Addy?"

I can play coy and pretend I don't know what he's talking about. But I'm through pretending. I stand on tiptoe and press my body against him, feeling his every muscle flex in response.

He's been waiting. For so long, he's been waiting. "I don't know if love is the right word."

Josh's face falls, the hurt as palpable as a heartbeat.

I press my hand to his heart and offer a reassuring smile. "You didn't let me finish. What I feel is so far beyond love, Josh. This is something I've never experienced before. Uncharted waters. But I'm not afraid. Not anymore. With you beside me, I'm not afraid."

I don't get to finish the rest of my admission as his mouth crashes against mine. Apparently, I've said enough. There's an urgency now, a searching as his tongue slides along mine. His hands run down my spine to grasp my ass and hoist me against him.

A small gasp escapes as my pussy grinds against his cock. He's so damn hard, and I'm soaking wet.

"I need inside you, Addy. Now."

Our tongues tangle as I nod my nonverbal agreement.

He sets me down at the foot of the bed as his hands pull off my dress.

"Christ, you're beautiful, Addy." Josh drops to his knees in front of me, burying his face against my skin.

My body is like a sealed box of tightly coiled springs, one that has never seen the light of day.

"Addy. I need you, Addy." He repeats these words again and again. I don't want him to wait any longer. I don't want to wait any longer.

I lead him to the bed, pulling him down on top of me. "You have me, Josh. Any way you want me. I'm yours."

Our gaze holds, and for just a moment, time stops. There's nothing beyond him and me. Nothing beyond this moment. No friends or family to intrude. It's him and me.

Josh knots his hands in my hair as his mouth claims me. He's holding nothing back.

Neither am I.

I wrap my hand around his length, arching my hips as I ease him inside me. Josh presses into me, deeper, and I feel him tremble.

I don't know why this gesture, beyond any other words or expressions, solidifies my importance in Josh's life. It's visceral, subconscious, and brutally honest. He needs me as much as I need him. I'm not sure how I missed it before, but there is no mistaking the urgency now.

"Addy," Josh chokes out, rocking into my body with hard, long strokes. "Fuck, you feel—fuck."

His movements become more aggressive, claiming every inch of me. Every moment of pent-up emotion is releasing now as I lift my hips against him, bringing him deeper. I scratch my nails down his back as the fire between us threatens to flame out of control.

I meet his gaze, feel his body tensing. "I want to feel you come, Josh."

His lips attack mine, covering them with nips and licks as I wind my hands in his hair and tighten around him. I want this man completely out of control for me.

Only for me.

"Come for me, Josh."

With a final primal thrust, he pumps inside me, and his climax releases my own. I gasp for air, my hands clawing the sheets, clawing him as every nerve ending in my body fires.

He collapses on top of me, our breath mingling as our hearts pound out of our chests.

"Holy shit, Addy. That was incredible."

"Nothing has ever felt so good as you inside me."

Josh lifts his head, grasping my lower lip between his teeth. "I agree. I plan on spending a lot of time here."

I stretch my body like a sated cat. "Can you just stay here forever?"

His playful smile turns sultry as his nose nuzzles mine. "Do you want me to stay forever?"

"Yes."

"Then, I'll never leave."

CHAPTER TWENTY-SIX

IT'S BLISS

*T*wo weeks. It's been two weeks, and the man is insatiable. Truly. Granted, so am I where Josh is concerned. Hell, I never realized I had a libido much less an overactive one, but even the slightest caress from this man has me fired up and gunning.

But it's more than amazing sex, although every time is back bending, sonnet spouting spectacular. Josh is the most affectionate man I've ever met—whether it's holding my hand, rubbing my back, dripping kisses along my shoulder and neck—as though touching me is as vital as oxygen for him. And his unreserved adoration spurs my own.

Before I met my gorgeous surfer, I thought public displays of affection to be a wholly unnecessary action. Now, I couldn't give two craps who's watching. I love being kissed by him, and surprising him with secret attack embraces and unexpected snuggles.

I've unofficially moved into Josh's cottage because neither of us can stand being apart. I still have my apartment, but we only drop by there when I need more clothing. He even cleared out space in his closet for me.

Even though this isn't the first time I've lived with a lover, it's all brand new. I've never been in love before, and everything looks shiny and new. It's incredible. I know, I sound like a damn fairytale princess, and I love every second of it. I waited almost forty years for these emotions, I'm taking full advantage.

Melissa and Sean are thrilled that I worked things out with Josh. Clint, for his part, hasn't said much of anything. Maybe he's finally learned to keep his yap shut, or perhaps it's because he's schtupping a graduate nurse. Either way, he's staying out of my business.

Hell, even my mother hasn't said anything negative, beyond the standard cautions of being careful in a new relationship.

Mr. Gibbs drops by a few times per week for dinner and card games, and I look as forward to his visits as I did time with my own father. He and his son fill a space in my heart that was empty for many years.

As for Josh's friends? Noticeably absent.

"So, are they avoiding us because they hate the idea of us being together?" I inquire with my nose in the fridge, gathering supplies for dinner.

Josh chuckles, shaking his head. "No. They're avoiding us because I threatened bodily harm if they didn't. I want some time alone with you, Addy. I've spent plenty of time with my friends. Besides, I still see them at work."

He's got a point. I, for one, do not miss Frank or his pointed barbs about my age. Besides, age doesn't matter anymore. When it's just Josh and me, the years between us doesn't exist.

I glance up from the stove and catch Josh's watchful gaze on me, a small smile playing on his lips.

"What are you smiling about?" I inquire, returning his grin.

He's by my side in two steps, wrapping his arms around my waist and pressing me close to him. "I'm picturing our future."

This man is a diehard romantic, another first for me. Clint and I discussed our future, but it was logistics and layouts. With Josh, it's all emotion, and his words set my soul on fire. Thankfully, I'm turned away from him, but there's no mistaking the pounding of my heart. "Oh, really? What does it look like?"

"I make you my wife on the beach at sunset. The sky is playing off the water and reflecting in your eyes as I promise to love you forever."

My eyes drift close. When he speaks the words aloud, I can see that future, too. Josh makes it so effortless. So easy.

"You're pregnant and absolutely radiant."

I chortle, giving him a light jab in the ribs. "So, that's why you married me. You knocked me up."

He pinches my ass, and I let out a squeal. "Stop interrupting. This is important. You're wearing this dress that shows off your amazing body—"

"Obviously."

"—and I can't stop looking at you. Pretty much how I am now."

I lean back into him, allowing the warmth of his love to find its way into every crevice of my heart. "I like your vision of our future."

"Me too. Now we just have to make it a reality."

"So, how cute is our kid?"

"They're gorgeous. Just like their mom."

"You've gone and done it now." I twirl in his arms, twining my hands around his neck.

"What's that?"

"Destroyed any chance another man has of winning my heart. No one comes close."

I TRY to coordinate our schedules as much as possible, but it's a challenge. Today, he's working, and I'm fantasizing about what I'm going to do that fine ass man as soon as he gets home.

I'm basking in the glorious afternoon sun when the doorbell rings. I stroll to answer it, expecting the mailman or delivery guy.

Instead, I find Chantelle on the stoop, her green eyes narrowing when I open the door.

"Chantelle, what can I do for you?"

"Have you moved in already?" She bites out the words. Apparently, she's done playing nice.

So am I. "That's none of your business. What do you want?"

"I have something to give to Josh." She thrusts a bag toward me.

"I'll see that he gets it." I take the bag and begin closing the door, but she's not moving. *Oh holy hell, what now?* "Is there something else I can do for you?"

"I was wondering what you're wearing Friday night."

My eyes narrow as my back goes up. Friday night? "I'm not sure what you're talking about."

"Oh, you must be working. Never mind."

I know women and their mind games. Little tricks they set to lure you into their net. I pride myself on never falling for said tricks. However, this is one lure that is too shiny to ignore. "I'm not working Friday."

Her hand flies to her chest, her eyes widening in mock shock. "I'm sorry. I shouldn't have said anything."

I know I'm going to regret asking this question. "What's Friday night?"

"Our sponsor is hosting a huge party in a new club in Laguna Beach. It's going to be a circus of celebrity and paparazzi. All of the models who are part of the partnership have to be there, of course. The models are allowed to bring their significant others, although most opt to travel stag. I know I'm not bringing anyone. I don't want some guy hanging on my arm when I'm surrounded by movie stars."

I nod, my mouth too dry to manage anything else at the moment. Not only have I not been invited to this shindig, I haven't even been informed that it was occurring. Double whammy. Lucky me. Still, I need to keep it together in front of Little Red Yoga Hood. "I hope you have a good time."

"Will I see you there?" The smile on her face is vicious. She's enjoying every second of my discomfort.

"I don't even know if Josh is going. He hates clubs."

Her brow quirks. "Since when? Josh always enjoyed the glitter of party life." She glances at her nails, clearing her throat. "Turning him into a regular homebody, aren't you?"

"That's what Josh prefers."

"No, that's what Josh *tells* you he prefers. Have a good day."

I watch her leave, tempted to grab the closest flowerpot, and chuck it at her head. Instead, I grab my phone and demand that Melissa meets me for an impromptu drink. Aside from work and errands, I haven't set foot outside Josh's house in the last few weeks. It's good to mingle with humanity, especially when they're not bleeding from the ears in your Emergency Department.

Twenty minutes later, my saintly friend is waiting for my anxious ass to arrive at the local watering hole, drinks at the ready. Bless this woman.

"How are you and Mr. Wonderful?" Melissa inquires, clinking glasses with me in a toast.

I can launch right into a diatribe about the hateful Chantelle, but I opt to focus on the good. Chantelle has already proven herself a meddler. I'm not giving her free reign in my psyche.

"We're great. He's amazing, Melissa. So attentive and caring. Totally unlike anything I've ever experienced before."

"And the sex?"

I sputter my drink. I should know Melissa is one to cut to the chase. "Insane, but in the best way."

"You're no longer an orgasm virgin."

"Definitely not."

"Congratulations. It's about damn time." She leans forward, studying my face. "But something is up. Am I right?"

Well, shit. Here I thought I was hiding it well.

I stir the straw in my drink, trying to figure out the best way to broach the topic. "It's probably nothing."

"Probably. But tell me anyway."

"Chantelle, you know, Little Red Yoga Hood, stopped by just before I called you. She had a package to give to Josh for their big party on Friday night."

"What party?"

I shrug, taking another sip of my drink. "I don't know. He hasn't mentioned it. According to Chantelle, it's part of their modeling sponsorship."

"Do you think it's another trick?"

"I believe her, but I'm a bit concerned that Josh didn't even mention it to me."

"Maybe it slipped his mind," Melissa offers.

"I don't think so. Chantelle mentioned that they're allowed to bring dates, but he hasn't said a word."

Melissa pats my hand, a perceptive smile on her face. "Chantelle wants to win back her ex-boyfriend. You're standing in the way. She will say anything to get a rise out of you."

I'm trying really hard, but my insecurities are getting a foothold. Again. "What if she's not lying? What if he can bring a date and he's opting not to bring me? What if he's embarrassed by us being together? We never go anywhere. Not restaurants, not clubs, not bars. Nowhere. What if—"

Melissa presses her hand to my mouth, silencing me. "Stop right now with this nonsense. Look, I'm sure it's perfectly innocent, but I suggest you go home and talk to Josh about it. See what he says. Don't pass judgement until you have all the facts. Promise me, Addy."

I nod, trying to maintain the euphoric glow I've felt in my time with Josh. "What if she's right?"

"Then Friday night, we will go out and do something even more fabulous."

I giggle. God, I love this woman. "I doubt that. They're hobnobbing with celebrities."

"Fuck celebrities. They're highly overrated. Drama queens every one of them. Actually, there's a great band playing downtown. Alternative rock with a funky edge. We'll have a blast."

"I don't deserve you as a friend."

"Don't worry. I'll send you a bill." Melissa sends me a wink before sliding the check in my direction. "Oh, look, here's one now."

"What a pal," I mutter with a smile.

JOSH POKES his head out of the kitchen the minute I turn the key in the lock. "Hey, beautiful. I was calling you. I didn't know where you'd gone."

"Sorry. I should have left a note."

He closes the distance between us, claiming my lips with a sensuous kiss. "How was your afternoon?"

"Good. I had a drink with Melissa. It was nice to get out."

Josh smiles, giving my ass a smack. "I'm sure it was. I'm making dinner."

I force a smile, trying to act casual. Operation 'do some digging' is about to commence. "I thought we might go out tonight."

Josh shrugs, his face unreadable. "We can, but I'm halfway through cooking."

I don't want to appear ungrateful. After all, the man hasn't done anything...that I know of...yet. "It smells delicious. Can I help?"

"Just sit there and be your sexy ass self."

I pull a bottle of wine from the fridge and pour myself a glass before perching on a bar stool. "Did you see your package?"

Josh's gaze sweeps around the rooms. "No. Where is it?"

"On the table." I swig back a gulp of wine. "Chantelle dropped it off."

With a sigh, Josh stops stirring the pot of food, setting the spoon to the side. "What did she say?"

I shrug, forcing a smile. Here goes nothing. "She asked me what I was wearing Friday night."

"Fuck," Josh mutters, and I'm reasonably certain he didn't mean for me to hear it.

"I didn't know you two were heading to Laguna Beach together."

"It's for work. There's this club opening—"

I hold up my hand. Once is more than enough to hear about their night out together with all the beautiful people. "She told me. My question is, why didn't *you* tell me?"

He's chewing his lip. That's never a good sign. "I didn't want you to get mad."

Slow inhale, slow exhale. Above all else, remain calm and resist the temptation to hurl wine bottle in his direction. "A tip for the future—not telling me that you and your ex-girlfriend are spending an evening together is *not* the way to ensure I don't get angry."

"Addy, it's not like that."

"I'm sure it's not." I finish off the glass of wine before heading to the fridge for round two. "Have fun." I'm waiting for him to invite me along, waiting for him to make it right. Waiting for him to reassure me that I'm not a fool for believing in him.

"You know I hate the club scene," Josh reminds me, curling his hands around my waist. "I'd far rather be with you. In bed. Naked. Kissing every inch of you." He skims kisses along my neck, but I'm in no mood for foreplay.

I push him off me, returning to my perch at the bar. "According to Chantelle, you enjoy the nightlife."

"That was a long time ago, Addy. I've changed." He tips my chin up, making me meet his concerned gaze. "Beautiful, if it bothers you that much, I won't go."

It hits me that Josh isn't going to invite me to the shindig, a realization that guts me. Time to fetch my emotional armor and put it back on. My heart isn't safe anywhere.

Forcing a smile, I shake my head. "I wouldn't ask that of you. This is important for your career. I hope you have a wonderful time." Shit. Now I sound exactly like I did when I was with Clint. "I'm going to take a bath. I'm not very hungry. If you'll excuse me."

I soak for the next thirty minutes, listening to sad songs and pondering if I'm foolish or naive. Or both. I don't want a repeat of my relationship with Clint, and no matter how polar opposite the men seem, I'm not sure of my place with either of them. Oh, I know my official place as a girlfriend, but regarding their hearts, I'm in the dark.

I finally climb from the tub, ready to curl up in bed with a novel. But when I open the door, I'm greeted by lit candles everywhere and the scent of roses perfuming the air. Soft instrumental music plays through the speakers, and Josh is waiting for me, right outside the bathroom.

He presses his fingers to my lips. "No questions. Come with me." He leads me to the bedroom, those long and talented fingers undoing my robe and skating along my naked body. "Lay down."

I open my mouth to speak, but his wide-eyed gaze stops me.

"Lay down, Addy," Josh repeats.

No sooner has my body hit the bed than I feel Josh's hands rubbing my shoulders. I release a low moan as he slides his oil-slicked palms along my spine with gentle pressure.

"You keep moaning like that, and I'll never get through this massage."

I burrow my head in the pillow, releasing a sated breath. The man's hands are seriously magic. "What's with the special treatment?"

"You're upset, and it's because of me. I never want to see that look of doubt on your face again. I saw it too much in the beginning of our relationship."

I tongue my upper lip, uncertain of how to respond. I know Josh can read me like a book, so he'll see through any falsehood, regardless. "Chantelle made me feel like I was in the way again."

Josh's lips nuzzle my nape, as his hands wind under my body, cupping my breasts. "Addy, who am I with? Who do I make love to every day that she'll let me? I'll give you a hint. It isn't Chantelle."

I turn over, capturing his gaze, my hands wandering along the planes of his chest. "What if we're the only ones who think we make sense?"

His lips tease mine, nibbling, and coaxing me into relaxed submission. "*We* are the only ones who count. If we think we make sense, no one else's opinion matters."

"What do you think?" I twirl a long lock of his hair, surprised by my boldness.

He nuzzles along my jaw, depositing soft kisses. "I think I would ask you to marry me, but I have my doubts that you'd say yes."

I'm glad I'm lying down. If I had been standing and he said those words, I would have collapsed to the ground. "What did you say?"

Josh grins, nibbling my fingertips as they stroke his beard. "You heard me."

"Marriage? Josh, are you sure this is a topic you want to broach? You're so young."

He groans into the pillow next to me. "Please don't start with the age equation again, Addy. You haven't mentioned it in weeks. Don't let it be an issue now."

"It isn't. Besides the age difference, we haven't been together that long."

"What does that matter? You were with your ex for four years and weren't engaged. Is there a specific timeline I should be following?"

"I'm just saying—"

"And I'm just saying that I want you to be my wife, Addy. I'm not asking you right now, but it is something I want you to keep in mind because I will be asking in the future."

His words set my heart and body on fire. He looks so earnest. He seems so genuine. And a life with this man sounds like paradise. Utter paradise. "Promises, promises," I tease, pulling his mouth to mine for a kiss.

Josh's gaze holds mine, and in it, I read every emotion in his heart. "I *will* be asking you, Addy."

"I don't want to lock you into something you might later regret."

That smile. It will be the end of me. He holds his wrists out in front of me, offering himself up for shackling. "Lock me in, Addy. Lock me in and throw away the key. I'll go willingly."

I giggle, wrapping my hands around his wrists as pseudo cuffs. "No shackles necessary, although it does give me an idea for later."

CHAPTER TWENTY-SEVEN

ANOTHER LINE CROSSED

I decide to pick up an extra shift on Friday night instead of spending time in a bar, wondering what Josh is doing. I'd much rather get paid to wonder what Josh is doing.

The Universe, my sadistic buddy, aligns to make it a night straight from the bowels of hell, and my shift is finished before I have a chance to look at the clock.

Thank you, Universe, that wasn't quite what I meant.

The only amusing part of the night? The deer-in-headlights look that Clint's new noodle wore the entire evening. Welcome to the ED, sweetie.

I yawn at least a hundred times on the short drive to Josh's house, but I'm wide awake as soon as I step foot into the empty cottage.

Josh isn't here.

I grab my phone, and sure enough, there's a message from my adoring boyfriend. It's hard to hear above the din of the music and crowd, but he sounds a bit inebriated. He mumbles something about staying in Laguna Beach and returning in the morning. He finishes his call proclaiming he loves me in four different languages, but I'm too far gone at this point.

My boyfriend stayed overnight in Laguna Beach with his ex-girlfriend.

I pace the floor, questioning my next move. Break every surfboard? That's an idea. Burn the house down? I'd likely go to jail. Get the hell out of here and go back to my apartment? That's the safest bet—for us both.

I grab some clothes and toiletries and make a beeline for the door. Internally, I'm giving myself a pep talk, keeping it together, not losing my shit until I know it's time to lose my shit.

My phone rings and I startle at the noise. "Hello?"

"Adelaide, it's your mother. Were you ever planning on calling?"

Figures my mother would call at half-past seven in the middle of a crisis. Her timing is impeccable. "Sorry, Mother. I've been busy."

"Still dating that young man?"

How the fuck should I answer that question? Likely not, but they'll never find the body? "Yes, we're still...dating. I guess."

She releases a loud sigh and a resigned laugh. "Men can be such dogs, can't they?"

What did she just say? I must be hallucinating at this point. "That they can."

"Do you want to talk about it?"

"I'm not sure what there is to talk about. It looks like everyone was right, and I got played for a fool."

"I take it his friends aren't fond of you?"

I choke out a laugh. "That's an understatement."

"I know the feeling."

I pull the phone from my ear. She's younger than my stepfather. How could she possibly relate? "You do?"

"Addy, I was a secretary. Your stepfather is the CEO of a multi-million-dollar company. He came from old stock and old money. They treated me like a scullery maid."

It's funny how you can know someone and yet never really see them. In all these years, I never knew how my mother suffered. "Why did you put up with it?"

"I loved him. It would have been much easier if I didn't. I also wanted to prove their rich, egotistical asses wrong. I wouldn't let them run me off. If I was to leave, it would be on my own terms."

"How long until they came around?"

My mother chuckles. "Most are dead in the ground and went into it still hating the idea of me. But, my husband loves the idea of me, and that is all that matters."

"I didn't know you struggled like that. I don't know how I missed it."

"You'd been through so much, Adelaide. Losing your father and then having to adjust to this new lifestyle. I wasn't going to burden you with any additional stress. You bore too much already."

Here come those tears again, but this time, they're welcome in the conversation. "I wish you had told me. I would have fought their pompous asses, too."

"Does he love you?"

"He says he does."

"Do you believe him?"

"I don't know."

"My darling daughter, strip away all the nonsense. His friends, family, and outside influences. Then look at him, just him, without any interference."

"That's just it. There never seems to be a time without interference. His friends are always meddling, just for kicks."

"Then kick back."

"I do have a mean roundhouse."

"I was thinking of visiting soon. Your birthday is in a couple weeks. I'd like to see you."

I smile because, for the first time in a long time, I'd like to see her, too. "I'd like that, Mom. I'd really like that."

My conversation with my mother and a shower work wonders on my psyche, but there's still a nagging pain in my heart. I don't know if Josh cheated last night, if Chantelle plied him with her looks and feminine wiles into something he may or may not later regret.

My exhaustion catches up to me, and I crawl into bed. I need to sleep. I need peace, too, but I'm less likely to find that anywhere.

I jerk awake, my gaze jumping around the bedroom. *What the hell time is it? It's only eleven. So what the hell woke me up?*

The banging at my door makes me jump again, and I stagger into the living room. I peer through the keyhole and see Josh on the other side, his foot tapping impatiently. Leaning against the door, I mumble, "What do you want, Josh?"

"Please let me in, Addy." I hear it in his voice. The trepidation. He knows he's in the doghouse.

"I'm tired. I worked last night. I'm going back to sleep."

"Addy, please open the door."

I bang my head against the door, feeling yet another headache brewing. "I don't want to do this right now."

"Do what? I called you more than ten times last night, and you never responded. Then I come home, and our bed isn't slept in. I have no idea where you are, and you won't pick up your damn phone."

Is this pretentious bastard actually mad at me? I fling open the door, my eyes blazing. "I'm sorry. Did I disturb your overnight fuck fest? I beg your pardon. It won't happen again." I push the door closed, but Josh is faster, shoving his way into the apartment.

"Addy, what the fuck is going on?"

"You tell me. What kind of work event turns into an overnight party? And how drunk were you last night?"

"I wasn't drunk at all. Our sponsor got hammered and spent most of the night puking. Chantelle was equally soused. I got to spend the night nursing both of them."

I'm sure he wants me to feel bad, but the mention of Chantelle's name only enflames me further. "Poor baby. It must be so hard being a model. You should try being a nurse." I know I'm being a bitch. A big one. But he spent the night with his ex-girlfriend, and I'm not about to let him off the hook that easily.

"Did you listen to the rest of your messages?" Josh bellows.

"I couldn't understand the first one, Josh. It was all garbled."

"I called you several times, asking if you would come to pick me up."

"What am I? Your mother?"

"No. You're my girlfriend. I thought the fact that I was stranded might entice you to come to get me."

My emotions are whirling like food in a blender. I don't know what—or who—to believe. I release a strangled groan, glaring at the ceiling. "Fuck you, Universe."

Then I turn on my heel and storm into the bedroom. Josh can let himself out.

I throw the blankets over my head, curling into the fetal position. The mattress sinks next to me, and I feel his arms wrap around me.

"What do you want?" I grumble.

He pulls the blanket down, exposing my head. "I want you to stop being angry at me."

"Fat chance of that."

"Addy, I didn't do anything."

I roll onto my back, glaring at him. "How do I know that?"

His eyes widen, clearly taken aback by my question. "I would hope that you trust me."

I focus my gaze downward, picking at the sheet.

"Addy, do you trust me?"

"This situation is making it pretty difficult to trust you. You spent the night with Chantelle."

"No, I spent the night vacillating between the club bathroom and cramped inside a car."

"With Chantelle."

His shoulders sag as his gaze becomes more searching. "You really believe something happened, don't you?"

"I don't know, Josh. But I can't risk it again."

"What does that mean?"

"Maybe we should—"

"Don't even go there, Addy," Josh cuts me off. "I'm not letting you break up with me, certainly not over my idiot ex-girlfriend."

My mind is tired. My heart, even more so. "I'm exhausted. I need to sleep."

His fingers stroke my cheek, my chin. There's so much love in his touch. But is it real or just the product of a talented actor? "Go to sleep."

I want to ask if he'll be here when I wake up, but I know the answer. He pushes off the bed, dropping a kiss on my cheek. "I'm going to pop into the shower. I'll be right back."

I nod as sleep hits me hard and fast.

"Hey, you feel better?"

I crack open my eyes. Josh is lying next to me, his fingers making lazy circles along my arm. "What time is it?"

"Almost three."

"Hmm. I'm still tired."

"You were out like a light, beautiful. I ordered us in some food."

I sit up, stretching out the kinks in my neck. Time to rejoin the world of the living. I go to the bathroom and splash water on my face and brush my teeth. Hey, I'm almost human again.

I return to the bedroom and crawl back under the covers. Okay, so I'm halfway to human. Another hour and a cup of coffee will set me straight.

My gaze falls to Josh, sipping from a mug of coffee and peering out the window, clothed in only a pair of boxer briefs. "I'm sorry you didn't have fun last night."

Josh smirks, nodding in agreement. "That's an understatement."

"Don't you love being around the beautiful people?"

He climbs into bed next to me, nuzzling my neck. "I love being around *one* beautiful person, and I'm with her now. I thought we could check out that cove later this evening. What do you think?"

Part of me wants to lie, claim I have plans for the evening. But Josh will see through it just like he does every falsehood.

"I'm not sure I'm up for hanging out tonight."

Our gazes hold, and then Josh gives me a soft smile. "Where's your laptop?"

"Random conversation change. In the kitchen."

He returns with the computer and climbs into bed with me, flipping it open.

"What are you looking for?" I inquire.

"Photos from last night."

"Wonderful."

"There's video, too."

"Even better."

"Shush. Just wait." He brings up several photos, scrolling through them. He looks amazing, but that's fairly standard for Josh. Unfortunately for my ego, Chantelle also looks amazing. "Here." He slides the laptop over, pressing play on a video.

The sound quality isn't great, but it's a hell of an improvement over the message Josh left me last night. It's a sound bite with a local reporter, asking about Josh's involvement with the company and his work with the veterans.

I can't help it. I'm proud of the work Josh does with our soldiers. I want the world to be proud of him, too.

Then the conversation segues. The reporter inquires if Chantelle is his date for the evening. Before Little Red Yoga Hood can answer, Josh negates the statement. He then proclaims that he's in a serious relationship with the woman of his dreams. Her name? Addy.

The video stops, and my gaze shifts to Josh. "You told everyone about me?"

Josh nods, snapping shut the laptop. "I did. It's like I love you or something."

"I really thought when you weren't home, that you and Chantelle—"

"Never. Not in a million years, Addy."

I smile up at him. "I'm glad because your face is too pretty to mar up."

Josh laughs, rolling on top of me. "I'm happy to hear I escaped a mauling."

"At least for now."

His fingers push my hair from my face, as he peppers me with kisses. "I love you, Adelaide Perkins. You need to get that through your thick skull."

I giggle, pushing him off me. He's right. I need to stop inventing problems where there aren't any. "Where's that food? I'm famished."

THE COVE IS beautiful and secluded, and although the night is chilly, Josh brought enough blankets and body heat to keep me warm.

We feast on an array of fruits and bread before snuggling together to watch the sun drop below the horizon.

"Was it worth it?" Josh whispers in my ear, his hands refusing to behave as they glide along my waistband.

"It was. Thank you."

"Do you like it here, Addy?"

"You mean the beach or San Diego?"

"San Diego. I know your contract is ending soon."

I nod, tucking my head against his chest to ward off the wind. "It is. I only have another couple of weeks."

"Have you signed up for another stint?"

"No, not yet." I turn and face him. "What's with the inquisition?"

"Just curious. Am I asking too many questions?"

"No. I'm an open book. Ask me anything."

"I have succeeded in life. Turning Addy into an open book." His fingers graze along my palm. "I have to go away for a couple days."

I chew my inner lip. "Another model sponsorship thing?"

"Something like that."

I can't pinpoint why, but his answer doesn't sit well with me. It's purposely vague. Clint was often purposely vague. But I also learned something from Clint and his illicit affairs. Give them enough rope to hang themselves. "I'll stay at my apartment while you're gone."

"Why? Mi casa, su casa. You know that." He pulls me tight against him, his lips pressing against my hair. "Have you ever been to Hawaii?"

"Great vacation spot."

"Great spot, period."

"I've heard it's beautiful, but I can't imagine living there. It's so far away from everything."

"Maybe that's a good thing. A fresh start where no one knows you."

The gnawing in my gut increases. "No one knew me here." I shrug, popping a grape into my mouth. "Besides, I can't fathom moving again right now. I've been living out of boxes for the last couple of months."

Josh falls silent, and I wish I was half the mind reader he is. Unfortunately for me, I don't have any idea what he's thinking.

"You're not planning on up and leaving me, are you?" I joke, leaning in to steal a kiss from those luscious lips.

He returns the kiss, but his smile lacks any mirth. "Never. I just wanted to see where your head is at."

I splay my fingers across his chest. "My head and my heart are right here. With you."

"Do you mean it, Addy?"

"Yes. I plan on spending my life with you. Now, you can't go running away after I said that."

"I needed to hear that."

My fingers drift down his stomach, and I hear his breath hitch. "Is there anything else you need, Josh?"

He can't hide the hunger washing across his face as he grabs my hand, nuzzling my inner wrist. His tongue slides further up my arm as he lowers me back into the cocoon of blankets. "I need inside you, beautiful."

"Then we better get home," I reply with a playful wink.

But Josh isn't in the mood to leave our beach locale. His body covers mine, his mouth nipping the line of my neck. "I need inside you. Now."

It's difficult to think as his hands become more presumptuous in their explorations. "You need to stop."

"Like hell I do," Josh growls as he yanks up my shirt, teasing my nipples with his tongue.

"We can't. Someone will see us."

"No one will see us." His fingers find their mark, sliding inside me, making me clench.

"Josh," I murmur, my voice somewhere between a gasp and a plea.

His fingers stroke along my folds, his thumb circling my clit. "Do you want me to stop, Addy?"

My hips arch against his hand, pushing him deeper. No way in hell do I ever want this man to stop touching me. "I want you, Josh. All of you."

With one smooth maneuver, he pulls off his pants, his cock pressing against my stomach. Those gorgeous eyes are even more mysterious in the low light, but I see the inner fire burning within. "All of me?"

I shove down my jeans and thong before wrapping my legs around his hips. "All of you," I repeat.

Josh slides inside me, taking his time to fill me inch by inch. Every thrust fills me, but I want more. I can't get close enough. His gaze holds mine as his body possesses every facet of my being.

I realize how desperately I love this man, how much I want to carry his child, and be linked forever to his heart. There are a million reasons why I shouldn't, but as I stare into those impossibly blue eyes, I can't think of a single one.

"I want it too, Addy."

"I didn't say anything."

"You didn't have to. It's written all over your face."

Shit. Please don't let me scare him off with my hormonal urges.

He thrusts deeper as his lips scald the skin of my neck. "I want it too, Addy. Just say the word." He's asking permission, ensuring he's welcome.

Deeper. Harder. Closer.

"Tell me I can," Josh growls in my ear, his hands cupping my ass to deepen every movement. "Say it. Tell me what you want."

My head shouts out a ton of warnings, but my mouth ignores every one. "I want all of you, Josh."

Another thrust. So deep. So united. Just like he told me in the beginning, I don't know where I end, and Josh begins.

"It feels so good," I manage, my breath coming in ragged gasps.

"I love you, Addy." He pulls out almost all the way before plunging deep inside me, and it's enough to send me over the edge.

My body shudders as I climax, every cell in my body on high alert. I see his face above me, straining to maintain control. I run my fingers along his jaw, holding his gaze. "I love you, Josh."

He comes on a bellow, growling with pleasure as he empties himself inside me.

I've never experienced something so intense, so erotic. Judging from the look on his face, neither has he.

We crossed another boundary tonight. I just pray he doesn't regret it.

Josh rolls off me and onto his back, his breath coming in short huffs. I sit, quiet, trying to gauge his response.

I don't have to wait long.

"If you're waiting for me to regret what just happened, Addy, you'll be waiting a long time."

A smile breaks across my face as I lay my head on his chest. "We haven't exactly been careful, but this is the first time we ever...the first time it wasn't an accident."

Josh twirls a lock of my hair around his finger. "Nothing has been accidental with you, my beautiful Adelaide. I knew from the moment I saw you stumbling across the sand that I would make you mine. You've always belonged to me. My heart recognized you immediately."

CHAPTER TWENTY-EIGHT

CANCEL ALL FUTURE PLANS

"When should I pick out a dress for the wedding?" Melissa jokes over the phone line, as I return her laughter.

"Not quite yet," I reply. I'm curled into a lounge chair on Josh's back patio, the gas fireplace removing the chill from the air.

"But it sure sounds like it's headed that way."

"It's headed that way." It took thirty-nine years, but I finally feel complete confidence in both myself and Josh.

Ever since that night on the beach, we have an unspoken bond between us. We're ready for the long haul, and we want that journey together. Those with any other opinions are free to keep their traps shut.

"Your nursing contract is ending soon. I assume you're staying here?"

The truth is that Josh and I haven't discussed our life post-contract, but I know he wants me with him. "Obviously. Josh's life is here. Besides, I love San Diego."

"Becoming a permanent SoCal resident?"

"Looks that way."

"So, what's the plan for your birthday, baby? Still on for the club tomorrow?"

I can't believe I'm turning forty tomorrow. I hold back a shudder at the thought. *It's just a number. A big, fat, stinking number. Can't I stay thirty-nine forever?* "Yes, but with slightly less alcohol."

"No worries, there. Josh won't let you get too soused."

"He won't be there."

"Why the hell not?"

"He's away."

"Where did he go?" Melissa presses.

The more questions she asks, the fewer answers I have. "I'm not sure exactly. Somewhere for a modeling gig."

"Please tell me Chantelle isn't part of that gig."

"I don't think so. Not this time."

"It's a bit odd that you don't know where in the world Josh is at the moment." I hear the trepidation in Melissa's voice. She knows me, and the last thing she wants to do is send me scuttling back to my cave of low self-confidence.

Trouble is, she's right. Josh was downright evasive about his trip. Hopefully, it's nothing. Just like every other time.

I hear the front door open. Josh is still away in parts unknown, so it's definitely not him. A thought flits across my mind, and my heart sinks.

Please don't let it be Frank.

A strange man steps onto the patio, startling us both. "Melissa, let me call you back," I murmur, disconnecting the call.

I stand, my heart beating erratically. I really don't want to be chopped into little pieces today. Or any day, for that matter. I peek through the kitchen window, but I know there's a snowball's chance in hell that I'll reach the knife block before he does.

"Can—can I help you?"

"Sorry to startle you, miss. My name is Russ. I'm looking for Josh."

"He's not here. He went away for a few days."

"Oh right. Hawaii." Russ snaps his finger as the memory returns to him.

Too bad the memory doesn't return to me. Then again, how could it? I had no clue Josh was in Hawaii. "Yes, I guess. He's away on a modeling shoot."

Russ's brow furrows with confusion. "Modeling gig? Josh told me he was headed to Hawaii to discuss that surfing sponsorship."

Are we speaking the same language? "Surfing sponsorship?"

"Yes, from what I hear, it's a done deal. He just had to fly down and sign papers." He whips out an envelope. "That's actually why I'm here. This is his deposit. Will you see that he gets it?"

"Deposit?" My God, I sound like a blathering idiot, but at the moment, I feel like one. Talk about being in the dark.

"I'm sorry to confuse you. First, I bust in on you, and then I unload buckets of information."

"You're fine, Russ. I apologize that I'm out of the loop." I'm real damn sorry at this point.

"I own this house. This,"—he shakes the envelope—"is his security deposit. He kept the place in great condition, so now he can use this money on his next adventure."

I accept the money with trembling hands, sliding it into a desk drawer, and thanking Russ before he lets himself out. I want to barrage him with a million questions since he seems to have a handle on what my boyfriend is doing with his life, but I remain silent. If Josh wanted me to know the details, he would tell me. Right?

Oh crap, what the hell is going on?

The doorbell rings, and I damn near jump through the ceiling. Did I miss the memo that everyone in the free world is dropping by unannounced today?

Okay, the last visitor had less than welcome news. What are the chances the Universe will send me two unwelcome visitors?

In reality—mine, at least, the chances are excellent.

When I see Chantelle standing opposite me on the vestibule, it takes everything in me not to slam the door in her face. "What can I do for you?" I inquire, leaning against the door frame. I'm in no mood for any of this woman's childish antics.

"I suppose congratulations are in order."

My eyes widen, and I glance over my shoulder, half expecting to find someone standing behind me with a Publisher's Clearinghouse check. "What are you talking about?"

"Play it coy. Can't say I blame you."

Okay, now I've earned the right to slam the door in her face. "I don't have time for this nonsense."

Chantelle places her hand on the door, preventing its closure. "Your plan worked. Congratulations. You must be *so* thrilled." The look on her face is pure venom.

The look on my face, I'm certain, is pure confusion. Assuming that this is another trick, I cross my arms over my chest. "What plan would that be?"

"Are you pregnant yet?"

Her question is so far out of left field, there's no way to prepare for it. "Excuse me? Who the hell do you think you are, coming over—"

"I'm someone who has Josh's best interests at heart. Unlike you."

I'm too old to get into a fistfight, but I'm not too old to be tempted to knock her block off. "What the fuck is that supposed to mean?"

"I repeat, are you pregnant?"

I lean in, my face inches from her. "I'm not having this discussion with you. My private life with Josh is none of your business."

"Then how about this discussion. Josh is considering giving up the opportunity of a lifetime, and it's all your fault."

My life, as I know it, slides out of focus with her accusation. "You better start making some sense."

Chantelle offers up a dry laugh. "You're a piece of work. Hell, I almost believe that you don't know anything about his sponsorship."

That's the second time in less than an hour that I've heard this term. Apparently, I'm the only person who doesn't know.

Her face softens, likely at my look of complete bewilderment. "Didn't Josh tell you?"

I feel my ego deflate alongside my heart. "No."

She clicks her teeth, eyeing me up and down. "Perhaps I'm mistaken. Maybe you aren't a threat at all."

"A threat to what?"

"Josh was approached by a few different surf companies over the last several months. They've watched his progression and his work with veterans and want him to be the face of their company. It's a huge deal. A ridiculous honor."

I'm glad I'm leaning against the door frame. I lack the strength to hold myself upright. "Wow." I know it's the worst comeback in history, but considering my world just got turned upside down, I'm proud that I'm still speaking English.

"What did you think he was doing in Hawaii?"

"I didn't know he was in Hawaii. Until today."

Chantelle clears her throat, and I can see the bitch is holding back a smile. *Way to get enjoyment at my pain, you yoga teacher from hell.* "He must have discussed the sponsorships. We *all* knew about those."

Everyone but me. The last to know, once again. I don't have the energy to fight Chantelle. Or Russ. Or anyone. "You can put your mind at ease. I'm not a threat. Just a passing fling, like you said."

"If you were pregnant, then he might consider taking you with him."

Universe, if I slap this bitch silly, all I can say is she had it coming.

I draw upon all my reserves, pushing myself off the door frame. "You and Frank can rest easy. I'm not pregnant."

I shut the door, not caring if the woman has any more news to lord over me.

As far as they're concerned, I'm done. The sad truth is, they're right. I pray Chantelle's accusations are false, but my heart knows the truth. When it comes to Josh's future, I am the only one who doesn't seem to be a part of it.

The writing has been on the wall for months. I was simply too foolhardy to read it.

CHAPTER TWENTY-NINE

TWO WEEKS & COUNTING

*A*fter Russ and Chantelle's visits, I can't stand being in Josh's home any longer, so I pack my things and leave. Hey, at least I'm saving Josh the hassle of removing me from his premises, not that it will be his home much longer anyway.

I cry myself to sleep and wake up the next morning on the first day of my forties, without a clue what the hell I'm supposed to do with my life. All I can say is what a banner year forty is turning out to be. Seriously.

Hey universe, might as well throw in some acne and the chickenpox. Make it a doozy all around. I'm kidding, universe. Give me a damn break.

And now, I'm in the middle of a night club, trying desperately to act as if nothing is wrong, while simultaneously being forced into celebration mode. Needless to say, I'm failing miserably.

My head and heart are drowning in the half-truths surrounding Josh. His lies make Clint look like Honest Abe.

"Hey, birthday girl, you want a shot?" Melissa waves a glass under my nose, and I take it, albeit grudgingly.

I really need to keep my head about me, but my heart is all for getting plastered. "Thanks."

"I know you miss Josh," Melissa says, tossing her arm around my shoulders. "When is he coming home?"

Never.

"Tomorrow." Time to change the topic. "How did you find this place, anyway? It's a bit of a drive."

"Nothing is too far for my friend on her birthday. Besides, the DJ is pumping, and the bartenders are heavy-handed friends."

Lord, love this woman. She's trying so damn hard. I, at least, need to make an effort.

She's right about the location. The club has a great atmosphere, even if most of the people are several years younger than I am.

"Do you have your bag of sex tricks ready for Mr. Wonderful's return tomorrow?"

"I'm ending things with Josh," I blurt.

Melissa's eyes widen. "Why? The man seems perfect, and he worships you."

I'm loath to admit that neither statement is remotely true. Instead, I use my tried and true excuse when it comes to Josh. The good old age difference. "I'm forty."

She shrugs at my answer. "Does tend to happen after thirty-nine."

"I'm serious."

"So am I. What's the issue?"

"I'm forty. He's twenty-seven. There are two decades between us." I hold up two fingers, wagging them at Melissa. "Two decades! I have to end it."

"Why does the age difference matter now? It didn't matter yesterday."

Oh, sweet friend, if you only knew how many things came to light yesterday, you would understand.

I finish off my drink, feeling it warm my belly. Countdown to inebriation starts now.

"Are you going to answer me?" Melissa prods.

I shake my head as the alcohol swirls with my misery, and I prepare to embark on the great journey known as drunk dialing. "I should call him and end it now. No time like the present."

Melissa grabs my phone. "Don't be an idiot. Have I mentioned that Josh worships you?"

"He doesn't. Trust me."

She waves her hand, dismissing my meltdown. "Think what you want. Josh isn't going to let it happen, regardless. He'll flex those muscles and smile with those damn dimples, and you'll be on your back and happy in no time." She hands me another shot glass with a flourish. "Until then, drink and be merry!"

I can't say if it's the alcohol or my moxie finally making an appearance, but I down the glass, bang it on the bar, and head for the dance floor.

What's the Buddhist saying? You can't control what happens to you, but you can control how you respond to it. I'm paraphrasing, but the core meaning is dead-on accurate.

I don't know if Josh's intent is to hurt me or just leave me behind. Regardless, I'm not letting him have the upper hand. This time, I'm prepared, and I'll strike before he has the opportunity.

The next hour passes, and I swear I've sweated out all the alcohol. That can only mean one thing. Refills.

I shimmy up to the bar, my hips swaying to the beat of the eighties music. Melissa was right. I needed a night out and maybe, just maybe, I won't have to run from San Diego with my tail between my legs.

The two of us wind around the dance floor, in desperate need of some fresh air. Stepping past an overly intoxicated man dancing with a mannequin, we ease our way outside. I only hope someone caught that nonsense on video.

I throw a final look over my shoulder, enjoying the feel of an honest laugh.

But my laugh dies a slow death as I turn around.

There, on the outdoor patio of the club, is Josh.

Josh, who is supposed to be in Hawaii.

Josh, who is standing with Frank, Mariah, and...Little Red Yoga Hood.

The thumping of the music reverberates against my body like bullets, but I'm frozen to the spot. My stomach turns, threatening a revolt. "What the fuck is he doing here? With...*her?*"

Melissa follows my gaze, and I see her jaw slacken from the corner of my eye. "I thought he was away?"

"That's what he claimed."

She gives me a small shove. "Don't just stand there. Go talk to him. Find out."

Finally able to move, I turn to my friend. "I'd like to go home."

"I'd like to know what's going on, so I'm going to speak to him."

My hand closes over her arm like a vise. "No. I'd like to go home. Please."

"It's barely ten o'clock."

I can't stand here any longer expressing my unquenchable urge to leave. I'm going, even if it means I have to walk home. "I'll call a Lyft."

She sees the panic in my face and nods in agreement. "Addy, come on. We'll go."

I slink out the exit, certain at any moment I'll feel Josh's hand on my shoulder, demanding to know where I'm headed. But I escape unseen. Perhaps it's a juvenile move, but after the deluge of information and truths I've been exposed to in the last twenty-four hours, I can't handle anything else. Not tonight.

Tomorrow, however, there will be major changes occurring.

The drive home is silent, save for the eighties station Melissa is blaring from the speakers. At least it's loud enough to drown out the screaming in my head.

She pulls into the parking lot, and I step out of the car, beyond ready to curl up with a bottle in my bed. "Goodnight. Thanks for being such a great friend."

"You're insane if you think I'm going to leave you here alone in this state."

"I'll be fine."

"I don't care. I'm coming up. Besides, you owe me a drink."

I relent, knowing that she isn't above shoving her way into the apartment using bodily force. "I'm going to take a shower. Make us a drink, will you?"

The water is borderline scalding, but I can't seem to get warm. There's ice in my veins, pumping from a heart that is closed for business. Permanently.

Melissa is chatting on the phone when I exit the bathroom, likely telling her husband that I'm in the midst of yet another nervous breakdown. I plop onto the sofa, accepting the glass of vodka with a forced smile.

I'll say it again. Forty sucks. Big time.

She ends the conversation, pulling her legs under her in a cross-legged position. "So, the plot thickens."

"How so?"

"The club wasn't Josh's first stop tonight."

I roll my eyes, taking another sip. "The story gets better? Can't wait."

"Actually, it does. And it doesn't." Melissa waves her hand.

"Josh stopped by the hospital looking for you. Instead, he saw Clint. Or rather, Clint saw him."

"How do you know this information?"

"Sean saw the whole thing. In fact, Sean followed Josh out to his truck after he stormed out. He's always thought that Josh was a good guy."

"No accounting for taste," I mutter.

"Apparently, Clint advised Josh to stay away from you. Fed him some crap about your mother and her money? Told him that if you two didn't reconcile, you were out of the will."

I feel the color draining from my face. I couldn't have heard her correctly. "Oh, for God's sake. Why would Clint tell Josh something like that?"

"It's not a big leap *why* he told him, Addy. Clint is jealous and desperate. People will do just about anything when they get desperate enough."

"Is that the entire story?"

"No. Josh asked Sean if he knew your whereabouts. Sean told him about the club."

I scoff into my drink. "You think Josh came to the club to look for me?"

Melissa nods, but I cut her down before she can say another word. "No. Why the hell would Josh bring his friends—who hate me, I might add—to the club to find me?"

"According to Sean, Josh was alone when he left the hospital. Maybe it's a coincidence that his friends were there tonight. It *was* a big party."

I used to believe in coincidences. Not anymore. Particularly not where Josh is concerned. Where's there smoke, there's fire. "I doubt it."

"Josh told Sean that he'd been calling you all evening, but you never answered."

"I turned my phone off for the night."

"Why would you do that?"

Time to let Melissa in on the truth. I get why she's team Josh. She isn't aware of the bevy of lies he's been handing me on a silver platter. "I didn't tell you about my visitors yesterday. Rather, Josh's visitors. One was his landlord, returning his security deposit. The other was Chantelle, warning me that I'd better not mess with Josh's future. In *Hawaii*."

"What the hell is going on?" Her expression is everything. I'm pretty sure I wore the same one yesterday.

"He's moving to Hawaii. Some huge surfing sponsorship. But he forgot to mention it to me. I'm only his girlfriend, ex-girlfriend —" I can't finish the sentence. I'll either burst into tears or vomit. "Do you understand now?"

"What I understand is that there's a ton of holes in this story. Holes that only Josh can fill in. But you need to speak with him in order to do that."

"No, thanks. Not in the mood."

Melissa rests her hand on my knee, giving it a gentle squeeze. "Addy, I'm going to tell you something that you won't like hearing, but it needs to be said."

"Great," I groan, burying my head in my hands. "More good news."

"Just listen. I think you're looking for reasons for your relationship with Josh to not work out."

My eyes bulge from my head. "Are you mad? Did you miss the part where I told you he's moving to Hawaii without telling me?"

"You don't know that. You invented this entire scenario in your head, and now, you're reacting to said scenario. But you haven't bothered to speak to the one person who can tell you what's going on."

"You don't understand—"

"No, *you* don't understand. I've seen how Josh is around you. That man would do anything for you."

"Except, tell me the truth." I finish off my drink. Time for the next round.

"What does the truth matter at this point? You don't even know the truth, but it hasn't stopped you from casting him out of your life. Sans discussion."

"Why are you acting like I'm the bad guy? This is about Josh and his inability to tell the truth."

"No. This is about you, Addy. You and *your* inability to stop fucking yourself over. That man is the single greatest thing to ever walk into your life, and all you're doing is pushing him away."

"I'm not pushing him away. He's moving on. Without me."

"According to a woman who wants to suck the cock of the man you're dating. I wouldn't put a whole lot of merit in her statements."

With a huff, I grab my phone and turn it on.

Maybe she's right. Maybe Melissa can see the situation for what it truly is, while my view is colored by fear.

My phone comes to life with a myriad of beeps. Josh has called numerous times, each message sounding more and more desperate.

I feel some of the anger drain from my body as I dial his number. I realize it's late, but I need to put his mind at ease. Hopefully, it will quell my anxiety, too.

"Jesus, I've been worried sick about you. Are you okay?" Josh's voice sounds hollow and thin as it competes with the surrounding din. Worried sick, huh? So concerned that he's still partying at the club. What a guy.

It's tempting to give him crap about partying—yet again—at another despised nightclub, but I don't have it in me. I feel like I've gone twelve rounds, and the primary opponent hasn't even stepped foot into the ring. "I'm sorry to worry you."

"Beautiful, where are you?"

"I'm home. I was out with Melissa."

"Stay there. I'm coming over."

"No. I'm really tired, Josh. I'm going to bed."

"So go to bed. I'll be right there to wrap my arms around you. I miss you, Addy."

"Sounds like you're having fun," I manage, hoping my voice sounds natural.

"Not really."

"At least the club has good music."

Josh offers a dry laugh. "I guess. Hang on one second."

I hear him speaking to someone, but I can't make out the words. It doesn't matter; I know intrinsically who the female voice belongs to—Chantelle.

"Sorry about that, Addy. I'm leaving now."

Tears prick my lids. "Just wait until morning. Come by then."

He huffs out a low groan. "You're killing me."

"I need to sleep. The last few shifts have been difficult."

"But you didn't work tonight. I know, I stopped by the hospital earlier this evening."

"Right. I meant last night." It's a lie, but in my opinion, a minor one compared to the whoppers Josh has been telling.

"I really want to see you tonight."

"I really want to sleep." I'm impressed with my composure. Outwardly, I'm cool as a cucumber, even as my insides threaten to implode.

"I'll leave you alone tonight, on one condition. You don't make any plans tomorrow. You're mine all day. All night. No questions asked. I'll be by early."

"That's fine."

"Don't sound so excited. Hey, it's going to be a great day. I have something really important to discuss with you."

I'll bet. I force a smile, wiping away the tears. "I'll see you tomorrow. Goodnight." I disconnect the call before he can reply, but even that short conversation exhausts my emotional reserves.

Melissa sits, waiting with bated breath, eager to know exactly what he said. "Well?"

"He's been worried about me. He wants to come over."

"I heard you tell him tomorrow. Can I ask why?"

I shrug, hearing my phone buzz again. "I'm an emotional basket case right now. I prefer to have some time to calm down so I can behave like a rational human being. I thought you'd be proud of me."

"I'll be proud of you when you stop thinking that gorgeous man is trying to hurt you."

I grunt, taking a sip of my vodka as I peer at my phone. Two texts. The first is from Josh. Not surprising after my abrupt end to our call.

I love you. I hate ending any conversation with anything other than I love you.

The other number is unknown, but my stomach sinks as I read the message.

Before you make any decisions, you should know the truth about the situation. Watch the video.

I know that whatever is contained in this message will either infuriate me, break my heart, or both. I also know I have to watch it.

So I do, and then I chuck the phone onto the couch like it's covered in maggots.

"Addy, what the hell happened?" Melissa snatches the phone, playing the video. "Jesus. Don't freak out, there has to be an explanation."

I jump to my feet, releasing a huff of indignation. "There *is* an explanation, Melissa. He's at a club with another woman, and they're far more than friends."

"Who sent this?"

"I don't recognize the number, but I'm assuming Frank."

"The man who hates you? Be careful there, Addy."

I grab the phone, shaking it at Melissa. "It's a video! I don't think Frank is talented enough to alter video; the man is a Neanderthal. But that is most definitely my boyfriend kissing another woman!"

"I know it looks bad—"

Is she blind? I want to skin him alive, but she wants to hold a come to Jesus meeting. "It doesn't *look* bad. It is bad."

"You're right. But then why bother with all the lovey-dovey crap?"

I shrug, finishing off my vodka. "Who knows? Maybe it's a game they're all playing for kicks."

"You don't really believe that load of bull, do you?"

"All I know is that I can't trust Josh. Not anymore. It's over."

"Addy—"

"It's over," I snarl, slamming shut the door of my heart.

Game. Set. Match.

At three that morning, I phone my mother. Granted, it's six o'clock in New York, but the early call still manages to rattle her.

"Adelaide? What time is it? Is everything okay?"

I sniffle, unable to hold back the tears. "No, mom. Things are not okay. I've decided to come home."

I hear her low groans as her half-sleeping brain processes my statement. "I know Clint is coming back to New York. Have you two reconciled?"

"No," I snuffle, wiping the snot from my nose. I must look a sight. "But I'm ready to come home."

"This sounds like a rash decision, my daughter. Do you want to talk about it?"

"No. I'm taking a page from your playbook."

"What's that, Addy?"

"Never let them know how much they've hurt me."

I end the call a few minutes later and place a second call to my travel nursing agency. I offer my thanks for my current contract but decline an additional stint in San Diego.

Two weeks and counting.

CHAPTER THIRTY

THIS HAS TO END

I wake up, crunched into an uncomfortable ball, my phone gripped in my hand. For one brief, delicious moment, I think that the events of the last two days are all a terrible dream.

But the dream fades to reality when I see the video clip in my messages. I must be a masochist because I torture myself with that video countless times.

I stretch, my muscles screaming from my odd sleeping arrangement. I need a shower and coffee, but the black gold wins this time.

I open my bedroom door and smell coffee brewing. The only problem? I didn't program my coffee pot last night, which can only mean one thing.

I stumble into the kitchen, stopping dead in my tracks. Josh is bent over a cutting board, chopping fruit and looking like the picture of innocence. Too bad for him that I know he's an adulterous lech.

"What are you doing here?"

He turns, a smile crossing his face. "Good morning, sunshine. I told you I was coming over early. I would have come over last night, but you wouldn't let me." He walks over to me, framing my face and pressing his lips against mine.

But instead of sparks, I feel nausea. Those lips pressed against Chantelle last night, an image that is forever burned in my brain. I push back, pulling my robe tight around me.

"What's wrong? Are you feeling okay? Partake a bit too much?"

Try as I might, I can't find any words to say to him. Part of me wants to toss something heavy at his head, but I lack the energy to make the effort. It's as if something died inside of me when I saw him kissing another woman. My heart won't allow me to feel too much. Not anymore.

I grab a mug and pour some coffee. One sip, and I realize it's his special blend. Of course, it is. "I'm just tired."

Unlike me, Josh is all sunshine and rainbows this morning. How lovely for him. She must be one hell of a kisser...among other things. I swallow back the nausea of that visual, focusing all my energy on the dark liquid in my mug.

"After breakfast, I thought we could lounge in bed or head to the beach and lounge there. Spend the day being lazy."

"Right," I mumble, not bothering to look up.

"I made reservations for dinner tonight. There's this amazing vegan restaurant up the coast that has gotten rave reviews, and I wanted to take you."

I lean against the counter, still weighing whether I should pitch my mug at his visage. Now he wants me out to dinner. To break up with me. How charming.

Josh meets my glare, his face questioning. "Does that sound okay?"

"Whatever," I mutter, walking into the other room. I need a

shower and a big glass of vodka. Coffee is not cutting it this morning.

Josh follows me into the bedroom, his muscular arms wrapping around me as his fingers slide under the waistband of my panties. "I know you're tired, but just the slightest hint of excitement would be appreciated. Haven't you missed me? I've missed you so much." He nuzzles my neck, and I hate how good his lips feel. I hate even more the lies falling from those lips.

I stay his hands, my entire body tense. "I'm not in the mood."

Josh backs away, his hands raised in mock surrender. "I see that. I get the feeling you don't want me here."

I offer a shrug as I grab some clothes from my closet.

"Addy, do you not want me here?" The first time, he was kidding. This time, he's serious.

I grab a towel and enter the bathroom, turning before I close the door. "You're already here, Josh. Besides, you want to speak to me. Might as well get it over with."

I step under the spray, letting the water course over me. I inhale slowly, willing myself calm. I'm failing. Miserably.

The door opens, and I let out an indignant huff. So much for privacy this morning. "Addy? I'm so sorry, but I have to run out really quick. There's something important I need to take care of."

"Whatever," I mutter. Apparently, I have a new favorite word.

The shower curtain flies open, and I'm face to face with Josh, his eyes searching and confused. "When I get back, we are going to discuss why you're mad at me. Again."

"Can't wait."

A muscle ticks in his jaw before he leans forward, his mouth claiming mine. He isn't asking permission as his tongue pushes into my mouth, stroking against me. It's a brief but powerful kiss, and it leaves me breathless. "Don't ever forget that you're mine."

He presses a final kiss to my lips before walking out the door, leaving me to wonder what—or who—is more important than us, once again.

❀

His errand takes a bit longer than expected, but he's back that afternoon, ready to take me to dinner.

I'm in no better mood than I was earlier, but at least I've got my emotional armor locked and loaded. He's not escaping this time.

The restaurant is beautiful, perched on a bluff and screaming of money. Good, Josh can afford it with his high-dollar sponsorship. He asks for a private table, no doubt to ensure that should I throw a fit, not many people will witness the event.

"A bottle of Taittinger, please," Josh requests before turning his attention back to me.

I hate that he looks amazing. He always looks wonderful, but he's dressed up in a button-down and slacks, hugging him in all the right places. I'm glad I opted to dress for the occasion as well, even if I half expect to be wearing the champagne by the end of the night. "You're gorgeous, Addy."

I force a smile. I have to maintain a neutral stance, or I'll devolve into a puddle of tears. "Thank you. I guess we're celebrating?" I nod at the bottle of champagne that the server is uncorking table side.

"I hope so." What an odd response.

After the server pours us both a glass, Josh lifts his in my direction. "We should toast."

I nod. Incredibly, I'm still able to function. "Might as well drink to my birthday."

"When is your birthday?"

"Yesterday."

His mouth drops open, gaping at me. "What?"

"Yep. I'm forty. Way too old for you."

He looks positively stunned. "Addy, how did I not know it was your birthday? Why didn't you say anything? I would have rearranged my trip."

Time to drop the bomb. "Oh, but you did make it in time. I saw you at the club with Frank and Mariah...and Chantelle."

"You *were* there last night."

"Yep."

"I don't understand. Why didn't I see you?"

"I saw you and your little girlfriend and opted to leave. Thanks for ruining my birthday, by the way."

His fist bangs the table, shaking the place settings. "Whoa. Wait a minute. First, I'm not with Chantelle, and second, how could I ruin your birthday when I didn't even know what day it was?"

"It's funny. You hate clubs, but you're more than happy to go to them with her. It took me a while to figure it out since I'm still fairly naive about love."

"I do hate clubs." He looks like he's been hit by a train. Welcome to my world, buddy. "I can't believe you didn't tell me it was your birthday. I would have planned something beautiful for you. Something so much better than that obnoxious hellhole."

"But yet, you were there, in that obnoxious hellhole. With her. The writing's on the wall, Josh."

Josh crosses his arms, his anger rising. "Is that so?"

"I'm too old. You're too young—"

"Not this shit again."

"It's true. With me, you don't frequent clubs, but with Chantelle, you'll make an exception."

"I wasn't with her! I was looking for you!" He yanks at his hair, his foot tapping wildly. "I should have been with you on your birthday, Addy. We should have celebrated together."

"Doing what?"

"I would have made you a special dinner on the beach, spent the night holding you and watching the stars."

"Because I'm not good enough to be seen with in public?"

"That's the most ridiculous thing you've ever said. We're in public right now."

"You and I both know why, too."

"I know why, but I think you have a far different version."

"Why is this the first time we've gone anywhere? We're always at your house or mine. Don't deny it, either."

A long sigh leaves his lips. "You're right. I'm sorry."

I expect a denial or a fabrication. I don't expect Josh's agreement, complete with an apology. The truth is so plain to see. I am a dirty secret. I always was.

Brave face, Addy. Never let him know how much he hurt you. "Thanks for being honest. Finally."

"We didn't go out to clubs or bars, but Addy, it wasn't because I was ashamed of you. You're beautiful. Intelligent. Kind. Funny. Sexy as hell. I was selfish. I wanted you away from the noise and the din. You and the ocean—my two favorite things in the world. I didn't want to share you. Share our time."

His words sound so genuine, his expression so real. But it's all a ruse. I have the proof in my purse.

I pick up the champagne flute, wiping away a stray tear. "What should we celebrate? I know. Let's celebrate Hawaii."

The color drains beneath his tan. Busted. "How do you know about Hawaii?"

"How is it that I *didn't* know about Hawaii?"

"Who told you?"

"Your girlfriend."

"My what?" Josh snaps.

"The same woman you kissed last night."

The expression crossing Josh's face is one I've never seen before. It's a mix of shock and horror. "I didn't kiss her, Addy."

I'm so tired of men and their mind games. "Don't lie, Josh. I detest cheaters, but I hate liars more."

"I'm not lying."

I shake my head, pulling out my phone. "You're just like the rest of them."

"Did you just lump me in with all the men in your past?"

I nod, flipping on my phone. "You did the same thing."

"How am I supposed to defend something I didn't do?"

This is like the fight I had with Clint. I'm tired of defending my righteous anger over their bad behavior. Fuck men.

I toss the phone in his direction, the video playing on repeat. Just in case he misses a moment.

"Well, I know where this came from," Josh bites out as he rubs his jaw, his foot tapping with such ferocity it's shaking the table.

"You're missing the point."

"Addy, so are you. Frank is setting us up. He doesn't want us together."

I take back my phone, giving it a smirk. "Apparently, neither do you."

Josh reaches across the table, grabbing my hand. "That's exactly what I want. Frank is furious at me, and he's trying to destroy the most important thing in my life."

"Which is what?"

"Us. You and me. Our future."

I want to scream that we don't have a future, but my voice fails me. Instead, I wipe a few errant tears and sip my champagne. I'll definitely need something harder than this if we stay much longer. "My contract is ending. My time in San Diego is almost up."

I expect him to feign sadness, but he squeezes my hand, offering a smile. "I know. Perfect timing."

"Yep." With that statement, I know where his heart is, and it isn't with me.

"You can go anywhere, right?"

I nod, not meeting his gaze.

"Addy, please look at me."

With a deep breath, I raise my head. This is going to hurt. Bad.

"This is not how I wanted this dinner to go." He stares at the table as if considering his next move. "But I know what I want, and I really hope—"

"I'm moving back to New York," I blurt. I have to deliver the death knell first. It's my last vestige of dignity in this situation.

His face contorts as he pulls his hands back. "When did you decide this?"

Wonderful, now he's going to act self-righteous. "Likely the same time you decided to move to Hawaii."

"I wasn't sure I was going—"

"You're going. This is a once in a lifetime opportunity. You have to go."

His shoulders sag. "My God, what he said was true?"

"Who?"

"Clint. He told me you two were reconciling and returning to New York. I called him a liar. Said you would never do that to me. To us. But you did."

"Do not blame me for this situation."

"Is it because of the money? I'll have plenty of money, Addy. I'll take care of you."

"I don't even know what you're talking about."

"You're going back with Clint because you need your mother's money." Holy God in heaven, the bastard really did spout that lie to Josh. Even worse, Josh believes him.

"Fuck you. I can't be bought. Not by him, not by anyone."

"But he said—"

"What Clint said is a heap of lies, fairly similar to what he's always said."

"So I'm not supposed to believe his lies, but you're allowed to believe Frank's? How is that fair, Addy?"

"I have video proof, Josh!"

"She kissed me, I didn't kiss her. I pushed her away."

"The video doesn't show that."

"It won't. Why would it? That would defeat what the bastard is trying to do. Please, Addy, I'm begging you."

"What am I supposed to say here? You know how bad this looks? How foolish I look for loving you? For believing you?" I wipe my tears, but there's more where those came from. "Go live your fancy life. You've earned it. I don't fit in there."

"You think any of this matters? I would give it all up for you."

"No, you wouldn't."

"Addy, stop telling me what I would or wouldn't do. I know my own heart. I would give up surfing for you. For us."

"I wouldn't let you."

"Maybe it's not your choice to make."

"What do you want me to do, Josh?"

"Love me, Addy. Love me like I love you. You see numbers and reasons why we can't be together. I see the love of my life."

The deluge arrives, tears streaming down my cheeks. "Yet you didn't include this love in any of your life decisions. You included everyone else. You made a fool of me, Josh."

"I didn't do it, Addy."

"Stop lying. If you ever loved me at all, please stop lying." I push my chair back, teetering to a standing position. "Goodbye, Josh."

"Where are you going?"

"I called a Lyft."

He grabs my hands, his expression frantic. "Don't do this, Addy. Don't leave."

"Hawaii really is the opportunity of a lifetime. I hope you enjoy it."

"No, you're the opportunity of a lifetime."

I cup his face, tears streaming down my own. "Take care of you."

"Are you really saying goodbye?"

I nod. "Yes, before we say anything we might regret."

"I don't regret one moment with you, Addy. Except for this one."

I can't stand here any longer. It's too painful. "This is me letting you go. You have your whole life ahead of you."

"All I want is you. But you won't let me have that. You never would."

With a final peck to his cheek, I dash from the restaurant, leaving all vestiges of my happiness behind.

CHAPTER THIRTY-ONE

THE TRUTH SHALL SET YOU FREE

I wake up, my throat sore and eyes scratchy from crying. I spent years holding back the tears, but yesterday, after I left Josh, every single one poured from my body. There was no stopping the deluge until I passed out from exhaustion.

As light streams through my window, I struggle to a sitting position, uncertain what to do at this point.

When my relationship with Clint dissolved, I had no issue moving forward. My time was invested, but not my heart. But with Josh, my heart is entwined and disentangling it is a sticky, ugly mess.

My phone beeps, and I grab it. Somewhere deep in the recesses of my soul, I hope it's Josh, but it's not.

It's Melissa. She's outside and coming up. No questions asked. Within seconds I hear the banging of the door and stumble to answer it.

"You look like shit," she observes, walking past me into the apartment.

"Thanks."

"I saw Josh last night."

I release a groan, collapsing on the couch. "Do I even ask how?"

"He was in the ED."

My eyes fly open. "Is he okay?"

"He needed some stitches, had a black eye."

"Oh, my God. Car accident?"

"No. He...beat the shit out of that friend of his."

"Frank?"

Melissa nods as she sets about making a cup of coffee. "He's in real bad shape."

"Josh or Frank?"

"Frank is fine. Josh is anything *but* fine. Physically he's okay, but emotionally, he's a train wreck."

"We broke up last night."

"I know. But to hear Josh tell it, you broke up with him."

"I had every reason."

"I know it looks bad, and Josh knows that, too. But I really get the impression that man adores you. I think you should speak to him."

"I don't know if that's a good idea."

"I also hear that you're heading back to New York."

I nod, taking the mug of coffee that Melissa offers. "Yes. Another two weeks, and I'm gone."

"Don't you want to rethink that?"

"No." Is she crazy? Why would I rethink it?

"What about moving to Hawaii with Josh?"

"Not a possibility. He didn't exactly invite me."

"According to him, you didn't give him a chance."

"That's just it. It's so easy to say the right things after the fact. But there, at that moment, at no point did Josh grab me and say he wanted me to come to Hawaii."

"It's your decision, but I still think there are things that need to be said. And I believe they'll eat at you until they are."

THE NEXT DAY, I'm sitting in my car outside Josh's house. I have his spare key, and I'm hoping I can return it without seeing him. Seeing him will be too raw. Too painful. My heart can't handle any more pain at the moment.

I climb the deck steps, lifting up the flowerpot to slide the key under.

"What are you doing here?"

I turn to see Josh, ever watchful, standing in the doorway. He looks like hell. One eye is blackened, and there's a cut on his mouth. "Are you okay?" I know it's a shit thing to say, but it leaves my mouth before my brain can stop it.

"No, Addy. I'm pretty far from okay."

"Does it hurt?" I motion to his face.

"Like you wouldn't believe." His voice is monotone, his eyes piercing through me. I mean his flesh. He means his heart. Without a word, he turns away from me.

"Josh, please—"

He whirls on me, his eyes flashing. "Please, what, Addy? You wanted me gone from your life. I'm gone. Okay?"

I nod, barely containing the tears.

"This is what *you* wanted, Addy. Not me."

"I didn't want this, Josh."

He grabs my arm, dragging me into the kitchen. He tosses a box in my direction. A ring-shaped box. "You know what I was hoping to celebrate the other night?"

My eyes remain focused on the box.

"An engagement. I want you to be my wife. I want you to be

the mother of my children. I want to spend every day with you. But it doesn't matter."

"If only your friends—"

"They're assholes, and they're gone. Frank and Chantelle are, at least. But they're not the reason. You are so wrapped up in the goddamn age difference. I couldn't love you enough to make the numbers disappear. I'm sorry I was born after you, Addy! I can't control it."

"I know. I just thought—"

"You thought that I was like every other guy. You never, not for one second, thought that I was the one."

"I did. I did think that."

"When? For a brief second? It never held. You were looking for an exit from the time I met you." His breathing is rapid, his movements erratic. "Why didn't you love me, Addy?"

"I do love you, but this situation isn't about love."

"That is *all* this is about. Believing in me. Believing in us."

"I did believe in us," I argue, each sentence from his lips harder to hear.

"No, you didn't. You put up with four years of mistreatment from that asshole. Four years of giving and not receiving. You wouldn't even give me the chance to prove I'm not like him."

I finally find my voice. "But you hurt me, just like he did."

"No, beautiful, you allowed other people to convince you that I had. Ever since I met you, I've been fighting an uphill battle. I tried to stop loving you because God knows it would be easier, but I couldn't do it. I still can't."

I break down, sobs racking my body.

"But I can't ride this rollercoaster anymore. I took the position in Hawaii. That way, you don't have to return to New York, or worry about seeing me around, reminding you of the mistake you made."

"You were never a mistake—"

"Wasn't I? You spent the majority of our time together, pushing me away. Listing all the reasons why we didn't make sense. Well, you got your wish. I'm walking away, Addy. I'm not coming back this time. Just know that no one in this world could love you more than I do."

He grabs me into an embrace as his lips find mine. It's excruciating and exquisite and over way too soon. "Goodbye, Addy. I wish you could have seen the plans I had for us."

THE NEXT TWO weeks are a blur. I work, come home and curl into bed with a bag of potato chips and ranch dip. I know it's a shit diet, but it's also a shit life.

I can't bring myself to go by Josh's house, even though I'm certain he's no longer there.

I work my final shift at Memorial, but the idea of returning to New York fills me with dread. Clint, on the other hand, is thrilled at the thought of moving back east and, for some reason, thinks our reconciliation is imminent. I don't have the strength to tell him otherwise.

Someone pounds my door and I groan. It takes every ounce of energy I have to move from the couch. I definitely need to start hitting the gym because my diet of champions is resulting in weight gain. Just what I need.

I swing open the door and close it again with a groan.

"Addy, please. I really need to speak with you."

I open the door just enough to peer through it. "What the fuck do you want, Frank? Come to gloat?"

"No. I came to apologize."

I cross my arms over my chest, my ire rising. "Really?"

"Can I please come in?"

I open the door and let him inside, pointing at the couch. That's as much hospitality as this asshole deserves.

"So? What do you want?"

Frank looks me over, but there's no animosity. Perhaps he truly is sorry, or maybe he's terrified I might kill him. I do have several weapons in the kitchen. "Have you been sleeping?"

"I don't see why that's any of your concern, but no, I haven't. I know you don't care to hear it, but I was totally in love with your best friend. I still am."

"We're not friends anymore. I can't say I blame him."

"I heard you two got into a fight. I always figured once you blackened each other's eyes that the beef was squashed."

"I fucked up, Addy. I deserved the ass whooping." Frank lets out a deep sigh. "I'm trying to fix the damage I've caused."

"I think it's too late for that."

"I hope not. Josh asked me to do one last thing for him." He produces a small box, handing it to me.

"What's this?"

"He didn't get you a birthday gift, so he asked our friend to make you something. She's a jeweler. It was a custom order, so it took a couple weeks."

Tears spring to my eyes, realizing that even after I broke up with him, Josh went out of his way to buy me a birthday gift. Opening the box, I smile. It's a gold necklace with two stars that fit together, forming a clasp. It's unique and beautiful, and so Josh. Tucked underneath, is a piece of paper.

With trembling hands, I read the words.

You are the brightest light in my life, Addy. I wish you hadn't walked away from me.

"I miss him so much."

"Go to him."

My eyes narrow in Frank's direction. "Is this another trick?"

"No, the only tricks were played by me...including the video."

My heart falls to my feet as I collapse in the chair. The video was the straw that broke the camel's back, the whole reason I held my ground. "What does that mean?"

"Chantelle and I set it up. She grabbed Josh when he wasn't paying attention, and he pushed her away immediately. He then spent the next few minutes berating her and—" He grabs out his phone, tossing it my way. "There. That's the whole thing."

I watch the video and see how the events truly unfold. I even hear Josh yelling at Chantelle.

"What the hell are you doing? I'm in love with Addy. Didn't you hear me announce that I'm asking her to marry me?"

"He meant it," I manage, my heart squeezing.

"Every word."

I pitch the phone at Frank, barely missing his head. "Are you insane? Seriously! You ripped us apart for what? Jealousy?"

"I know it was wrong. I thought you were just an attraction, and he'd get over it. We had plans. I was supposed to be in Hawaii with him. I was never the surfer that Josh was, but we had an agreement. I would ride his coattails and work at a surf shop on Oahu."

"What the fuck does that have to do with me?"

"He meets you, and suddenly, all he wants is to get married and have a family. There wasn't room for me. I saw the plans we had slipping away. So I decided to intervene."

"Intervene? Who do you think you are? How does Chantelle play into all this?"

Frank shrugs, a remorseful look on his face. "She's a gold digger. She always had a thing for Josh, but after she ran into him and realized his future potential, she wanted a slice too."

I fall back against the cushions, sobs wracking my body. "I could kill you both."

"That's pretty much what he said, too."

"Why tell me now? It's too late. He's gone."

"Mariah spoke with Josh the other day. He's miserable. I owe it to the man who was always a friend to me to reunite him with the woman he loves."

"He could have moved on by now."

"Addy, he wanted to marry you. He hasn't moved on." He slides a slip of paper across the table. "That's his address. Use it."

* * *

Melissa, the only person I actually enjoy seeing lately, drops by later that afternoon, complete with takeout and beer. Have I mentioned what a saint she is?

"Well, you're free. What's your next move?"

I push the paper to Melissa, watching her eyes widen.

"Good move. I approve," Melissa replies, handing me a beer.

"What if he doesn't want me?"

"There's no guarantee. I'm pretty damn sure Josh wants you. But the only guarantee you'll have if you *don't* go is that you'll never know. What do you have to lose?"

"My heart, my sanity, my dignity."

"But what do you have to gain?"

I smile. She's right. "The love of my life." I set the beer down, opting for a glass of water.

"You okay?"

I nod, taking a sip. "Yeah, just a bit sick to my stomach lately."

"Are you pregnant?"

"No," I reply, laughing off the question. "I'm too old to get pregnant like that."

"Oh my God, you're a nurse. You know that's a bullshit answer. Were you two careful?"

I flush, shaking my head. "Define careful."

"Oh, Jesus, you *are* pregnant."

"I'm not. Honest. I'm just having a few bad weeks."

"So, what about Clint? The man is parading around discussing your future in Manhattan."

"It's all a fallacy. I never agreed to reconcile with Clint. Not now or ever. I gave him four years. Four years too many, it turns out."

"Yeah, you could have been out here four years ago, hanging with me, bonking Josh."

"He would have been so young then. No!" I laugh, realizing it's the first time since my breakup. "He's still so young."

"Get over that age crap, once and for all. I'm not kidding. I don't think he'll stand for it again."

"I haven't even decided if I'm going."

Melissa sends me a wink, downing her beer. "Yes, you have."

CHAPTER THIRTY-TWO

GOODBYE SAN DIEGO

*B*ut the truth is that I'm not 100% certain I should follow Josh to Hawaii. After everything that happened between us, is there room for reconciliation?

I opt to sleep on it, except that my sleep is now colored by dreams that would make Dali blush, and my stomach still isn't cooperating. When the sun streams through the window the next morning, my hand is clasped around the necklace from Josh.

I can't live without him. Well, I suppose I *can*, but I sure as hell don't want to try.

It hits me like a bolt out of the blue when I allow my stubbornness to subside long enough for my heart to step in. I start packing that moment, gathering my life once again into a collection of cardboard boxes. With any luck, my next destination will be my final one.

In the midst of the chaos, I call my mother. I know she'll be disappointed, but I also know that she'll understand. She's understood me for far longer than I realized.

I swear, I can see her knowing smile when she answers the phone. "You're not coming back to New York, are you?"

A humble chuckle escapes my mouth. "You know me pretty well."

"I may wear the cloak of social acceptability, but deep down, you and I are cut from the same bolt of cloth. I'm glad you two reconciled."

I clear my throat, a wave of uncertainty washing over me. "We didn't exactly reconcile. In fact, Josh moved to Hawaii."

"Hawaii?"

"Yes. He got a ridiculous surfing sponsorship. I still don't understand all the nuances, but it's something he's worked for most of his life."

"I'm not following, Adelaide."

"I'm going after him."

Her bark of surprise cuts across the phone line. "Does Josh know you're coming?"

Every question should be breaking down my resolve. Instead, it's reaffirming my decision. "No. I'm winging it, Mom."

I can't read her silence. Finally, she elicits a chuckle. "Brazen. We really *are* alike."

"How so?"

"When I met your father, he wanted to take a job in Seattle. He didn't invite me to go, but I decided that I wouldn't let that man slip through my fingers. So, I showed up on his doorstep."

"What happened?"

"I shocked the hell out of him. And his maid, whom I thought for a brief instant, was his new lover."

"But it all worked out."

"Obviously. And despite losing him, I'm grateful every day that I got on that plane."

A chill washes over me. "What if Josh says no, Mom?"

"Then, you still tried. You can't ever look back and have any regrets. Love is worth that kind of effort." Another chuckle. "I have to run. Rotary Club meeting. Call me when you land; I'll book a trip to Hawaii."

I hope my mother is right. I pray that I'm not too late. I know it's only been a couple weeks, but everything with Josh moved at lightning speed. What if his heart moves on from me just as swiftly?

Time to focus on the task at hand. I have one final conversation waiting in San Diego and judging by the knocking at the door, he's here.

Clint scans the room, taking in the jumble of half-packed boxes. "Damn, you didn't waste any time. I thought we were staying for the next couple of weeks, at least."

His overarching assumptions border on the ridiculous. "You can. I'm not."

"No, I'll call the hospital in New York. I miss the city, although this has been interesting. A real learning experience."

I bite my tongue at his statement. I highly doubt he's learned much of anything from this experience. "I'm surprised you want to leave. Word on the street is that you're knocking boots with a graduate nurse."

His face blanches, but he quickly regains his composure. "It was just sex."

"Isn't everything with you?"

"We weren't together, Addy. As I recall, you were banging some surf kid."

"His name is Josh, and he's not a kid."

"Regardless. I'm not apologizing." What a prick.

I burst out laughing, pulling a box into the living room. "You really are pretentious, you know that? I don't want you to apologize. Relax."

Clint releases a huffed breath, forcing a smile. "Sorry. I need to learn to hold my temper."

"And your tongue."

"Either way, I'm not sleeping with her anymore. I'm thrilled to head back early, but have you got a place lined up for us yet?"

Oh, this is going to be fun. I shoot him a sympathetic stare, patting his chest. "You're on your own with that one."

"Addy, you know we'll reconcile eventually."

"Actually, no. I'm not going back east."

"Where are you going?"

"Hawaii."

"You're chasing after that kid?"

I nod as tears brim in my eyes. "Damn straight. I'm running after than man and begging him to still love me. He's the best thing that ever happened to me. "

Clint runs his hand over his hair, his jaw slack with disbelief. "Addy, just stop. I know you're upset—"

"You're right, but not for the reasons you think. I'm upset I was too foolish to realize what a gift I had in Josh."

"What makes you think he still wants you? Chances are he's slept with a few beach bunnies by now. That's how men are, Addy."

"No. That's how you are. Not all men are like you. I know that now. Some men love with their whole hearts and aren't afraid of jumping in headfirst. But you're not like that."

"Thank God," he scoffs.

"Yeah. Thank God you showed me your true colors back east."

"Addy—"

"I'm serious. If you hadn't, I never would have moved to San Diego and met the love of my life. So, thank you. Now, if you'll excuse me, I have a shit ton of packing to do before the movers arrive."

"You're serious."

"Deadly. I know what I want, and nothing will deter me from it. And I want Josh."

CHAPTER THIRTY-THREE

HELLO, HAWAII

So, I may have second, third, and fourth guessed my decision the entire flight to Hawaii, but I'm here. In Oahu.

I grab my suitcases, half shocked that they arrived in one piece, and jump into a rental car for the drive to Ke Nui Road. I did my homework before I left San Diego. I know that the North Shore is the surfing hub of Hawaii in the winter months, and where the professional surfers and the companies that represent them live. Seeing Josh's address along that road gives me a burst of pride.

He's made it. His dream came true.

Now I can only hope that I'm still part of that dream.

It's a scenic—and at time heart-pounding drive across the island. I'm lucky I have an inside advantage. I sent Josh's Dad a text as soon as I landed. He's going to scope out his son's whereabouts so that I won't be traipsing all over the North Shore looking for him.

My phone beeps. He's at the beach. I chuckle. Why am I not surprised my Neptune is surfing the waves?

I blast upbeat pop songs on the drive. It's by far the most beautiful place I've ever been, and I've traveled to some of the most luxurious spots around the globe. There's a rough-hewn natural feel to the land, and the laidback pace makes San Diego look like it's on speed.

My hands shake as I park the car, and I'm afraid I'll lose my breakfast even before I step onto the sand. For a split second, my mind screams to turn around and return to the safety of my previous life. But this time, my heart overrules any objections.

I glance at myself in the mirror. It's funny, despite my stomach issues, I look good. My skin glows, and the dress hugs my curves. Maybe a diet of potato chips isn't such a bad idea, after all.

I stroll down the sand, marveling at its softness and the surreal beauty surrounding me. When I see the water, tears spring to my eyes. *This* water is the color of Josh's eyes. *This* is his home.

I fall into the sand, pulling out my camera and scanning the surf. It only takes a moment to find him. He rides the crest of the wave, as effortless here on these mammoth waves as he was in San Diego. Repositioning myself, I snap off a few shots, earning some nods of greeting from passersby.

After several shots, I flip through the photos. They're so beautiful they look fake, but I know that amazing man and incredible ocean are the most real things I've ever witnessed.

I'm a safe distance. What that means is I can see Josh, but I doubt he can see me. I'm capturing his ride without his knowledge that I'm there, a voyeur into his private moment. He's in his element. No doubt, this is where he belongs. I'm so glad he didn't choose to stay in San Diego, particularly not because of me. I could never live with myself if he made that decision.

He emerges from the sea, his surfboard tucked under his arm, the wetsuit hugging every inch of his delicious body. Showtime.

It's now or never, Addy.

I jump to my feet but stop dead in my tracks.

A gorgeous woman of about twenty-five jogs up to him as he walks out of the wave, her blonde locks, and tanned skin a perfect complement to his own. She touches his bicep, giggling. I remember that sound. Josh made me giggle like that too.

Then I see him return the smile and wrap his arm about her shoulder. My gut clenches. When her arms thread around his waist, it's time to go.

I'm too late.

What a fool. I should have known. A man like Josh only comes around once, if you're lucky.

My emotions seize up, and I sink back to the sand. Even though I knew this outcome was possible, I never really thought I'd be living it. I didn't think Josh would forget me that quickly.

Being wrong sucks.

At least I have some photos, and I think they capture Josh's power and grace. I'll be sure to email him copies when I arrive wherever the hell I'm going next, because I know I can't stay here. This may be the most populated of the Hawaiian Islands, but it's still way too close for comfort.

God, I'm going to wind up in New York with my tail between my legs. I can see Clint's smirk now. The pretentious prick.

With my final vestiges of courage, I gather up my camera and secure it into the bag before pulling my hair into a messy bun. I kept my long hair down, figuring it looked more romantic. Now practicality comes into play. And stealth. I need to beat a hasty exit before Josh sees me.

I refuse to look in his direction, afraid if I do, I'll see some sex-driven beach scene straight out of a Hollywood movie. Wonderful, there's that nausea again.

"Addy?"

I freeze mid-step. Maybe I'm hearing things.

"Addy? Is that you?"

Nope. Definitely not hearing things. I pivot on the sand to find Josh less than twenty feet from me and closing the distance. Fast.

He reaches my side and grabs my arms, his face a mixture of shock and confusion. "You're here. In Hawaii."

"Yeah." I look past him and see the lithe blonde watching the scene with a great deal of interest. Wonderful. A broken heart *and* a catfight. What better way to spend a morning in paradise?

"What are you doing here?"

I want you to love me, but it's too late. "I wanted to watch you surf."

His expression changes. Softens. It's almost imperceptible, but I see it. As always, Josh sees right through my mask and straight into my heart. "You saw me ride the waves in San Diego a ton of times."

I manage a rueful laugh. "I did, but I wanted to see you in your new home. Josh, you look amazing. Totally in your element."

The statuesque Barbie catches up to us, dropping an arm on Josh's shoulder. Wow. There is an actual physical pain when your heart shatters, a fact I'd have been happy never to experience. Funnily enough, her gaze is curious but not defensive. Then again, she likely doesn't see me as a threat.

"Hi there." It's my best attempt at a greeting. After all, it's not Barbie's fault I'm an idiot extraordinaire.

"Aloha."

Of course, she uses the local lingo without it sounding forced or trite. She's a damn sea nymph.

I turn my attention back to Josh. "I got some great pictures. I'll email them to you. I better get going. Have a nice day." I nod at the Barbie doll. Blinking back tears, I force a smile for Josh. "It was great seeing you again."

I feel them both watching me as I turn and begin the long trudge off the beach. I can't even do that gracefully. God, I suck.

"Are you seriously going to leave like that?"

I pause, keeping my back turned to him as my heart rate speeds up like a locomotive.

Josh spins me around, forcing my chin up.

"Were you just going to walk away from me? Again?"

"I-I wasn't—"

"No way in hell, Addy. You don't get to walk off like that."

"It's too late," I manage to blurt, chewing my bottom lip.

"For what? You came here for a reason, and I deserve to hear it. Tell me, Addy. Tell me why you came to Hawaii."

I want to ask him when he became so sadistic, but the look in his eyes stops me. He's right. He does deserve to hear it.

Even though it's too late.

"I love you, Josh. And it doesn't matter if you're in Hawaii or China or Mars because I'll go anywhere you are, just to be near you. I don't care that you're thirteen years younger or thirty years younger because I adore you. I love who I am when I'm with you. I know that I spent our entire time pushing you away, but all I want now is to hold on to you and never let you go."

Tears stream down my face as I wipe them away with the palm of my hand. "I've never cried so much in my life as when you left. You make me feel *everything*. I never knew love like this existed, and now, I know I can't live without it."

I shrug, throwing up my hands and offering a sad laugh. "So, there you have it. Everything that's in my heart. I hope I didn't anger your girlfriend. I didn't know. She's gorgeous. You two look perfect together, and I wish you both every happiness."

Josh stares at the sand, but I see the smile breaking across his face.

What is so damn funny? I spill my guts, and he's amused? That's cute.

"My girlfriend?" he asks with a chuckle. "I would think we *do* look alike. She's my cousin, Addy." He turns his head. "Hey, Sarah, come here. This is Addy."

The willowy blonde bounds back over, pulling me into a hug. Unexpected. "Addy? Wow, I've heard so much about you! You're here! I told you that she'd come."

"You're his cousin?" I swear, if a breeze blows, I'm going to fall down.

"Yep. Teaching this greenhorn how to surf something other than ankle biters."

"My mother's family is from Hawaii. She moved to the mainland to be with my father. But this one," Josh jokes, grinding a noogie into her head, "grew up in paradise."

"I'm just glad he's finally here. I'm so glad you're both here." With a wave, she runs off down the beach.

"Your cousin?" Do I kill him or kiss him first? Decisions, decisions.

There's that smile again. "Yep."

"I thought—"

He offers a sheepish grin. "Sorry. I wanted to watch you squirm. *Just* for a minute. A dick move, I know, but you did rip my heart apart. Granted, I can't blame you after what Frank and Chantelle put you through."

"Are we even now?"

Josh crosses his arms over his chest, peering down at me from his full height. "That depends."

"Do you still love me, Josh?"

"Addy, I never stopped loving you."

Here goes nothing. "Will you consider loving me forever?"

The corners of his mouth quirk up, despite his best effort to remain neutral. "Are you going to stop with the age shit?"

"Yes."

His eyes widen. He knows I'm full of shit.

"I mean, I'll still have the occasional hang-up because I'm really good at those."

That did it. The smile widens now, as Josh chuckles. "You are exceptionally talented at those."

I grab his hands, smiling up at him. "Love me. Let me love you."

"Are we making it official?"

"That has so many meanings. I don't want to presume—"

"Addy." Josh is warning me in the most loving way. Don't retreat now.

"Absolutely official. Rings and dresses and everything."

"I have to wear a dress?" I really am going to kill him. But only after I've kissed every inch of him. Then I meet his gaze. His banter is light-hearted, but I see the happiness in his eyes, and I know it reflects my own.

I put my hands on my hips, sending him a fake glare. "We're having a moment here."

"Sorry." He pushes a lock of hair behind my ear, his trademark gesture that warms my soul. "I love you, my Addy."

So, I'm taking that as a yes?"

When his lips claim mine, I have my answer.

CHAPTER THIRTY-FOUR

MY HOME

*O*ur kisses are always intense, but this time, I'm taking the lead, leaving no doubt in his mind how I feel. We lose ourselves to the moment, biting and sucking, our tongues sliding together.

His hands tangle in my hair, tight almost to the point of pain, as he pulls me against him, soaking the front of my dress. "We need to be alone. Now."

"Agreed," I rasp, my hands sliding along every plane of his torso.

He stops, his hands cupping my face, his eyes drinking me in. "You're really here."

I stand on tiptoe, pressing my lips to his. "Forever."

With a happy whoop, Josh swings me into his arms, and I feel at peace with the world until my stomach threatens to unload every bite of airplane food. "Sweetie..."

He sets me back on the ground, his gaze searching my face. "You okay?"

"Can we stop swinging? My stomach has been off for the last

couple of weeks. I'm sure the jet lag and airplane food aren't helping."

"Uh-huh." The corners of his mouth quirk as he drops a kiss on my head. "Let's go home. You must be exhausted."

I link my fingers with his as he leads me up a private path to the rental house. It's beautiful, and I'll be sure to explore every nook and cranny, right after exploring every one of his nooks and crannies.

Josh hangs up his board before leading me into the house. "I've got to take a shower and you," he hooks a finger in the bodice of my dress, pulling me toward him, "are coming with me."

I know it's only been two weeks, but watching Josh strip that wetsuit from his tight body brings every damn hormone I've ever had to life. I don't even try to pretend I'm looking anywhere else. I'm drinking up every inch of him with my eyes.

"See something you like?" Josh jokes, standing in front of me, his naked body a work of art.

"Where do I begin?" I opt to perform my own little striptease, letting the dress slide down my body, wasting no time pushing him back against the shower wall and claiming his mouth again.

"Look at you," Josh murmurs in a heated whisper, his hands gripping my ass and pulling me against him.

"I know what I want."

"Show me." The look in his eyes, I can't deny this man anything.

I perch on the built-in shower bench, grasping his hips and turning him toward me. I grip the base of his cock, feeling it strain in my hand. My mouth closes over the tip while my fingers stroke along his length.

A heated groan rises from his chest, his hands bracketing the shower walls.

I take him completely into my mouth, my tongue stroking the

underside of his shaft as his body bucks toward me. I gaze up at him, watching the exquisite heat move across his features as I coax him to his release.

"Fuck no, I need inside you," Josh demands, pulling me off the bench and bending me over. With his fingers wrapped around my hips, he plunges into me, pushing my legs apart to take him deeper. He's taking everything he can get, claiming every inch of me.

I arch my back, milking his shaft and driving us both out of our minds. His fingers find my clit, and I writhe against his hand, sobbing out a release. With a heated groan, he empties himself inside me.

He pulls me to him, grabbing the soap and lathering up my body. He just screwed the hell out of me, but now, he loves every inch of me. His hands glide along my stomach, his beard tickling my neck as his tongue paints designs on my skin. "I missed you so much."

We doze in each other's arms for the next couple of hours. Well, I assume that Josh slept. I was out like a light the moment my head hit the pillow. The combination of jet lag and erotic stimulation was more than my body could handle. Time to recharge, so I can have another go.

I wake to the sea breeze blowing in the window, carrying with it all manner of tropical smells. With a stretch, I pad down the hall, looking for the kitchen. I've heard Kona coffee is the bomb. I'm putting that theory to the test.

"Hey, beautiful."

I will never get tired of hearing this gorgeous man speak those words or getting to ogle his half-naked body.

And he knows it.

With a wink, Josh slides a mug of coffee in my direction. "You keep looking at me like that, and I'm marching your sweet ass right back to the bedroom."

"Promises, promises," I tease. "I'm sure you're busy. I don't know your schedule, but I'll stay out of the way. Go wander the beaches."

"I'm free the next couple of days. Don't think, for one second, I'm letting you out of my sight." He sighs, running a hand through his hair.

"What's wrong?"

"It's going to be tricky to get out of my contract here. But I'm going to call them and see what I can do."

"Why would you do that?" I ask, winding my arms around his waist.

"To get us back to the mainland. You wanted to return to New York."

I grab his face, planting a hard kiss on that delicious mouth. "I love you."

"I love you, too."

"You're not canceling the contract. We aren't going back to the mainland."

His eyes brighten. "You'll stay here?"

"I'll stay wherever you are, for as long as you want me. And beyond that, because I won't let you get rid of me."

Josh sits me on the counter, and I wind my legs around his waist. Our earlier kisses were urgent, but this one is all about tasting, exploring, taking our time. "Thank you."

I bite my lip. I dread the answer to my next question, but I need to know. "Josh, can I ask you something? I won't be angry regardless of your answer—"

"Nope."

"I didn't ask you yet."

He turns the full force of his gaze on me. "I didn't sleep with anyone else."

"You didn't?"

"No. My cousin tried to set me up, though. I went on one date." He grins at my scowl. "Stop glaring. Sarah didn't know about you until later that evening."

"Oh." My chest tightens, but what else can I say? I pushed the man away from me. He had every right to seek solace elsewhere.

"Sarah knew I was depressed, so she asked me to hang out with a few of her friends. It was a nightmare. I spent the night pining about you until I got drunk, and then I started talking about you."

"Josh, you don't drink like that."

"I know. But after I landed in Hawaii without you, I spent the first week in a bottle."

"Oh, God."

"Not pretty. I realized at that moment that unless it was you, I wasn't interested."

"I could pretend to be upset about that, but I'm not."

His gaze pierces me through his dark lashes. "Did *you*—"

"No! I cried and ate a ton of potato chips and dealt with this stupid stomach bug. Maybe it's all the chips screwing with my stomach." I run my fingers across his lips and through that soft beard that I always crave against my skin.

Josh smirks, nibbling on my fingertips. "How long have you had this stomach bug, beautiful?"

"I don't know. Off and on for a few weeks? But I was also eating like crap."

"Well, we'll get you back to eating healthy. It's important."

I nod, accepting a piece of fruit that he offers. "Deal." I look down, fiddling with the hem of my dress. "I'm sorry I believed all the lies that Frank told. He said you're not friends anymore. I feel awful if I ruined that."

"You didn't ruin it. He did. And no, after I broke his nose, it's safe to say the friendship was doomed."

"That's why it looked crooked. Frank did seem sorry for what he'd done."

"Addy, he tried to ruin the most important thing in my world out of jealously and spite. He and Chantelle both. I don't have any love for either of them."

"Trust me, I feel the same way. Did he ever apologize?"

"He did, but it was too little, too late. I was thousands of miles from you. I didn't know if I'd ever see you again." He clears his throat as if trying to throw off the cloud covering the moment. "But I'm glad that wasn't the case. I'm sorry I assumed you were reconciling with Clint. He said—"

"Oh, I know what he said. He's a pretentious prick. That's my new nickname for him." I giggle. "Our first official date was a real doozy. Talk about a fun dinner. Can we do that again sometime? Like the fifth of never?"

Josh laughs. "Talk about a terrible proposal."

My heart catches at his words. "You didn't actually ask me, so technically it doesn't count as a proposal."

"I guess it doesn't."

"It would have been amazing if you'd given me a chance to say yes."

His fingers trace along my thighs, drifting higher and higher up my leg. "So...if I ask you to marry me now, am I guaranteed a yes?"

My heart flutters at his question, but I opt for a bit of banter. "Hmm. I just don't know. Maybe?"

"Maybe? Addy, you'd better agree to marry me, or I'll be forced to tie you up and drag you to the courthouse."

"Well, when you put it like that, how can a girl say no?" My lips seize his, our tongues gliding together, our bodies pressing together and becoming more and more heated.

"I don't think that counted as a proposal either," Josh comments, his hands cupping my breasts.

"I'll take it."

His mouth attacks my neck as his hands pull the straps down on my dress. "I need you naked."

I shimmy out of the dress, making certain his mouth is never far from mine.

Josh takes a step back, his gaze washing over my body. I catch his eyes focused on my bra, rather my boobs spilling out of my bra. "Potato chips," I state, pointing at my breasts.

"What?" Josh laughs.

"I gained a little weight from eating potato chips. Lucky for me, some of it went to my boobs."

"Come here." He holds out his hand, urging me to follow.

Not an issue. I'll follow him through the gates of hell.

Josh hands me a small paper bag. "Go to the bathroom."

I peek inside the bag, my eyes widening. "Pregnancy tests?"

"Yep."

"Is there something you want to tell me?" I joke.

"I picked them up while you were asleep. I have a feeling your stomach bug has nothing to do with potato chips or airplane food."

"I don't know, Josh. I'm forty. It's not that easy to get knocked up."

His lips press to my shoulder as his arms wrap around me. "True, but your future husband is a virile twenty-seven-year-old. You never know."

With a smirk and a smack on the ass, I shoo him out of the room and pee on the tests. All four of them. He's lucky I had to go to the bathroom. Again.

Now I'm nervous, bordering on terrified, bordering on excited. I exit the bathroom and hold up three fingers. "Three-minute warning."

"Come here." He pulls me down onto his lap, his face tucked in my shoulder.

I'm a ball of nervous energy. "Maybe I should have a drink."

"What? No. If it's negative, then we'll go get you a drink."

"If it's not?"

"Then I'll take you to the bedroom and make love to you for the rest of the day."

"Why do I hope it's positive?"

"I know I do."

I see it in Josh's face. He means it. Everything he's ever said he's meant. His words make me want this baby as much as he does. The buzzer sounds, and we both jump.

"You go look," I urge, hopping off his lap.

"You sure?"

"Yes." I stare at the tile floor as he disappears into the bathroom, realizing how fantastic it would be to have a child with Josh. He'll be an amazing father.

The floor creaks, and I look up into Josh's face. His neutral, expressionless face.

I swallow against the disappointment in my throat and force a smile. "I guess I'm drinking early this morning, huh? I told you it was all those potato chips."

He grabs my hands, leading me to the bedroom. "No drinking."

My heart stills in my chest. "Wait. What?"

"No drinking for the next nine months."

"Oh, my God. We're—"

"Having a baby." Then he smiles, and it's a smile I've never seen before, bright enough to light up the universe and keep me warm forever.

I gape at Josh, my brain trying to process the news. "We're pregnant?"

"Yep. I told you that your virile stud wouldn't let you down."

My laugh bubbles up from way deep inside me. It's a soul laugh—a laugh that I spent decades of my life looking for and one that I found in Josh's arms. I link my hands around his neck, tangling my fingers in his golden hair. "I believe you have a mission for the day, sir."

His grin changes from ecstatic to smoldering as he pulls me to him. "This has been the longest few weeks of my life. Never again, Addy. I may never let you out of my sight again."

"Sounds like a plan." His lips press against mine, and all the heartache falls away. I'm home.

Josh is my home.

EPILOGUE

ell, Josh came close to getting his wish of three children before he turned thirty. The day my husband reached his fourth decade, we had two little boys, both carbon copies of their Dad. My favorite pastime is watching them play along the sandy coastline as they skip stones and search for shells. They love the ocean with the same passion as their father. Josh is already talking about teaching our eldest, Owen, how to surf. My camera is at the ready for that moment.

Josh gave me the option of moving back to the mainland before Owen was born, but I declined that idea. I knew that our dreams would flourish here in Hawaii, and they have.

He made up for the terrible proposal with a glorious one the day after I arrived in Hawaii. He drove us to Waimea Waterfall and asked me to spend my life with him. I think he already knew my answer, but my excited squeal sealed the deal.

He and Frank did reconcile, but their friendship is irrevocably damaged. Lucky for Josh, he has an entirely new crew of buddies to hang around with, not that he's ever far from my side. He much prefers spending his downtime with me, our boys, and the stray cats that adopted our family.

His Dad moved down when he found out he was going to be a grandfather, and I think being near Lisa's family again is therapeutic for him. He even charmed the pants off my mother when she came to visit. She jokes that should things go south with her husband, she's moving to Oahu. It's not out of the realm of possibility.

Clint got married to Debra of all people. I hope they're coexisting in some level of upwardly mobile hell. I guess it wasn't such an illicit tryst, after all.

As for me, I gave up nursing and pursued my love of photography, with Josh's blessing. He was a nervous nelly during both of my pregnancies, so he didn't want me anywhere I might get injured. Some might think it's annoying or overprotective. I just call it love.

"Hey, beautiful." Josh drops to the sand beside me, offering up that radiant smile I will never tire of seeing.

"To which of us are you referring?"

He leans over with a smirk, pressing his lips to my swollen belly before moving up to claim my mouth. "Both of you. Obviously."

Yep, our third child is due in a few months. A little girl.

I guess you can say that everything worked out according to plan.

Love's plan.

AFTERWORD

Hello lovelies,

I hope you are as crazy in love with Josh and Addy as I am. I adore this story—the heat, the love, the raw honesty. It holds a very special place in my heart.

I hope their story made you laugh, cry, and sometimes want to throw the book across the room. Life—and love—is often like that, but in the end, it's always worthwhile.

I love to hear from my readers and encourage you to subscribe to my newsletter or to email me at m.l.broomeauteur@gmail.com. If you have questions, ideas or suggestions, I'm all ears!

It would be great if you could spread the word about this book, particularly if it touched you in some way. Reviews on sites like Amazon, BookBub, and GoodReads are very welcome and appreciated.

Best wishes for a life well-lived. Until we meet again.

M.L. Broome

Connect with M.L. Broome

Sign up for her newsletter!
https://www.mlbroome.com/
BookBub
http://bit.ly/BookbubMLBroome
Facebook Author Page
http://bit.ly/FBMLBroome
Facebook Readers Group
http://bit.ly/BroomeBadassBook
Instagram
http://bit.ly/IGMLBroome
Amazon Author Page
http://bit.ly/MLBroome
GoodReads
http://bit.ly/GoodReadsMLBroome

ABOUT THE AUTHOR

I'm a bohemian spirit with a New York edge. I adore dressing up and kicking back, a nice glass of wine with an equally stunning view, and experiences that make the soul—and mouth—water.

When I'm not writing or holding one-sided arguments with my characters (spoiler alert—they always win), I love losing myself in nature on my

North Carolina farm, one of my rescue buddies at my side.

Life is beautiful...so are you. Don't forget to look up.